Praise for Lin Anderson

'A real page-turner'   Ian Rankin

'A cleverly crafted nail-biter with spectacular suspense. An all-consuming, one-sit read that I absolutely loved. Brilliant book'   Helen Fields

'An engrossing Highland tale, with layer upon layer of intrigue, skilfully drip-fed by a classy writer' Mari Hannah

'Forensic scientist Rhona MacLeod has become one of the most satisfying characters in modern crime fiction – honourable, inquisitive and yet plagued by doubt and, sometimes, fears . . . As ever, the landscape is stunningly evoked and MacLeod's decency and humanity shine through on every page'   *Daily Mail*

'Lin Anderson is one of Scotland's national treasures . . . her writing is unique, bringing warmth and depth to even the seediest parts of Glasgow. Rhona MacLeod is a complex and compelling heroine who just gets better with every outing'
                                         Stuart MacBride

'Vivid an   *Guardian*

THE
PARTY
HOUSE

Lin Anderson is a Scottish author and screenwriter known for her bestselling crime series featuring forensic scientist Dr Rhona MacLeod. Four of her novels have been longlisted for the Scottish Crime Book of the Year. Her short film *River Child* won both a Scottish BAFTA for Best Fiction and the Celtic Film Festival's Best Drama award and has now been viewed more than one million times on YouTube. Lin is also the co-founder of the international crime-writing festival Bloody Scotland, which takes place annually in Stirling.

By Lin Anderson

THE RHONA MACLEOD SERIES
Driftnet
Torch
Deadly Code
Dark Flight
Easy Kill
Final Cut
The Reborn
Picture Her Dead
Paths of the Dead
The Special Dead
None but the Dead
Follow the Dead
Sins of the Dead
Time for the Dead
The Innocent Dead
The Killing Tide

STANDALONE NOVELS
The Party House

NOVELLA
Blood Red Roses

THE
PARTY
HOUSE

LinAnderson

PAN BOOKS

First published 2022 by Macmillan

This paperback edition published 2023 by Pan Books
an imprint of Pan Macmillan
The Smithson, 6 Briset Street, London EC1M 5NR
EU representative: Macmillan Publishers Ireland Ltd, 1st Floor,
The Liffey Trust Centre, 117–126 Sheriff Street Upper,
Dublin 1, D01 YC43
Associated companies throughout the world
www.panmacmillan.com

ISBN   978-1-5290-8452-8

1 3 5 7 9 8 6 4 2

A CIP catalogue record for this book is available from the British Library.

Map artwork by Hemesh Alles

Typeset by Palimpsest Book Production Ltd, Falkirk, Stirlingshire
Printed and bound by CPI Group (UK) Ltd, Croydon, CR0 4YY

Visit **www.panmacmillan.com** to read more about all our books
and to buy them. You will also find features, author interviews and
news of any author events, and you can sign up for e-newsletters
so that you're always first to hear about our new releases.

This book is dedicated to my father, former Detective Inspector Bill Mitchell, who brought his family to live in the Highland village of Carrbridge

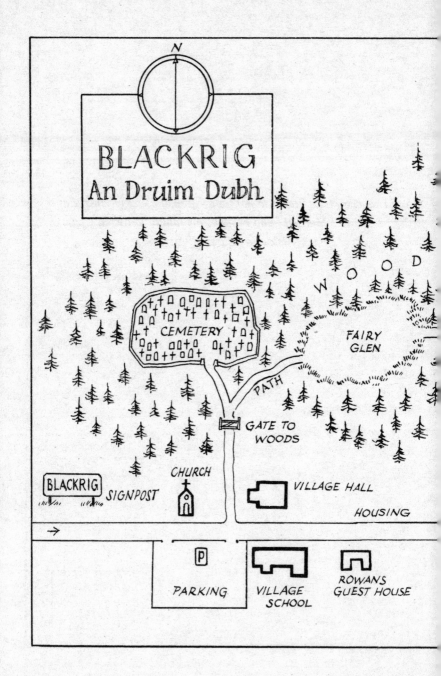

AN LOCHAN UAINE

○ HOT TUB

SAUNA

BEACH

ANCIENT PINE FOREST

ARD CHOILLE

GROUNDS OF THE PARTY HOUSE

ANCIENT PINE TREE

L A N D

TRACK

MOORLAND

BEANACH

HILL

WOOD PATH

HILL

ROUTE TO ARD CHOILLE/BEANACH

FORRIGAN

HILL AND MOORLAND

ROADSIDE   HOUSING

DEAD END

BLACKRIG ARMS

VILLAGE SHOP

Ard Choille
THE PARTY HOUSE
-HEMESH·ALLES-

Ailsa

Before

Eleven o'clock and the sky was still light. In Glasgow it would be dark by now, she thought.

She hadn't wanted to come here, to this dead-end village in the Highlands, but here she was.

You could have run away again, a small voice reminded her.

No, I made a deal. Come here, stay clean. Go to art college in September.

She'd hated it at first. Folk looking at her as though she'd just dropped in from outer space. They were friendly enough, she had to admit that, especially the local boys, who'd fought for her attention from the outset.

She smiled, remembering the fun she'd had with that, playing them off one against the other. It was a game that had kept her sane at the beginning. Made her feel good about herself. She'd even tasted some of the wares on offer, and found a few to her liking.

Especially when they took place here in the heart of the woods.

She ran her eyes over the circle of carvings that stood sentinel among the trees, thinking again how beautiful they were. The birds fashioned from stripped pine, some in flight,

1

others resting quietly on a branch. Her favourite was the owl sitting watching her from atop a tree trunk pedestal.

He was so real that she often found herself talking to him.

Then the woodland creatures . . . A roe deer, she could imagine taking off to bound away through the trees. A pair of majestic wolves nearby which might pursue it. Even imagining this didn't worry her, because she had no doubt who would win that particular race.

Her eyes were now drawn to the centre of the circle and the father and mother of all the carvings . . . literally. The green woman of the woods, together with the green man.

Until it was explained to her that they were a symbol of rebirth, she'd had no idea what the green faces staring out of the leaves and twigs were. Initially, she'd found them rather spooky. Once she knew they represented the cycle of new growth that occurred with every spring, her attitude to them had changed.

She'd starting bringing her sketch pad here and, sitting on this tree trunk, she'd drawn all of the carvings, then added a few imaginary ones of her own.

It was here she'd first encountered him. In fact, it was he who'd explained the carvings to her.

She was startled from her reverie by a burst of music escaping from the distant village hall as someone opened the back exit. Raucous shouts followed from the guys who were hanging about on the steps, drinking and smoking.

She'd already run that particular gauntlet when she'd left the ceilidh, with plenty of offers to walk her home. All the way to her family's cottage, Forrigan.

The familiar faces of Josh Huntly and his assorted mates had met her at the door. She'd already danced with Josh and a couple of the others, including the shy Finn Campbell, but hadn't taken anyone up on their offer, knowing full well a walk wasn't what they had in mind.

Been there. Done that. No longer interested.

She checked her phone, but the waited-for message hadn't arrived . . . yet.

She took a deep breath of the night air, filled with the scent of pine. The June weather had been warm and dry. Even here, the normally boggy ground and its three amber peaty pools had partially dried out.

The rain will come, everyone said. Hopefully soon enough to prevent a fire in the pinewoods or the moor.

She tried to imagine such a fire . . . the crackling of the bone-dry heather, the whoosh as the pine needles flared up, the hot sweet smell of smouldering peat.

It should have frightened her, but it didn't. Not until she thought of the green woman and man ablaze. The leaves and winding branches that made up their bodies a mass of fire. Like back when they'd burned women as witches. That was an image she didn't like.

The crack of a twig underfoot caused her to turn in anticipation.

She rose to greet him, hearing his footsteps cross the needle-strewn forest floor, feeling a surge of desire.

Her smile, at first warm and welcoming, slowly shifted to something very different as she realized the footsteps were multiple, and none of them were likely to be his.

Greg

Now

Blood hit the mirror in a fine spray.

Cursing, he grabbed a towel and wiped his face, his hand and then the mirror.

So much blood for such a small cut.

He was examining the damage when a sleepy Joanne appeared beside him to kiss the wound.

'There,' she said. 'All better.' She laughed. 'For a man who can cleanly butcher a deer, you seem a little careless with your own face.'

There was a smear of blood on her lips. He put his mouth on hers, tasting it. This is what it had been like since the moment they'd met in London. This gnawing hunger for her, which had never abated.

Taking her in his arms, he lifted her on to the surface. She laughed as he moved to position himself between her legs.

Later, when he was finally dressed, she asked if he might pick up a few things in the local shop for her.

He assumed an amused smile. 'I'm out on the hill all day. You could take a walk down yourself?'

She didn't look keen to do that. 'Caroline doesn't like me,' she said with a wry smile.

'I told you, it's not personal. Besides, you don't strike me as a big fearty.'

'What's a big fearty?' she demanded.

'Something you're not.' He kissed her firmly. 'There are venison steaks in the fridge. I'll cook them when I get back.'

He headed out to the Land Rover, releasing his two labs, Cal and Sasha, from their kennels to jump into the back.

In the glen below, where Blackrig nestled, the morning sun had burned off most of the mist, although faint spirals of it still rose from the surrounding pinewoods like spirits escaping the dawn.

Settled now in the Land Rover, he glanced in the rear-view mirror to find Joanne, still in a state of undress, observing his departure. He hooted the horn in response to her wave, and thought back to the moment they'd first met.

Greg

Then

Alighting from the Caledonian Sleeper in the early morning, he'd been greeted by a solid wall of heat and city smells.

It had been hot overnight in the single-berth cabin, so much so that he'd eventually lain naked in the bunk, rising early to wash and dress before his coffee and croissant had been delivered by a cheerful guard.

Gaining the platform had felt like stepping into an oven. He'd almost forgotten just how sweltering it could be down here during the summer months.

It wasn't his first time in London, but the virus had prevented his annual visit to advertise the Blackrig Estate at the Highland Game event. Lockdown had hit the estate and its associated hunting and fishing visitors hard.

Now it was time to start it up again. So, as head ghillie on the small Highland estate, he was here to spread the word that visitors were welcome at Blackrig once more.

Walking towards the exit, he found himself dodging the swarms of people that filled the concourse, his brain still wired into the two-metre rule, or a coffin's length apart. True, a few folk in the crowd were still wearing masks. As for the rest, it looked like the mass deaths had already been forgotten in the UK's capital city.

Not so in his own neck of the woods, he thought. Not everyone in Blackrig was happy about opening up again to tourists. And there was a very good reason for that.

Greg shoved that thought to the back of his mind and concentrated on finding his way to the conference hotel. He would have preferred to stay in the open air, however muggy, but despite his earlier plan to walk to the venue, he found himself heading for the tube, since it was clear the crowded streets were no less busy than what he was likely to meet below ground. Plus he would get to his destination quicker.

Having seen very few people during the previous eighteen months, except when he'd ventured to the village shop or encountered locals out for a walk in the woods or the hills, he now found himself intrigued by the faces of the people sharing the carriage with him.

Especially the women.

Colin Aitken, his assistant ghillie, had warned him that would happen. 'You've been sex-deprived for yonks. Make sure you find someone quick. You've got a lot of time to make up and you're only there for a few days.' He'd looked so wistful as he'd said it that Greg had almost offered to let Colin go to London in his place.

Now, seated between two brightly dressed attractive women, Greg was glad he hadn't, although he wasn't sure if he could deal with making the moves that might take him further than just chat with any woman he met at the event.

Walking the hills or lying in bed alone, he'd fantasized plenty about sex during lockdown, but fantasies were just that – fantasies – and not real life.

Reaching the hotel, he checked in and made his way up

to his room, pleased to find it sufficiently air-conditioned to make him think he was back in Scotland. The event material had been delivered, along with a bottle of whisky to welcome him. Had it not been so early he would have poured himself a dram.

His mobile buzzed shortly after that, suggesting Colin had been tailing him.

'You're there?'

'I am,' Greg assured him.

'What's it like?' Colin sounded eager.

'It's London. Hot and crowded.'

'Women?'

'Thousands if not millions of them,' Greg told him.

'Lucky bastard. Remember, they'll all have been in lock-down too.'

'Sadly, it'll be mostly hunting and shooting men that I'll be meeting with. All well up there?'

There was a moment's hesitation before Colin said, 'Caroline says there's a rumour going round that we're planning to open up the Party House again soon.'

It wasn't a rumour. In fact, it was one of the reasons he was here. There was alternative accommodation for small weekend shooting parties on the estate, and he was planning to focus on that. Mostly because he wasn't happy himself about the thought of the Party House being used.

'They'll have to do it sometime,' he reminded Colin. 'It makes a lot of money for the estate owners.'

'There'll be trouble if they do,' Colin said darkly.

There was no answer to that, so Greg didn't attempt one. 'I'll be back in a couple of days. Don't mess up before then,' he ordered.

Colin was young and keen, but he had his daft moments.

Which was partly the reason he hadn't sent him down here in his place.

Realizing how hungry he was, he decided it was time to check out the restaurant, plus take a look at the itinerary for the weekend.

That was when he first saw her.

She was sitting just inside, working on a laptop, a coffee alongside. She looked up at his approach, gave him a studied look, then smiled.

'Greg Taylor, Blackrig Estate?' She rose and held out her hand. 'Joanne Addington, here to do a piece for *The Field*.'

Surprised she should know his name, he found himself saying, 'Have we met before?', thinking maybe at some drunken do, at a previous event.

'Only on paper.' She waved the list of contributors with their photos at him. 'In this one you're wearing a kilt.' She looked him up and down.

'Company policy, but only in the evening,' he said, matching her smile.

She pulled her laptop towards her a little. 'Join me, please. I don't know anyone here, except you now.'

And that's how it all began.

Greg

Later, he would question the way she seemed to have picked him from among all the other men who'd been there that weekend, just as he would question many things. But at that moment he was pleased to be the chosen one, because it didn't matter who'd made the first move, since what followed had closely matched his own lockdown fantasies.

And those fantasies had brought her here to Beanach, his home on the estate. Something he hadn't imagined possible. Yet on their last day in London, he'd found himself inviting her to Blackrig, now that lockdown was over. To his surprise, she'd immediately accepted.

'I'd love to come, and soon. It sounds like a perfect place to write.' She'd drawn him to her at that point, 'and do the other things you've promised.'

And so, ten days later, he was picking her up off the Caledonian Sleeper at Inverness.

Watching her step onto the platform of the quiet station, he remembered his own reaction to the difference between their two worlds. She stood for a moment, as if doubting her decision to come here, before he called out her name. Then, catching sight of him, her face broke into a wide smile and, picking up her bag, she headed towards him.

He remembered thinking how little luggage she'd brought

with her, and wondering if that was an indication of how long she planned to stay.

They loosely embraced rather than kissing, signifying perhaps the space that had grown between them during the previous ten days.

'No kilt, I see,' she quipped. 'Although you do look like a gamekeeper.'

'I'll take that as a compliment,' he said, lifting her bag. 'The Land Rover's not far.'

Once on the open road, silence replaced the casual chit-chat they'd engaged in as they'd walked to the car park.

He was conscious now of the dwindling signs of settlement and the increasing emptiness as they headed west. He decided not to pester her by talking, but left her to gaze silently out of the window at the beautiful but daunting landscape.

Eventually she said, 'This is amazing.' She turned a stunned gaze on him. 'I had no idea that it was so beautiful.' She shook her head. 'Of course, I've seen lots of photographs, but they don't do the Highlands justice.'

He smiled his joy at that. 'Wait until you see the view from Beanach.'

'That's your home. You told me Beanach was Gaelic for "blessing".'

'I'm impressed you remember that part of the evening,' he said honestly.

She laid a hand on his thigh. 'I remember all of it.'

After that he'd given her a running commentary on the hills, lochs, rivers and hamlets they'd driven through, which she seemed truly interested in. When they took the final turn-off towards Blackrig, he explained that the main road ended at the village. 'There's no other route in.'

He slowed as they reached the English–Gaelic sign for

Blackrig. Laughingly, she attempted the Gaelic version, An Druim Dubh, with little success.

He corrected her. 'You'll have to learn to roll your Rs and ignore half the letters,' he added with a smile.

As they passed the now-discarded road barriers sporting the words KEEP OUT, PANDEMIC and LOCKDOWN, he explained.

'We had problems with campervans, and folk from south trying to outrun the virus,' he said. 'Hence the barriers, which were manned twenty-four seven.'

'And did it work?'

'Up to a point,' he said.

Entering the village, he gave her the short, express tour. 'On the left, the church and the village hall. On the right, the Blackrig Arms, our local hotel and pub, and the primary school. The older pupils have a bit further to travel, back the way we came. Plus the all-important village shop, which saved us during the pandemic when we couldn't get to the supermarket in Inverness. I need to stop for milk,' he added, drawing up outside the little shop, where a large chalked sign displayed the message: VISITORS TO BLACKRIG MUST WEAR A MASK AND SANITIZE HANDS BEFORE ENTRY

Joanne looked askance at it as she climbed out of the vehicle. 'Maybe I should just wait outside?'

'No, I need to introduce you to the village and this is the quickest way.'

He kissed her firmly on the mouth before putting her mask on. Then, squeezing some gel into his own hands, he massaged hers and led her inside.

He knew there was every chance that Caroline would be behind the Perspex screen, and he wasn't wrong. She looked up on his entry and gave him a big smile, then she caught sight of the masked Joanne.

'Joanne, this is a good friend of mine, Caroline, who runs the shop and helped to keep us fed and watered during the pandemic.'

'Pleased to meet you, Caroline,' Joanne muttered from behind her mask.

'Joanne'll be staying with me up at Beanach for a while.' He smiled encouragingly at Joanne.

'Really?' Caroline took a moment to process this bit of news. Greg could almost hear her brain working. *So, he went south for the weekend and ten days later she arrives to stay with him.*

'Where have you come from?' Caroline said, now giving her full attention to the incomer.

With a quick glance in Greg's direction, Joanne answered, 'London.'

Caroline shot Greg a look that told him clearly what she thought of that.

'And how long are you here for?'

'Not sure, yet.' Joanne glanced at Greg again, who smiled in return, hoping that signified he was open to suggestion.

'We heard rumours that the Party House was opening up. Is that true?' Caroline said as he paid for the milk.

'It's not been confirmed,' Greg told her.

'Folk don't want that place let. Not now. Not ever.'

Once outside, Joanne handed him her mask. 'What's the Party House and why are folk so mad about it?'

He didn't want to tell her. Even having the words of explanation in his head filled him with dread, but she would hear about it eventually, and it was better coming from him.

'Six people in the village died from the virus. Malcolm's wife from the hotel, a teenage boy, two young children and two infants.' He heard the catch in his voice. 'We were in lockdown, socially distancing, even out on the hills and in

13

the woods. We set up the barricades, did everything right, then the estate owners brought in a party of folk from London by helicopter to the Party House. They brought the new strain with them, which was affecting children badly, and it killed six people before it was contained. That's why locals don't want it to open up again.'

He felt her shock, and reached out to take her hand.

'How awful,' she said. 'No wonder Caroline didn't like me being here.'

They'd reached the Land Rover and he opened the door for her.

'It's not you personally,' he said.

The truth was Caroline wouldn't have liked any woman who came to visit him, but now wasn't the time to mention that.

'It's just hard, after everything that's happened, for Blackrig to open to visitors again.'

She stayed silent as he started up the engine and, drawing away from the shop, took the single-track road that would eventually lead them to Beanach.

He'd known things would be different here from London, and yet, he reminded himself, she had chosen to come. He had to assume that she wanted more of what they'd had together there.

It was time to see if he was right.

Having made his decision, he immediately left the track and entered the outskirts of the nearby woods, startling a roe deer which darted away through the undergrowth, its white tail bobbing ahead of them.

'Where are we going?' she shouted, gripping the door handle.

'You'll see,' he said.

Coming to a halt, he got out, opened her door and, grabbing her hand, urged her to come with him.

'Where?' she said, sounding unsure whether to be alarmed.

He smiled reassuringly. 'Come with me, *please*.'

The sun drifted down through the mix of pine, silver birch and rowan as he led her even deeper into the woods. The scent of rowan blossom and the murmur of feasting bees filled the air.

He'd told her what it would be like here, but now she could see and smell it for herself. The bustle of the city no longer existed. She was in a different world. His world. He saw her smile, and knew she was pleased by that.

Eventually they arrived at the place he'd described to her. The place he wanted her to see. The place where he wanted to make love to her.

The tall Caledonian pine was multi-branched, twisted and ancient. Scots pine trees were known to live for up to seven hundred years, he'd told her. This one, his favourite, would have stood here for at least five hundred. 'Think what it would have seen.'

'This is the tree you told me about?' Joanne said, touching the lichen-covered trunk and looking upwards at the two thin strips of leather that hung from the lowest branch. She laughed. 'Are they there for me?'

'At your request, if you remember?'

'I do.' She smiled.

This wildness is what they remembered of each other. It was what they'd shared during those heady days in London. This was why she had come here, so that he might keep his promise.

Both naked now, he lightly touched her mouth with his, then slid slowly down, circling her breasts, pulling at her nipples, down to breathe softly against the springy hair until her body rose towards him. When she called out in pleasure, he pulled himself up beside her.

'Okay?' he said.

'Better than okay.'

She reached up to catch hold of the leather strips and, leaning back against the trunk, urged him to continue.

This was the desire she'd revealed to him. To make love like this in a forest. Far away from London, from everyone. The lockdown fantasy that she'd replayed for him countless times.

As he took her hands in his own, she kissed him fully on the mouth.

'That was worth coming here for,' she said with a smile.

'Your wish is my command.'

As they made their way back to the Land Rover the sound of a gunshot split the air.

Greg halted, trying to judge where it had come from, who might be shooting, and at what.

It was open season on stalking, but they had no shooting parties booked in, so it had to be Colin keeping numbers down, or possibly a local lad trying his hand at poaching.

Even as he considered which it might be, the injured deer appeared, crashing wildly towards them in its fear. Greg pulled Joanne into the shelter of a tree.

The shot had failed to kill, whoever had fired it, which meant the creature would wander round in pain until it was put out of its misery.

'What will you do?' Joanne said.

'I'll get you home, pick up the dogs, find it and kill it.'

When they reached the cottage, he ushered her inside.

'Think you can manage until I get back?'

She'd looked around and smiled.

'I'm sure I can,' she assured him.

Joanne

Now

She waved goodbye as the Land Rover headed off, and heard him sound the horn in reply. Even after the vehicle disappeared from view, she continued to stand at the door, enjoying the sun on her face, thinking about being here and how she felt about that.

She realized that she felt safe. The safest she'd felt in some time. They'd talked about how they'd each coped with lockdown and it was clear that Greg's story had been very different from her own.

Of course, she hadn't been entirely truthful about her own experience. Instead, she'd painted a picture of being shut up alone in a city flat without a garden for months on end.

She'd stopped there, unwilling to say any more. At which point Greg had drawn her into his arms and told her she was safe here to do whatever she liked. Plus she would have him for company.

Although, you don't really know him, she thought. *And he definitely doesn't know you. Or why you're really here.*

An image of their most recent coupling sprang to mind, and with it that recurring sense of excitement whenever he was around. Something she hadn't foreseen.

But that, she thought, was par for the course. You met someone new. You slept with them, then you got to know them, and very quickly found out you didn't want to be with them for anything other than sex. And maybe not even for that.

She came back inside and fetched her mobile. Checking her messages, she found three from Lucy, one from last night and two this morning. Lucy was obviously keen to know how things were 'up there, in the wilds of Scotland'.

Joanne poured herself a cup of the freshly brewed coffee Greg had made, and sat down at the kitchen table to return Lucy's call.

The mobile was answered almost immediately.

'Good morning,' Lucy said. 'I thought you would never call me back. I assumed you must be off-grid.'

'I'm not in the wilderness,' Joanne said.

'But you're near it,' Lucy said dramatically.

'I'm a twenty-minute walk from the village.'

'Which, let me guess, has three houses, a pub and a shop.'

'A few more things than that.' Joanne found herself standing up for Blackrig.

There was a pause as Lucy digested this, then her bright voice declared, 'So, how is your gamekeeper?'

'It's called a ghillie,' Joanne said. 'He's away to work and I'm here in his cottage, called Beanach, which means "blessing" in Gaelic.'

'Listen to you,' Lucy whooped. 'Going all native on me.'

'It's pretty special up here,' Joanne said. 'Especially after the London version of the plague.'

'So, I take it your ghillie isn't a disappointment?'

'He wasn't a disappointment in London and now he's on his home turf . . .'

Lucy groaned in what Joanne imagined was jealousy. 'I wish you'd taken me to the Highland Game thingy. Maybe I would now be swanning around a Highland estate.'

Frivolities over, Joanne moved to more serious matters.

'Is everything all right down there?'

'Yes. No one has come looking for you, and if they did, I would say you were off on an assignment, but I wasn't sure where.'

Joanne considered this for a moment. 'Thank you, Lucy.'

'No problem. Since I have no idea where you are, except that it's somewhere in Scotland.' She carried on. 'So how long do you plan to stay?'

Joanne had no idea and said so. 'It depends on what happens with Greg. He's keen at the moment, but who knows how long that will last?' She thought about what had happened yesterday and Caroline's reaction to her. 'Plus I think he's got history with the woman who runs the village shop. She was throwing me daggers when we went in yesterday.'

'Did he explain why?'

'No.' Joanne thought about telling Lucy the sad tale of the pandemic, but realized she might discover where exactly she was via that information, which wasn't a good idea.

'Who hasn't got a history?' Lucy said.

Joanne made a noise which signified her agreement.

'Well, keep in touch, Lady Chatterley. And stay safe.' Lucy's voice broke a little at those final words, and Joanne knew exactly why.

'You too,' she said. 'Sending hugs.'

She put down the phone, noting that her hands were trembling a little. The first call was always going to be the most difficult, and it had gone well. Or okay, at least.

With the whole day in front of her she decided she would shower, dress and then take a look round Beanach, both inside and out.

They said you could tell a lot about a person by the way they lived.

Greg had given her a quick tour the day before, so 'she wouldn't get lost', he'd said with a smile. 'It's a Highland cottage, so I don't think that will happen.'

There were two attic bedrooms, one his, the other he said he used as a study and for estate work.

She decided to take a proper look round the bedroom. Greg had said his late father had worked for the former laird, so this had been his family home. By the age and style of the furniture, it looked as though nothing had been changed since that time.

She glanced in the wardrobe at the neatly stored clothes, mostly work related, or casual. His kilt and accessories were hanging there, of course, but no dress suits. So it appeared Greg wasn't into dressing up in anything other than his kilt on special occasions.

She felt a bit odd about checking out the contents of the oak tallboy but, bracing herself, did so. What she was worried about finding, she wasn't sure, but the drawers contained just the usual socks, underwear and T-shirts.

In fact, it was all perfectly normal. Greg appeared clean, reasonably tidy, and didn't have anything lying about which might indicate he was weird or a threat to her in any way.

The final place she checked was his bedside cabinet, where she found a small cloth pouch which held a gold ring that looked like a man's marriage band.

Had Greg been married at one time? If so, he hadn't mentioned it. She couldn't blame him for that, since she hadn't mentioned anything about any of her former relationships either.

So there was the first mystery which she couldn't solve without revealing that she'd been rummaging through his things.

In that moment she thought of what Greg might discover were he to search her place. The thought troubled her so much, she chose not to enter his study, but took herself downstairs and outside.

What was she worried about? She had no reason to suspect Greg of having any other motive for inviting her here than what was plain to see.

She, on the other hand, did have an ulterior motive for accepting his invitation. She was the one with the secrets. Starting with her reaction to Greg's story of the virus deaths in Blackrig, which she'd already been aware of, although, in fairness, her shock at his emotional retelling of the tale had been genuine enough.

She'd known about them because she'd read about it online, when checking out Blackrig, but the piece had entirely missed out the role the Party House had played in those deaths.

She'd been truthful when she'd told Greg she could write here. What she hadn't told him was what she planned to write about.

Greg

Greg steeled himself before going in, knowing Caroline was liable to be even more obvious in her displeasure when she saw that he was alone. She was busy serving someone, so he went and picked up the items Joanne had mentioned she'd forgotten to pack and took them to the counter.

Caroline waited until her other customer, Mrs McVitie, had left before she turned her wrath on him.

'You knew they had a team up at the Party House getting it ready?'

'No,' he said honestly. 'I have nothing to do with letting or maintaining the place and I only see the visitors if they want to go shooting or stalking.'

'This can't happen. Have they no respect? It's a death house to us. They broke the law by bringing folk there and killed six people. Four of them babies. Have you forgotten that?'

The look she'd shot him when she'd said 'babies' cut him to the quick, as she knew it would.

When he remained silent, she said, 'There's a meeting about it tonight in the village hall. You work for the bloody estate, so I'm assuming you'll be there?'

Greg nodded. He would have to go. Colin too, if only to gauge the degree of mounting anger against their employers, Global Investment Holdings.

She seemed to soften a little at that, and gave him a smile to remind him that they had once been more than just this. Greg waited, imagining the next comment would be about Joanne, but it didn't materialize, even as she bagged the obviously feminine items he'd come in to buy.

As he departed the shop, he wondered just how soon he would be told what Caroline thought about Joanne. Or alternatively, and much worse, when Caroline would decide to tell Joanne all about him.

That thought unnerved him the most.

Back in the Land Rover, he texted Joanne and told her he'd picked up what she'd wanted from the shop, so there was no need for a trip to the village. Then, checking the time, he headed for the Party House.

Cresting the hill, he could make out Beanach up to his right, and on the left the little track he'd driven down with Joanne. The tree he'd taken her to was very near the grounds of the so-called Party House, although the house's original name was in fact Ard Choille, which meant 'high wood'. And it was obvious why when it came into sight.

A pale silver wooden structure that blended perfectly into the surrounding mature birch trees. Built on three levels with a live birch at its centre, it resembled a big treehouse with encircling balconies from which to watch the sun rise and set. The front of the building looked down on open grass to a green-coloured lochan, known as An Lochan Uaine.

It was from its white sandy shore that he and everyone else in Blackrig had learned to swim. It had been their summer playground until the late Lord Main, who'd had Ard Choille designed and built, had died, and the new owners, Global Investment Holdings, had denied access to the house grounds and ruined the shoreline with a

Scandi-type wooden sauna and a concrete plinth which housed an open-air hot tub.

One of the many indignities the new owners had imposed on the people of Blackrig.

Greg noted the surrounding grass had been cut and the area spruced up. It was obvious from the garden at least that the house was being made ready for visitors.

It was all very well for him to deny that he had any responsibility for letting the house, when it was probably his visit to London that had generated its occupation in the first place.

He turned at the sound of a vehicle, to find Colin's jeep coming to join him.

'So it's true, then?' Colin said on approach.

Greg nodded. 'There was an email early this morning. A party of eight, apparently, from London. They're bringing a caterer with them. Arriving off the Caledonian Sleeper early tomorrow, then hired cars are bringing them from Inverness.'

Something he hadn't mentioned to Caroline, or Joanne for that matter.

'It's a mistake to do this so soon.' Colin looked worried. 'Folk won't like it.'

'What can we do?' Greg said. 'Lockdown's over. It's perfectly legal.'

'And it makes Global Investment Holdings upwards of twenty grand,' Colin said.

'We need to be at that meeting tonight,' Greg said. 'Plus be up here first thing tomorrow to see what they want to do while they're here.'

Greg

The village hall was the heart of the small community. Used for weddings, birthday and anniversary celebrations, for summer and Hogmanay ceilidhs, for school recitals and prize-givings.

It was a place for wakes too, but not for those six deaths, because it hadn't been allowed. All the community could do was to line the road between the church and the nearby graveyard in the woods, masked and two metres apart, to watch the hearses go by. Four of them carrying tiny coffins.

Greg and Colin had taken their place at the back of the hall, choosing to stand, knowing the rows of seats would swiftly fill up. Room had been left at the front for the bereaved families, and it was clear by their faces how raw their loss still was.

As four members of the community council mounted the stage, including Malcolm, who was the current chair, there was a roar of disapproval from the crowd, silenced by a male voice who shouted, 'Malcolm's wife died too.'

Greg didn't recognize the owner, but his protest worked. It wasn't Malcolm or the other members of the committee they were after, but the owners of the estate.

'We're fucked,' Colin whispered by his side.

The first person to speak from the floor was the mother of Tracey Scott, the youngest victim at only eight months old.

'How is it that if a car had driven at speed through our village, killing our children, the driver would be charged? If a man had shot them all, he would go to prison. How can the estate owners not be charged for wilfully breaking lock-down and killing people?'

It was the question that had been asked multiple times, and never answered.

'Because rich folk can do whatever the hell they like, whatever the consequences,' someone shouted, after which he turned and glared at Greg and Colin.

'Jesus,' Colin whispered. 'We're dead men.'

Greg shushed him as Malcolm began to speak.

'I have contacted Global Investment Holdings and explained about our concern at having visitors to the Party House so soon, giving our reasons. They assure me that they will not be seen in the village and will bring their own catering staff with them, so will be self-contained.'

'Rubbish,' someone shouted. 'They'll be meeting with those two at the back of the hall.'

All eyes turned to Greg and Colin.

'We have no influence on what happens with the Party House,' Greg said evenly.

'But you were down in London not long ago advertising it,' someone shouted.

Greg knew he couldn't deny this, so there was no point in trying. Joanne's presence at Beanach was clear evidence of his London visit.

'I've worked on the Blackrig Estate most of my life, as my father did before me,' he said. 'If I leave, Global Investment Holdings will just bring in someone else, and they won't be local. How will that help?'

'He's right,' a voice shouted. 'At least Greg's one of us.'

The murmurs surrounding them now were more concili-atory. Colin threw him a look of thanks. 'Maybe we won't get lynched after all,' he said with a weak smile.

'Not tonight, anyway,' Greg said, hoping that was true.

He'd spotted Caroline in the throng, but she hadn't looked round until then. Now she nodded her approval and threw him a small appreciative smile.

The relative calm that followed his speech was sadly short-lived.

At that moment, the back door to the hall was flung open and a babble of angry voices entered, causing everyone to turn.

'Here we go again,' Colin muttered as six young men, led by Josh Huntley, marched into the room.

Greg took a deep breath. This, he realized, was much more serious than the mood of the crowd in the hall. Checking out Josh's gang, he registered that every one of them had a close connection to the virus deaths, and all were as angry as their leader.

Josh's voice was ice cold as he accused the owners of the estate of murdering his wee sister Jenny. 'Those rich arseholes broke the law.' Josh turned his gaze on Greg and Colin. 'And they're fucking going to pay for it.'

That brought everyone to their feet. Some shouting their agreement. Others, like Malcolm, trying to calm things down. Greg caught the quick glance a worried Malcolm threw him, indicating that they should slip out the front way before they became a target.

'Come on,' he gestured to Colin. 'We can't do any good here.'

Using the commotion as cover, they made their way along the back wall and slipped out of the front entrance, closing the door behind them.

'Jesus,' Colin said as they headed for their vehicles, the fracas in the hall still audible. 'What the fuck do we do now?'

'I'll inform our bosses,' Greg said.

'There's no way they'll cancel.' Colin shook his head. 'They're booked on tonight's sleeper.'

Colin was right, but the estate owners had to be told how difficult the situation might be for the intending visitors, after tonight's performance.

'Was Harry there?' Colin said.

Greg had checked for their local policeman, who lived ten miles away. 'He wasn't in the hall. Maybe just as well with Josh busy making threats.'

Driving back to Beanach, Greg suddenly remembered with pleasure that Joanne would be there waiting for him. Then he realized how late it was and, even worse, that he'd promised to cook for her tonight.

He would have to make it up to her in other ways, he decided.

Opening the door quietly, he found her seated at the kitchen table, back to him, working on her laptop, seemingly oblivious to his arrival. He stood for a moment, enjoying both the image and the scent of her.

He moved to stand behind her, slipping his hands down the front of her top. She gave a little moan as he found her nipples. Swiftly closing her laptop, she pushed it to one side and, turning, lay back across the table, welcoming him.

When it was complete, he drew her up and into his arms, and felt her breathing ease against him.

'That was some homecoming,' he whispered into her hair.

She laughed. 'I agree.'

Later, as they ate the venison steaks he'd cooked, he told her about the meeting.

She looked concerned. 'What do you think will happen now?'

He shook his head. 'I honestly have no idea.'

He hadn't mentioned the accusation thrown at him about his London trip, but by her expression she'd known her presence here would have been a factor.

'It's probably best if I don't show my face in the village while I'm here. I don't want to make things more awkward for you than they already are.'

He wasn't sure how to respond to that. Was she planning to go, and soon? He found himself despondent at the thought.

'What if I keep you captive?' he said. 'So that you're always here, like tonight, waiting for me?'

She smiled. 'Maybe it's my turn to tie you up,' she suggested.

That was something he wouldn't mind, and he said so.

Greg

Looking out across the lawn at the Party House, he remembered the last time it had been occupied. The bright lights, the laughter, the loud music that had drowned out every true night sound of this magical place.

Back then, there had also been a full moon laying its rays over the green lochan and turning the beach to gold. Steam had been rising from the hot tub, he remembered, and naked bodies running about.

Including his own.

He allowed the memory of that night to take over. Felt himself high and drunk, running across the grass in pursuit of the naked body of Marion. Taking her into the trees.

The memory was so sharp, he could taste her again. Her and all the whisky and champagne he'd consumed that night. Earlier, to his shame, he'd played the gamekeeper for them, kilt and all, just as they'd demanded. Their toy.

Why?

He'd told himself it was to keep his job, and that was half true, but only half.

Perhaps it had been reckless abandon, like a soldier in the midst of war, but this time the enemy had been insidious and invisible as well as deadly.

And always the excuses for himself. Surely they wouldn't

have come here if they were ill with the strain that was even more deadly than the original, especially for children?

But they *had* come and they *had* been infectious.

And he had carried the virus from here into Blackrig. The killer they sought tonight in the village hall had most likely been him.

You don't know that. You were never ill.

'But I was the only one to come here and mix with them,' he said into the silence.

His admission of guilt drifted out over the green water and was swallowed by the surrounding trees.

Being at the meeting tonight had simply served to remind him of what he feared the most. That he had been the one to carry the virus into the village. That he, not the estate owners, should be taking the blame.

And so, while Joanne slept, he'd risen and dressed, and walked up here to do – what? Pay penance before the next visitors arrived? Feel sorry for himself rather than for the grieving parents in those first two rows?

He swore under his breath. Maybe he was here out of relief that he had never been found out. Never had to face the consequences of his actions.

When he caught the distant sound of voices, he thought he was still replaying his memories from before. Then, as they came closer, he realized they were real and present.

Instinct took him back among the trees as the voices grew in strength, accompanied now by the noise of advancing footsteps.

He knew at once by the voices that they were local and conjured up a vision of the angry gang led by Josh who had threatened retribution at the meeting.

As the six figures burst whooping and hollering from the

trees, he saw that they were wearing balaclavas and brandishing what looked like metal bars, and maybe even axes.

What the hell were they planning to do?

He knew he should step out now and challenge them, but their fury suggested he might be their first victim.

His first thought was that they would go for the house, but it was all locked up. Might they climb up onto the lower balcony and force entry that way?

But it became quickly obvious that wasn't their intention.

The noise rang in his ears as the first blows fell. The two axes, one wielded by a figure he thought was Josh, were up on the plinth and systematically smashing the hot tub.

Another masked figure joined them, giving a whoop of joy as he proceeded to urinate on the wreckage. Then the rest joined in, shrieking and pissing, as Josh paused to examine his handiwork.

Greg held his breath, hoping that would be enough to satisfy them, but his hopes were soon dashed.

The hot tub smashed, they now began destroying the concrete slabs on which it stood. They didn't last much longer than the hot tub. Grabbing at the broken pieces, they set about bombarding the remains of the hot tub with the rubble.

Eventually the whooping and hollering stopped and cans and bottles appeared, as the gang finished off the alcohol which had propelled them here in the first place, tossing their empties into the wreckage.

All Greg could think about now was whether they'd had enough of destruction or whether there was yet more planned and this was only the opening skirmish.

His eye went to the sauna, only yards away. Would that be next on the list?

He saw a light flare, and for a frightening moment imagined

they were about to light a fire. Maybe even set the wooden sauna building on fire.

Jesus, if they did that, it could set the whole tinderbox of the woods alight.

But that, it seemed, wasn't their intention. They had sat down to smoke and consume the remainder of their drink. They were talking, but Greg was too far away to make out what was being said.

One of them – Greg thought it might be Billy MacKenzie, whose nephew Ben had also died from the virus – had taken to examining the ruins in closer detail.

'Jesus, fuck! Look at this!' he shouted.

They all crowded round, keen to see, preventing Greg from having any view, even after someone produced a head torch.

The swearing, however, made it clear that it was something horrendous.

They were standing in a huddle now, talking excitedly, trying to make up their minds what to do with what they'd found.

Josh eventually took charge, and his orders were to get out of there and quick.

And to keep their fucking mouths shut about it, he declared, as they swiftly abandoned the scene, moving back into the woods in shocked silence.

Greg waited until all sounds of them had faded into the distance before approaching the shattered plinth. The moon, half hidden by a cloud now, could scarcely illuminate the extent of the damage.

The smell hit him first, easily distinguishable from the piss and alcohol they'd doused the area with.

You couldn't deal with death on the hills the way he did

and not immediately recognize the scent of decay, but this was no deer, sheep or bird carcass he could smell.

Greg retrieved his head torch from his pocket and, putting it on, switched on the circle of light to search for the source.

The black plastic had been cleanly cut open, probably by Billy, when he'd spotted the mysterious bundle.

The smell, so much stronger now, made him retch and he swiftly turned away, but not before he had made out tendrils of long blonde hair and the remains of a ravaged human face.

Greg

Opening the front door as quietly as he could, he headed straight for the shower. No way could he get back into bed beside Joanne smelling like this.

Despite soaping himself all over he imagined he could still smell and taste the scent of decay in his mouth and nostrils.

Eventually he emerged to dump his clothes in the washing machine and, donning a fresh pair of boxers, he went straight for the whisky bottle and poured himself a large one, drinking it down in one go.

It had to be her. That's what his brain kept repeating. Who else could it be?

But how had she got there?

He stopped that line of thought. It was too dangerous a route to go down.

He sat at the table and poured himself another shot.

He found himself suddenly furious at Josh for having gone to the Party House. For having smashed up the hot tub. For finding her.

Hadn't they had enough horror? Hadn't they dealt with enough death?

Yet here it was, back again. He sipped the whisky this time, trying to think through what he would do.

Should he call the police? That thought left him cold. He

couldn't reveal he was up there, saw Josh and his mates destroy the hot tub, and did nothing to stop them. Maybe he could miss that bit out? Pretend he was on the lookout for poachers and just happened upon the damage . . . and the exposed grave.

No. He shook his head as though convincing himself. He couldn't say anything.

When Ailsa went missing, every male in the village had fallen under suspicion. Him included. Even the gang there tonight. No wonder they were so freaked. They wouldn't report it, and neither could he.

His next thought was for Colin, who would arrive there first thing. Colin hadn't known Ailsa. He wasn't living in Blackrig when she went missing. He was never a suspect. It was better that Colin discovered the scene, he decided.

Colin would radio him, of course. He would act surprised and horrified and tell Colin what they needed to do. Colin was an innocent in all of this. No harm would come to him. He wouldn't even need to give a DNA sample, like they all had to do last time, because he hadn't been there five years ago when Ailsa had disappeared.

Colin hadn't known Ailsa at all.

He would tell Colin that he would inform the estate of the find. Hopefully the Party House booking would be cancelled, the guests sent home or found alternative accommodation on a neighbouring estate.

The estate would call the police.

He might be able to manage the opening to this story, he realized, but he would have no control over the way it played out.

If it *was* Ailsa, the investigation team would be back here again. Just as they had been when she'd disappeared.

They would all be back in that nightmare. Only this time they would have a body.

And a body changed everything.

Rousing himself, he finished his whisky and, going quietly into the bedroom, he slipped into bed alongside Joanne. He wanted to reach out and touch her, but didn't, in case she woke and asked him where he'd been.

As far as he was aware, Joanne didn't know the other story of Blackrig. The one he hadn't chosen to tell her, despite the fact he'd had a star role.

The disappearance of seventeen-year-old Ailsa Cummings.

Joanne

She lay as still as possible, breathing deeply and evenly as though asleep. The smell of whisky from Greg's breath, the damp scent of his skin, made it obvious he'd showered on his return from wherever he'd gone to, and seemingly required a drink.

It was also obvious that he was keeping his distance and definitely didn't want her to wake up and perhaps question him.

Where had he been that he needed to shower, and why had he been drinking whisky in enough quantity for it to be obvious?

They'd gone to bed together around eleven, and she'd swiftly fallen asleep, satiated by making love more than once, with a good meal in between.

Greg had happily come to bed with her, saying he would have to be up early, because the visitors were expected off the overnight train, and he would be required at the Party House to greet them.

After which he'd given her his full attention, until, of course, he'd disappeared from their bed sometime after they'd had sex and four in the morning, when she'd woken up.

She'd eventually risen and gone to look for him. Finding he wasn't in his office, she'd headed downstairs, only to find both the kitchen and sitting room empty. The Land Rover being still parked out front, and the dogs in their kennel, his absence didn't look like it had anything to do with work.

At that point, both intrigued and a little alarmed, she'd walked the short distance to Beanach's larder, only to be met by the ripe smell of the hanging deer carcass he'd shot on the day she'd arrived, but nothing else.

What had Greg been doing that had required a shower and also, by the distant sound of the washing machine, a need to wash his clothes?

As her mind went into overdrive, she found herself comparing Greg's actions to someone who was having an affair, showering to rid themselves of the smell of a lover.

There was little doubt in her mind that he and Caroline had been an item at one time. Perhaps they still were? Hence Caroline's response to her own appearance in the village shop.

Greg had mentioned that Caroline had been at the meeting in the village hall. Had they arranged something between them, then?

She immediately told herself she was being stupid. Greg was a gamekeeper, who had to go out at night on occasion. Maybe he'd been worried about poachers after they'd seen the deer shot. Or maybe he'd gone hunting himself and got blood on his clothes.

One thing she was certain about . . . her new lover did not want her to ask him where he'd been and what he'd been doing. At least, not at this moment.

She decided she would leave it until morning, to give him a chance to tell her that he'd gone out last night and why. If he didn't say anything, she could ask him outright, of course. Perhaps make a joke of it and watch his reaction.

Then again, what if he started asking her questions, such

as why she'd immediately closed her laptop when he arrived home unexpectedly, and distracted him still further from what she'd been doing by offering herself up to him.

What if he asked her outright what she was writing about, or why she was really here?

What would she say then?

Hearing the now steady sound of his breathing, she made a decision. She wouldn't question Greg about his absence or even mention that she knew about it.

She had her own reasons for being here and had no idea how long she would need to stay, or how long he would permit her to.

That was what she had to concentrate on, and that would require her to keep him as happy about her presence at Beanach as possible. Whatever that took.

Greg

He'd eventually dozed off, entering a nightmarish dream that was worse than being awake and thinking.

When his mobile rang at dawn, Colin's name on the screen, he got up and went to his study before answering it.

The torrent of words that met him, interspersed with a series of 'fuck's, caused him to remember the role he must play here, so he ordered Colin to stop, take a breath, then tell him exactly what was wrong.

Colin's voice was shaking as he tried to do as asked.

'I went to the Party House first thing. I was worried . . . and I saw it.'

'Saw what?' Greg demanded.

There was the sound of a swallow, then the choking words . . . 'The hot tub's all smashed up.'

'What?' Greg demanded. 'Who the fuck?'

'That's not the worse part,' Colin stuttered.

'What then?' he demanded.

'They broke the concrete slabs and there's something buried in the sand.' Colin ground to a halt.

'Fuck's sake, Colin. Get a grip. What exactly did you see?'

'It's wrapped in plastic, but I saw the face. I saw the fucking face.'

'What do you mean, a face?' He made himself sound irritated.

41

Colin came back in. 'It's a lassie. Her hair . . . it's a dead lassie buried under the hot tub.'

Greg, trying to sound newly shocked himself, asked if Colin had called the police.

'Not yet. I called you first. Maybe it's that girl. You know, the one that disappeared—'

Greg interrupted him. 'Shut up and listen, Colin. You need to cover the area, before the guests come. Use one of the big tarpaulins. That way it won't be visible. If the cars arrive from Inverness before I get there, tell whoever's in charge that the hot tub's been damaged so it won't be in use. As soon as the scene's protected, call the police. I'll phone the company now and explain there's been an incident in the grounds and the police have been informed. They can decide how to deal with it after that.'

Colin sounded calmer now as he accepted his instructions.

Greg told him he'd done well. 'I'll be with you shortly.'

He was quietly congratulating himself on the fact that his plan, constructed last night, had been the right one, then he realized that Joanne was standing at the study door.

How long had she been there and how much had she heard?

'What's wrong?' she asked.

What should he tell her? He made a split-second decision not to include the body, which would immediately drag up the Ailsa story. Something he wasn't keen to mention until he had to.

'Someone's vandalized the hot tub at the Party House, and the guests arrive this morning. We're trying to sort something out.' He hoped that would be enough for the moment. 'I have to speak to the owners, then head up there.'

He could tell by her expression that she thought the phone

call had been worse than that, so chances were she'd been there when he'd had to shout at Colin to pull himself together.

'Sorry, I need to phone the estate owners,' he said to distract her. 'Maybe you could put on some coffee?'

After he heard her go downstairs, Greg shut the study door and attempted to make the call, only to have it go to voicemail with, 'The office is currently closed. Please leave a message.'

Greg recorded a brief piece regarding vandalism in the grounds of Ard Choille, and that the police were involved, then rang off.

Dressed now, he went downstairs, to be greeted by the smell of fresh coffee – Joanne had done as asked. She'd also made him a bacon roll to take away.

He thanked her with a kiss. 'I'm not sure how long this will take.'

'Don't worry. I can occupy myself,' Joanne said with a supportive smile. 'Shall I take something out of the freezer for dinner?'

'I've fresh salmon in the outside larder if you fancy a change from meat,' he said. 'Good job you're not vegetarian.'

'Who said I'm not?' The look she gave him had him worried for a moment, before she laughed. 'Go to it, Mellors. I'll see you when you get back.'

'I'll look forward to it, Lady Chatterley.'

Joanne

She watched the Land Rover depart, giving it her usual wave and receiving a hoot of the horn in response.

Back in the kitchen, she sat down to consider what had just happened.

Greg hadn't been exactly truthful about his conversation with a traumatized Colin. She knew that because she'd stood out of sight and listened. And whatever had freaked Colin had been more than just an attack on the hot tub.

And why had Greg avoided telling her what that something was? Could it be because he didn't want her to know at all, or just not until he'd viewed whatever it was for himself?

Then another scenario suggested itself.

Might Colin's call be related to what Greg had been doing in the middle of the night? The reason why he'd had to shower and wash his clothes when he came back? Why he'd needed a stiff drink?

It had been clear when he'd returned from the council meeting that he didn't want this group of visitors to arrive. That he thought they were opening the Party House up too soon after the virus deaths.

She stopped herself there.

She just couldn't see Greg vandalizing the property, knowing that the blame would likely land on Josh's gang because of their behaviour last night. Greg wouldn't do that.

She chided herself at this point. Let's face it, she had absolutely no idea what Greg was capable of, outside of sex, which was how they'd spent most of their time together.

She thought back to yesterday evening. How rattled she'd been when she'd suddenly realized he was right behind her and might see what she'd been writing.

She'd immediately shut down her laptop and presented herself to him to make sure he wouldn't ask. And it had worked.

Hearing a car approach now, she rose swiftly and went to the window, wondering if Greg had forgotten something, only to see it was a police car.

Still in her dressing gown, she answered the door.

'Morning, Miss. PC Harry McGowan. I'm looking for Greg?'

'He just left five minutes ago, to go to the Party House. Colin called first thing about some vandalism, he said.'

'Right, Miss . . . ?' He waited, obviously looking for a name.

'Addington,' she offered. 'Joanne Addington.'

'Ah, Greg's visitor from London. A short break, is it?'

Joanne felt herself bristling, despite the smile on the policeman's face. 'Lockdown's over,' she found herself reminding him. 'It's perfectly legal to travel about the UK.'

He nodded. 'Well, I hope you enjoy your wee holiday, Miss Addington.'

As he headed for the car, Joanne went back inside and shut the door, aware that she had begun to blush under his keen stare. Why should she apologize for being here anyway? Or say how long it was for?

She realized she was annoyed because he was a policeman, and she didn't want a police officer to know anything about her, or her whereabouts.

Then you shouldn't have answered the door.

If she hadn't, the likelihood was that he would have just walked in. After all, Greg never locked the door, as apparently no one else did in Blackrig.

Watching from the window, she saw the police car turn onto the track to the Party House.

What the hell had happened up there?

She decided it was time she found out.

Greg had given her a small set of binoculars and a telescope for when she went walking, telling her, 'The binoculars are for scanning. The spyglass to magnify.'

She was pretty sure she could see the grounds of the infamous house from the top of the hill behind Beanach, especially via the telescope. Joanne decided to get dressed and make use of it.

Greg

As he pulled up short of the tarpaulin-covered hot tub, a fraught Colin came hurrying towards him.

'They're here already. Two carloads plus caterers. I explained about the damaged hot tub. The one who says he booked the place told me they don't care. They'll stay anyway. He's called Aidan Stratton.'

At that name, Greg swore inwardly. Stratton was CEO of Global Investment Holdings and they'd met before. Greg had no doubt Stratton would remember that.

'And the police?' he said.

'I called Harry,' Colin confirmed. 'He says he'll take a run up.' He hesitated. 'I didn't mention . . . *it*. You can't see it unless you pull back the plastic.'

Greg had a terrible thought. 'Tell me you didn't touch the plastic?'

Colin went as white as a sheet. 'Jesus Christ. I wanted Harry to spot her first. Now I'll have to tell him I did. He'll wonder why I didn't mention a body on the phone.'

Greg's brain was already racing after hearing Stratton's name. Now this.

'Just tell Harry you touched the plastic.'

'But if my DNA is on it—' Colin's eyes widened in horror.

'Fuck's sake, Colin, you didn't live here when she disappeared.'

'So you *do* think it's the missing lassie?'

Greg was saved from answering as a tall blond man in his thirties emerged from the house and came striding towards them.

'That's him. That's the one I spoke to,' Colin said under his breath.

'Wait here for Harry. I'll go and speak to Mr Stratton,' Greg ordered, having no wish for Colin to be there when Stratton recognized him, which he undoubtedly would.

Stratton's grip was firm and his gaze direct as he took Greg's hand. 'Your man told me about the damage. We'd prefer to stay despite that.' He halted there, before saying, 'We've met before, I believe. The last time we were here.'

Greg waited, wondering how much Stratton recalled, considering how wasted the man had been.

'I remember,' Stratton continued. 'You came to our lock-down party. You were with Marion, I believe. Think it was the kilt that got you an invite.' He was eyeing Greg, waiting for him to acknowledge the fact that he too had broken the law.

Greg gave a brief nod. 'I did stop by to check on you, yes. Is it the same group?'

'If you're asking if Marion's with us, the answer, sadly, is no.' He pulled a 'sorry' face. 'All different women this time, but just as pretty. Only Brian and I were here last time. The other men are business acquaintances.' He smiled.

Greg changed the subject. 'The police will want to examine the damage.'

'It won't stop us having fun, I can assure you. In fact, it'll add to it. The wilds of Scotland, restless natives, et cetera.' He gave a little laugh.

All Greg could think about was the body, but it would be

up to the police now to decide if the occupants of the Party House could stay.

Seeing the approach of the patrol car, he turned and, excusing himself, went to speak to Harry.

'I called in at Beanach,' Harry said as he climbed out of the car. 'Met your visitor. *Very* nice.' He raised an eyebrow. 'Your London trip paid off, then, in more ways than one.' He glanced from Greg to the Party House and back again.

'I tried to stop them coming, but they were on the night train. They may want to leave once you've taken a look.'

Harry, picking up on the signal between Greg and Colin, said, 'What's going on?'

'Come and see,' Colin said, looking relieved that Greg was encouraging him to be truthful.

'So why the tarpaulin?' Harry said on approach. 'Too messy for the visitors to see?'

'Greg told me to cover it,' Colin said, swiftly passing the buck.

Greg didn't care. He was too intent on what would happen when the tarpaulin was pulled back.

As Colin removed the stones holding it in place, Greg mustered himself to help pull it off, the image of what he'd viewed last night being slowly revealed.

'Good thinking on the cover,' Harry said as the damage together with the abandoned weapons came into view. 'Hopefully we'll pick up some fingerprints from all of this.' He turned to Greg. 'You were at last night's meeting, I take it?'

Greg nodded.

'So you heard the threats Josh Huntly and his gang made?'

'Josh wasn't the only angry person in that room,' Greg told him in an effort to avoid pointing the finger.

Moments crept by as Harry checked out the shattered basin and commented on the smell of urine. When he began to slowly walk the perimeter, Greg nodded at Colin to reveal what he'd found.

Colin, panicking now, shook his head. That wasn't going to happen.

At that precise moment, Harry hunkered down and gave a little whistle.

'Fucking hell, did you see this?' He looked up at Colin.

'See what?' Colin said stupidly.

Greg, while groaning inwardly, prepared himself to express horror at what Harry had just found.

Joanne

Her spirits lifted as she climbed the hill behind the house. Above her, small white clouds patched a sky so blue it was hard to believe it was real.

Reaching the top, she turned to look down on the panorama that was Blackrig, nestled in its wooded glen. The single road running through. The small church, the village hall, the school, the shop, the little hotel. The other white houses that lay scattered across the surrounding hills, including Beanach.

A world that looked secluded and safe. Until the invisible enemy had arrived.

She thought of a parallel English story, which she might use in the piece she was writing, about the little village of Eyam, in the Peak District. In 1655, the bubonic plague had been brought to Eyam from London in a flea-infested bolt of cloth.

There, the villagers had closed themselves off to prevent the plague from spreading to the surrounding area. One woman had buried six of her children and her husband.

According to Greg, something similar had happened in Blackrig. The locals, with no idea initially how the new variant had reached the village during strict lockdown, hadn't tried to flee. They'd remained isolated, supporting one another, and had still buried their children.

It was only later the people of Blackrig had discovered that the virus had been brought from London to the Party House.

No wonder they were still angry about it reopening. She couldn't blame them for that. Nor for their concerns about visitors arriving in the village . . . visitors like her. Adjusting the spyglass, she sought and found the walled local graveyard nestled among the trees. A little further west lay a clearing with what looked like dark peaty pools and fallen mossy trunks.

There were other shapes there too – animal carvings, she thought. A roe deer and a pair of wolves. Others she couldn't make out even with the spyglass.

Greg had mentioned there was a carving trail in the woods, so she assumed this must be it.

She would go there on her next walk, she decided, explore the woods and maybe visit the graveyard. She could clearly do that without ever showing her face in the village.

Turning, she now focused on the road from Blackrig to Beanach, searching for the rough track through the pine-woods Greg had taken her on, when he'd brought her from the station.

She could recall the experience in detail. The almost over-powering scent of the trees as she'd emerged from the vehicle. Greg's hand firmly taking hers. The realization of how strong he was. How isolated they were. How she didn't know what this man would be like in his own environment, with no one around to hear what he said or did.

How she'd feared that she'd made a mistake coming here. That Greg might be taking her into the woods to harm her. That no one in London knew where she was, so no one would come looking for her here.

And yet despite all of that, Greg's hand, encasing hers, had also strengthened her desire for him.

As the spyglass now found and focused on the ancient pine tree in its own little clearing, she relived the moment when she'd realized Greg had listened to her drunken woodland fantasy . . . and had created it here for her. Any fear she'd had about his true nature had left her at that point.

So why was it back gnawing at her now? Was it because he'd gone out in the middle of the night and had avoided telling her? Or why whatever he'd been doing necessitated him having a shower and washing his clothes?

She abandoned that line of thought as she noted that the track they'd taken to the ancient pine eventually emerged from the woods onto a big open grassy area in front of what just might be the infamous Party House.

A silvery grey, like the birch trees that surrounded it on three sides, the house looked like something out of a fairy tale, encircled as it was by walkways and balconies, with what was undoubtedly a real tree emerging from its roof.

It was then she noticed that two more police vehicles, one a van, were heading up the road from Blackrig towards the house.

That's weird, she thought. Greg hadn't said the vandalism was serious.

She contemplated trying to call him, then decided against it. Instead, she would head for the track through the woods and take a closer look herself.

Twenty minutes later, making sure to keep out of sight, she chose her vantage point, directing the spyglass on what she saw was a recently erected forensic tent near the strip of sand at the edge of the nearby lochan, with white-suited personnel milling about.

What on earth had happened that required such activity? Surely they couldn't be here because someone had damaged a hot tub?

She swung the spyglass towards the house to discover two big 4x4 vehicles parked outside, plus what looked like a caterer's van. On the middle front balcony, a group of men and women were visible, apparently chatting and drinking champagne as they viewed what was going on in the grounds.

So the visitors had already arrived and they didn't look remotely concerned about taking up residence near a crime scene. In fact, it resembled a party.

Spotting Greg's Land Rover parked next to PC McGowan's cop car, she scanned the area looking for Greg and thought she spotted his figure up near the house.

Even as that thought occurred, she heard the crack of a twig behind her.

Realizing there was no way she could leave quickly enough to avoid a challenge, she slipped the spyglass into her pocket and turned to face whoever was about to emerge from the trees behind her.

Greg

Spotting the glint of the glass from the nearby woods, he'd come to check who was spying on them. His first thought as he circled round to approach undetected was that it might be one of the gang from last night's rampage, here to view the fallout of their escapade.

If so, he planned to give them a piece of his mind. Maybe even tell them he'd been a witness to their actions, before ordering them to fuck off or he would tell the police exactly who had destroyed the hot tub.

That would be preferable to a reporter who'd discovered there was a major crime scene at Blackrig's infamous Party House.

But who would inform the press? Not Harry, but once the call went out to Inverness about a body being discovered, someone at HQ might well pass it on to a newspaper for an agreed payback. The most likely informer had to be Aidan Stratton. Getting the Party House in the news again would be seen by him as a plus at any time.

His own anger at the imagined intrusion had grown with every step and was at its height as he approached the fantasy tree where he and Joanne had coupled so wildly on her arrival.

That's where he cracked a twig loud enough for the watcher to hear. He'd halted then, listening for the attempted getaway, which he intended to pursue.

In this he was wrong. The spy remained where they were, even though it was clear that they'd heard his noisy approach.

Startled now himself, he realized the slight figure wasn't one of the six men from last night, or a reporter, but that of Joanne, who now turned to look at him.

It was difficult to say who was the most embarrassed by her discovery, Joanne or himself.

'Greg, I was just looking for you. I saw your Land Rover . . .' She drew to a halt, and he knew it was because of the anger suffusing his face.

'What are you doing here?' he heard himself demand.

He could see he'd made a mistake right away by her expression. Her embarrassment had gone, defiance replacing it.

'I was out walking on the hill with the spyglass *you* gave me. I saw the Party House and more police vehicles arriving. You said there'd been a bit of trouble. That looked like big trouble. So I came for a look.'

He heard himself evading the truth, which seemed to have become a habit of late. 'The hot tub was attacked and destroyed. The owners wanted the damage examined properly.'

'And that's why all those police officers are there? For damage to a hot tub?'

Greg reminded himself that it would be all round the village like wildfire soon. Plus it would no doubt reach the national news. So why not tell her?

'They found something under the hot tub.'

'What did they find?' she demanded.

He hesitated, hating having to say it. '*Possible* human remains.' *There was no possible about it.*

Joanne looked stunned. 'They found a body below the hot tub?'

He nodded, thinking how much worse 'a body' sounded than 'human remains'.

'How long has it been there?'

Greg shook his head, although he was pretty sure of the answer.

'Could it be that girl who disappeared?'

'How do you know about that?' he said sharply.

'I did some research on Blackrig after you told me about the virus deaths and the Party House. The story came up.'

Of course it would. He shouldn't be surprised. Nor should he be surprised that she'd done her homework. He wondered exactly when she'd checked out Blackrig. Before she came here? Or only after he'd told her about the virus deaths?

Or even before she'd met him?

He was suddenly reminded of how she'd greeted him as he'd entered that London dining room. How he'd had the notion that she hadn't been there by chance.

Greg forced himself to relax. Joanne wasn't a part of any of this. And it wasn't her fault she'd seen the police presence.

He apologized for his sharpness. 'The village is mad that there are folk in the Party House again. I suspect someone came here to destroy the hot tub, hoping it would mean the visitors wouldn't come . . .' He tailed off.

'Did they see the remains?'

'I don't know,' he said, adding another lie to the increasing list.

'So who spotted what had happened?'

'Colin saw the damage when he checked the place this morning. He was freaked because the visitors were due to arrive.'

'And the body?'

'Harry was the one to spot the remains.'

'My God.' She shook her head. 'That poor girl.'

As she studied him, he realized she was looking for his reaction to such a grisly discovery. His main feeling being fear, he'd been doing his best to stifle it.

When he could produce nothing of note, she said, 'If this is a bad time for you, I could go back to London?'

And there it was. The thing he'd feared from the moment he'd seen her standing there. He realized it was the last outcome he wanted, despite everything that had happened and what might yet happen.

'I don't want you to go.'

She considered that for a moment, then her expression softened. 'I passed our tree,' she said. 'At least I think I did, but the leather straps were gone.'

'I hung them there for your arrival,' he told her. 'Maybe better that we choose another tree until further notice.'

When she smiled, he felt his heart lift. At another time, he would have taken her there and then, and by the way she was reacting, she felt the same.

The animal attraction was still strong, he decided, maybe even stronger than before. Was that caused by being so close to death?

He eased away from her.

'There's a ceilidh in the village hall tomorrow night. It's the first gathering since we got the all-clear on the virus. I'm not sure if it'll go ahead now. If it does, I'm on behind the bar with Caroline. Will you come?'

He watched as she mulled this over, sensing his mention of Caroline might tip the balance, which it was intended to do.

'Of course I will.' She planted a kiss on his lips.

The buzz of an incoming text stopped him responding.

He glanced at the screen. 'I have to report to the big house.'

'Then I'll head back to Beanach.'

'I should be home by five,' he promised.

He waited for her to disappear along the track before he took the shorter route to Ard Choille. His anger at finding her there in the woods had dissipated but it was clear they'd both revealed aspects of themselves, kept hidden up to now.

It would have been wiser to encourage her to leave Blackrig. Especially now that the body had been discovered. Things could only get worse. For him and every male that had been in Blackrig the night she disappeared.

Because the face he'd seen last night had been Ailsa, and he had no doubt the forensic examination would confirm her identity soon enough.

Then it would all start up again. The nightmare of five years ago. The suspicions and the gossip. Blackrig torn apart by accusations. Both founded and unfounded.

Emerging from the trees, he passed the forensic tent. According to Harry, they could be in there for the next twenty-four hours. Excavating the body, forensically examining it in situ, before it was taken away to the mortuary for further examination.

'The killer will have left his mark,' Harry had said solemnly. 'And they'll find it.'

Greg avoided glancing in as the tent flap was drawn aside for someone to exit.

There was no point thinking about that yet. He had other problems to deal with first. Stratton had asked him to come up and organize some shooting for his visitors. Greg suspected it was more likely that he was to be grilled on what was happening in the garden.

He braced himself as he banged the stag's head knocker on the front door.

Above, on the balcony, he heard the laughter and chatter cease momentarily before Aidan's disembodied voice shouted at him to come on up and meet the gang.

Steeling himself, Greg entered to a rush of memories from the last time he'd been in this house. Then, it had been in the evening and the entrance hall had been filled with shadows. Today it was bright with sunlight from all sides, which caught the silver bark of the banisters.

It was, he thought, gazing upwards, just like climbing into a treehouse. When he reached the first floor, the woody smell he loved was almost smothered by expensive female scent and male cologne.

He stood for a moment, taking in the expensive decor, which had been much altered from that of Ard Choille's creator. Seeing the change again made him feel sad. He braced himself before stepping through the open glass doors and onto the balcony.

Silence fell as, champagne glasses in hand, they all turned to examine him. No kilt on this occasion, but the looks still suggested he might be some exotic creature they'd just come upon in a foreign environment.

He decided to study them just as intently.

The four women were all beautiful in a polished manner. Smooth and sleek, bodies toned and curvaceous, just as Marion's had been.

Aidan stepped forward. 'Ladies, this is Greg, who's our head ghillie here at Ard Choille. A man to be trusted with your secrets.' He cast a knowing smile in Greg's direction. 'And this is . . .' He pointed to each of the women in turn as the names Poppy, Jessica, Naomi and Viola fluttered past

Greg, accompanied by interested smiles, especially from Naomi.

The women, he decided, seemed friendly enough. The men, on the other hand, were observing him as one might a handyman who is required, but whose presence is not really welcome.

The two strangers were introduced first. Greg gave each a brief nod.

'And, of course, you remember Brian Chalmers.' Aidan's smile reminded him yet again that all three of them had been here the last time, and therefore complicit in the breaking of lockdown.

Introductions over, Aidan got down to the real reason Greg had been called up here.

'So, what exactly have they found in my garden? Surely more than some damage to the hot tub?'

'Do tell us if it's a body,' the one called Viola trilled.

He suspected Aidan was already aware of what had been found and that this meeting was all for show, so they might continue with the vicarious excitement, hopefully with a few more added details.

'They found human remains in the sandy ground under the hot tub,' he confirmed.

Viola's hand flew to her mouth in exaggerated surprise.

'Male or female?' Aidan said with interest.

Greg shook his head, indicating he didn't know, which of course wasn't true.

He found Aidan studying him intently.

'So, we have an actual crime scene within viewing distance of the house. How extraordinary,' the woman called Poppy said.

'You'll be glad to know that I've checked with the police,'

Aidan said, 'and they confirmed we were free to stay, since they've secured the crime scene.' He gave Greg a satisfied smile. 'I'll let you know later if we'll need you for the afternoon.'

Summarily dismissed, Greg found that the anger he'd swallowed while in the room was now threatening to overwhelm him. He held it in until he reached Colin, when he finally allowed the stream of invective to escape.

'Wow! That bad?' Colin said warily. 'I take it they're staying on, then?'

Greg nodded.

'And are we needed?'

'Our Lord and Master will let us know.'

Joanne

I shouldn't have asked outright if it was the body of the missing girl. He didn't like that.

The image of Greg's furious face when he'd realized that she had been spying on them returned to trouble her. She hadn't seen him angry before. Annoyed perhaps, like this morning when he'd realized she was within earshot of his call with Colin.

But when he'd found her in the woods, he'd been outright furious, his knuckles clenched white. If the interloper had proved to be a man, she could imagine Greg punching him.

She'd eventually been saved by the call from the Party House, although her effort to defuse the situation by mentioning 'their tree' had seemed to ease the situation a little, followed by her offer to leave if things were difficult for him at this time.

Something, it seemed, he definitely didn't want.

Her swift walk had brought her to the tarred road into Blackrig. Joanne stood for a moment, contemplating whether to return to Beanach immediately, as she'd told Greg she intended, or to visit the village woods instead.

She was definitely keen to view the carvings at close quarters, but that wasn't the only reason the lower woods now beckoned.

From the moment Greg had reluctantly confirmed that

human remains had been found below the hot tub, she hadn't been able to set aside the possibility that they might be those of the teenage girl who'd gone missing from those woods five years before.

She also suspected Greg thought the same, despite his unwillingness to say so.

From her research – of which there was far more than she'd admitted to Greg – the missing girl had last been seen leaving a dance in the village hall to walk home through the woods. There had been no mention of where her home was exactly, except to say it was twenty minutes away on foot, and it had been midsummer, which meant it was still light when she'd set off.

Of course, the police and a band of local volunteers had conducted an intensive search of the woods and the surrounding area, which had gone on for days, but no trace of her had ever been found.

There had been numerous rumours as to what may have happened, including that she might simply have run away. Apparently Ailsa had done that in the past, when her family were living in Glasgow. In fact, it had been reported that her parents had brought her to Blackrig to get her away from a bad crowd in the city.

Joanne came to a halt, realizing by the signpost that this was a pedestrian entrance to the managed woodland that surrounded the village, and from here she might reach the carving trail and the cemetery, eventually emerging onto Main Street next to the village hall.

Taking the needle-strewn steps into the trees, she was immediately struck by how different these surroundings were from the woods near the Party House. There, the trees had been much older, a remnant of the ancient Caledonian Forest.

Here, young, tall and straight, they reached for the sky, their bases buried in a wondrous carpet of heather and what looked like fruiting bushes of future dark-purple berries.

Setting off along the clearly marked path, the blue of the sky visible among the softly swaying treetops, she could understand why walking home this way, in the brightness of a northern midsummer's evening, would have held no qualms for Ailsa.

She thought of the girl's photograph used in the search. It was obviously a selfie, plucked from an Instagram or Facebook account, showing a pretty pouting face and long blonde hair.

There had been half-a-dozen witnesses, who'd all confirmed that they'd seen her leave by the back door of the hall and set off into these woods.

The big question remained. Was she really heading home? Or was she intent on meeting someone?

The village had had its fair share of tourists that night, some staying at the hotel and in the scattered B&Bs round about. Many of the visitors had been at the dance. Then there were the local men, all of whom would have known Ailsa.

Reaching a fork in the path, and choosing the route to the carvings, Joanne quickly found herself heading steeply downwards through denser tree cover and undergrowth. Minutes later, she emerged into the open space she'd viewed through her spyglass.

Joanne caught her breath in wonderment.

The hollow, enclosed by the ancient-looking trees, was dotted by dark peaty pools and fallen moss-covered trunks, with here and there a carved creature, some of which she'd seen from the hill at Beanach.

What she hadn't spotted was the centrepiece of this display.

Two larger intricate carvings, which she immediately recognized as symbols of new life. The green man and woman of the woods.

Joanne took a seat on a mossy log and breathed it all in.

She could imagine this would be where couples would meet and, she acknowledged, it more closely resembled her own woodland fantasy than the place Greg had chosen for her.

Using her mobile, she took a series of photographs for the piece she was working on. The article she hadn't mentioned to Greg. The one she would likely publish under her pseudonym and not Joanne Addington.

She was disturbed in these thoughts by the sudden arrival of a black Labrador, who immediately bounded over to greet her.

'Hello there. Who are you, I wonder?' she said, rubbing the glossy coat.

It was a female voice that answered. 'Her name's Heidi.'

Looking up, she found Caroline observing her. 'Greg gave her to me. She's one of Sasha's litter.'

'Oh,' was all Joanne could think of saying. 'She's lovely.'

'I hear there's trouble at the Party House,' Caroline said. 'I take it Greg's up there?'

Joanne had no idea how to respond. What would Greg want her to say?

She decided to feign ignorance. 'Colin called him this morning. No idea what the problem was,' she lied.

Caroline didn't respond, but continued to observe her as though she were a goldfish in a bowl. Caroline's bowl.

The mark of the intruder now firmly branded on her brow, Joanne decided her best defence was escape.

'Well,' she said, glancing at her watch, 'I'd better get on.'

'Where are you heading?' Caroline demanded.

'Just a wander in the woods. It's lovely, don't you think? Especially this place.'

Caroline gave the glade a cursory glance. 'It's a place where young folk come to fuck,' she said pointedly. 'Everyone in the village has had sex here at some time or another. Especially when we were teenagers.' She indicated the green man and woman. 'Just as well not all of us fell pregnant.'

Joanne was pretty sure that was a loaded remark, but didn't hang about for further enlightenment.

'It was nice meeting you,' she offered as she made for the path out of the mossy dell without looking back.

Her heart was pounding, and not because she was currently climbing a hill. What the hell was Caroline alluding to with the sex and pregnancy references? And she'd made a big thing about Heidi being an offspring of one of Greg's dogs.

She'd felt Caroline's eyes boring into her back as she'd climbed towards the main path, the waves of dislike as powerful as they'd been in the shop, the day she'd arrived.

So, she was right. Caroline and Greg had been a thing.

Well, she obviously wasn't with him now, which was probably why she was so pissed off.

Deciding she would keep the cemetery for another day, Joanne chose the Main Street route, hopeful that by leaving the woods altogether she could avoid meeting Caroline again.

Minutes later, she passed through a gate and onto a pathway, with Main Street visible ahead. And there, yards away on her left, was the back door of the village hall. This was where Ailsa had last been seen as she'd left to walk home. Six youths had given statements that they'd been standing here together when she'd set off into the woods around ten thirty.

The drill of her mobile broke into her thoughts. Since only two people had this number, she expected either Greg or Lucy's name to be on the screen. Instead she found an unknown caller.

Unnerved by this, she tried to find an explanation for it . . . spam, of course, being the most likely one. Staring stupidly at the screen, her heart racing, she finally reached for the dismiss button, just as Caroline appeared alongside her, waving her own mobile.

'Greg just called me. He says they've found a body in the wreckage of the hot tub. He thinks it might be Ailsa Cummings.' There was a pause as she checked for Joanne's response to her announcement. 'You do know about Ailsa?'

So Greg had called Caroline about the possibility that it might be Ailsa, yet he'd refused to discuss it with her.

Having already lied to Caroline about her knowledge of what was happening at the Party House, Joanne was at a loss as to how to respond, then decided attack was now her best line of defence.

'I'm glad he told you,' she said evenly. 'I didn't want to break his confidence until he made up his mind what he should do.'

She was rewarded by a surprised look from Caroline, which swiftly turned into one of annoyance.

'Greg and I have always shared things,' she said. 'We grew up together here in Blackrig.'

Joanne smiled. 'It's important to have friends you can share things with. Especially in a small community like this. Now I'd better get back to Beanach. Greg will be expecting to find me there.'

And with that she left Caroline, hopefully open-mouthed, although she didn't look back to find out.

Now she was sure. Caroline and Greg had been a thing and Caroline was apparently under the impression they still were.

What about Greg?

Had he invited her here not imagining for a moment she would take up his offer?

She considered what had happened between them up to now and decided that it didn't feel like that. Plus he'd seemed genuinely keen that she should stay on, despite the circumstances.

And, she reminded herself, *you came here for other reasons beside sex.*

Greg

Greg rang off, unsure now whether he'd done the right thing in warning Caroline that the police had found a body, and that it might be Ailsa's.

You owe Caroline, he reminded himself, *especially with anything to do with Ailsa Cummings.*

Besides, in a community the size of Blackrig, the discovery of a body would become common knowledge soon enough. He couldn't imagine for a moment that Josh and his gang would have kept it a secret for long.

As for Colin, it had been difficult enough getting him to wait until Harry appeared on the scene.

No, Caroline had to be told first, and by him, if only to keep her on side about that night.

Glancing at the balcony, he noted that most of the women appeared still to be there and continuing to consume champagne. He wondered, and not for the first time, why the folk that came to the place seemed to be here just to party, rather than enjoy their surroundings.

He was also dubious about taking anyone from Stratton's group out on the hills if they were inebriated, although he couldn't see himself able to deny the CEO of the company he effectively worked for. Stratton had made it evident often enough that what he wanted he got.

He thought once again that it would have been wiser to

leave the estate when it'd changed hands, but he loved this place, despite what had happened in the last few years.

You might live to regret not leaving, he thought. *Especially now.*

A swift glance at the forensic tent and associated police vehicles reminded him that all hell was about to break loose in Blackrig. Just like five years ago, a major investigation team would appear, but this time they had a body, and you didn't need to watch TV crime dramas to know that changed everything.

Especially for him.

His anxiety mounting, he noted that the women on the balcony were all scrutinizing him. The one called Viola blew him a kiss. Pretending not to notice, he focused instead on Aidan, who'd now emerged from the house and was striding towards him.

'Ah, Taylor. Just myself and Brian heading out. We'll be ready for you in half an hour.'

'Colin will be taking you out today,' Greg said evenly.

Stratton threw him an annoyed look. 'Surely you will be the one to take us?'

It didn't sound like a question, more of a command, which made Greg enjoy giving his recently thought-up answer even more.

'The police want me here as a representative of the estate until the body is processed and removed. I'm liaising with PC McGowan on this.'

Anger darkened Stratton's face. He wasn't used to being thwarted, but it was obvious arguing with the police might be something he wasn't keen on doing.

Greg wondered at that moment whether the police hadn't been keen on Stratton's group taking up residence on what was essentially a crime scene.

'Sorry, but I think we'll have to comply with their request,' Greg said, to rub it in.

'No matter.' Stratton shook his head in dismissal. 'We shall make do with the boy, then. What's his name again?'

'Colin.'

'Well, I do hope he knows what he's doing.'

'He does,' Greg assured him.

'We'll be down in thirty minutes. Make sure he's ready and waiting.'

'Of course,' Greg said as an infuriated Stratton turned on his heel and took himself back to the Party House.

Finding Colin still hanging about awaiting instructions, Greg gave him the bad news.

'You are joking!' Colin's expression was so traumatized, Greg considered changing his mind, but didn't.

'They're safer with you. If I have to listen to Stratton's bloody voice again today, I'm liable to shoot him rather than a stag.'

'Okay, boss, but you owe me one.'

'More than one,' Greg said with a thankful smile.

'Oh, I almost forgot,' Colin said. 'A Detective Snyder has arrived. He's with Harry in the incident van up at the gate. Harry says he'll likely want to talk to us about finding the body. You'll need to tell him I'm out on the hill with the Party House folk.'

So offloading Stratton hadn't turned out to be such a good idea after all, Greg thought, as he made his way to the entrance. Still, their story was simple enough. Colin had covered the wreckage with a tarpaulin on his orders and called PC McGowan, who, on examining it in closer detail, had spotted the body. If Snyder asked any awkward questions, he would brief Colin in advance of his own interview.

Approaching the open door of the incident van, Greg steeled himself. This discovery of the body was only the initial skirmish, but it would involve lying by omission. Once the murder investigation began, the lies would only get bigger.

He wondered if this Detective Snyder had already made himself acquainted with the previous investigation. Fear gripped him momentarily. Could he remember exactly what he'd said back then?

At that moment Harry emerged from the van, looking pretty serious.

'Detective Inspector Snyder's inside. He wants to talk to you about finding the body.'

'I didn't find it,' Greg reminded him. 'You did.'

'That's what he wants to talk to you about.'

Harry stood back for Greg to enter.

Joanne

Main Street was like running the gauntlet, she thought, as a third person crossed the road on spotting her approach.

It might have been less stressful to return to Beanach by the woods after all.

She turned as a head popped up in a neighbouring garden, and a voice called out, 'Don't mind them, dear. Folk have got used to keeping their distance. It's hard to break the habit even when they tell you it's all over.' The elderly woman gave her a wide smile. 'You'll be Greg's visitor up from London?'

Joanne nodded, giving her name.

'Nice to meet you, Joanne Addington. I'm Kath Webster. My son Malcolm has the Blackrig Arms.' She paused. 'I don't suppose you fancy a cuppa? I've just about had enough of weeding. Or my back has.'

When Joanne hesitated, she added, 'We can have it here in the garden if you like, or we can go inside and really give them something to talk about.'

Joanne laughed. 'I'd like that very much. Thank you.'

'Good, come away in, then.'

Minutes later, Joanne was seated in a sunny front room with a large ginger cat eyeing her sleepily from the back of a neighbouring couch.

'You're in luck,' the woman said, entering to place a tray

on the nearby coffee table. 'I just got a fresh delivery of scones from the pub. Malcolm keeps me well supplied with goodies from the kitchen.'

During the silence that followed, while they both munched their scones, Joanne considered why she'd really been invited in. Was she to be questioned on her and Greg or what had happened at the Party House?

It turned out to be neither, in fact.

Joanne relaxed as Kath did all the talking, and she began to learn things about Greg and the village.

'Greg and his dad have lived at Beanach for as long as I remember. His mum, Elspeth, died when he was ten. Cancer.' She shook her head in memory of that. 'His dad, Jim, was a gamekeeper on the estate. That was in the days when Lord Main owned Blackrig. Like many of the young folk, Greg went away, then came back when his dad died. Took over from Jim.' She checked with Joanne. 'He didn't tell you all this?'

'Just bits and pieces,' Joanne fibbed.

Kath nodded. 'Aye, he's not a great talker. Keeps himself to himself, just like his father.'

She was silent for a bit and Joanne thought she was trying to decide what she would say next. Eventually she continued.

'A few folk left after the terrible time when Ailsa Cummings disappeared. Then we lost five of our children to the virus, brought in by folk who should never have been here in the first place.' Her voice rose in anger. 'Rich folk who thought the law didn't apply to them. Like our current owner.'

'I thought six people had died,' Joanne said, puzzled.

Kath nodded. 'Five children, plus my daughter-in-law, Mairi. She was our district nurse.'

'Oh, I am sorry,' Joanne said, feeling terrible to have

brought it up. She waited a moment, then tried to bring the subject back to Ailsa.

Kath scrutinized her. 'Aye, I know about the body up at Ard Choille and that it's likely to be that poor lassie. Bad news blows through Blackrig like a north wind.'

Joanne waited again, knowing Kath would likely say more if given time.

'It's a sorry tale. Her parents brought her here to get her away from Glasgow. She was supposed to be going to art college in the autumn. All excited about it she was. We used to take a walk together in the woods now and again. She always had her sketch pad. Would suddenly take a seat and start to draw.' She paused. 'She did a lot of sketches of the carvings in the woods. The green woman and green man in particular. Gave me one of the woman as a present, if you'd like to see it?'

Joanne nodded, feeling slightly uncomfortable as the girl she'd only thought of as an intriguing story suddenly began to feel real.

Having left the room, Kath now reappeared with a framed drawing and handed it to Joanne.

The image was so powerful, it made her catch her breath.

'Good, isn't it?' Kath said. 'I feel I can see the real Ailsa when I look at it. Not those silly selfies she used to take of herself.'

They sat quietly for a moment, before Joanne ventured to ask, 'What was Ailsa like, really?'

Kath gave a little smile. 'An exotic butterfly, especially to the local lads. She played them along, of course, though you couldn't blame her for that. I liked her. I liked her very much.' Her face clouded over. 'The police were convinced one of the village boys had something to do with her disappearance, but there were holiday folk here then too. Some thought she'd gone back to Glasgow, maybe with one of the visitors.'

She halted there briefly, before continuing. 'The whole thing set the village against itself. Everyone was under suspicion, especially the men. The police swabbed them all for DNA, but they never found a body, so they'd no evidence that she'd been harmed.' She shook her head, apparently remembering the horror of it all. 'Her poor parents couldn't stand it here after that and when the searches ended they upped and left. Just like that. The house belonged to the estate. It's still shut up.'

'Where is the house?' Joanne said.

'Just to the east of Beanach, but not easy to spot from the track. It's marked Forrigan on the map.'

So it was close to Greg's place.

Joanne looked up to discover Kath's concerned eyes on her.

'Now they've found what they think is that poor lassie, it'll be bad here again,' she said. 'Especially for Greg. I hope you'll stick around for him.'

Greg

He looks like the real thing, was Greg's first thought as the detective stood up to greet him. Tall and broad with eyes that strove to take in everything about you at a glance.

'This is Greg Taylor, head ghillie here at Blackrig,' Harry introduced him. 'Colin, his assistant, is currently out with a shooting party.'

'Detective Inspector Snyder,' the man confirmed. 'Please take a seat, Mr Taylor.' He waved at the chair opposite him at the small table, then nodded to Harry that he could go, which he hastened to do.

Snyder leaned back in the chair and completed his study of Greg before saying, 'First things first. I wondered if there was an estate office we might make use of for interviews? As you can see, this space is not ideal.'

'I'm sorry. This is a small estate. I run things from my study at Beanach, where I live.'

Snyder nodded. 'I see. I passed a building next to the church on my way through Blackrig. I take it that's the village hall?'

'It is,' Greg confirmed.

'Then we'll headquarter there. Who do I get in touch with about that?'

'Malcolm Webster, who has the Blackrig Arms, is chairman of the community council.' He offered him Malcolm's number. 'However, there's a ceilidh being held in the hall tomorrow night – the first since we've emerged from lockdown – but there are a couple of rooms at the rear you could probably use.'

Snyder stood up and, taking the number Greg had given him, stepped outside.

Greg strained to listen to what was being said, but it was obvious Snyder had gone far enough away for that not to be possible.

Eventually he re-entered and, resuming his seat, said, 'The ceilidh's moved to the pub. We'll require the full use of the village hall until further notice for the murder inquiry.'

There it was, the word they'd all been avoiding, himself included.

His heart pounding, Greg nodded without comment.

'So, when did you become aware of damage to the hot tub?'

'When Colin, my assistant, called me early this morning. He was worried because visitors for the Party House were arriving on the Caledonian Sleeper shortly.'

'Is that the property's name?'

'Sorry, no. It's actual name is Ard Choille—' He was about to explain that the locals called it the Party House when Snyder interrupted him.

'Ard Choille meaning "high wood" in Gaelic, an apt name for it.'

'You speak Gaelic?' Greg said, surprised.

'My family are from Barra. So, I take it the locals have christened it otherwise because?'

'Folk come here to party. Sometimes annoyingly so.'

'So there's ill will towards the place?'

Greg wondered just how much the detective already knew from Harry, and decided to keep it simple.

'They're not keen on it since the new owners took over,' he admitted.

'PC McGowan said there was trouble at the hall last night, which Mr Webster confirmed. You were there, I believe?'

Greg indicated he had been.

'Would you like to give me your version of events?'

'Locals were angry at the Party House opening up again. Global Investment Holdings had folk from London staying there against lockdown rules. One of them brought the new variant of the virus. The one that killed kids. Five children from Blackrig caught it and died.'

Snyder was silent for a while, before he said, 'It must be difficult for you, seeing as you work for the estate.'

'I'm also a local born and bred. They know I can't change things.'

'Though you might want to?'

When Greg didn't respond, Snyder said, 'When was the hot tub installed?'

'When the new owners took over. Before that there had just been a paved area next to the beach.'

Greg could almost see the timeline being written in Snyder's head.

'When Colin called you this morning, what did you do?'

Slightly thrown by the sudden change of direction, Greg had to think for a second before replying. 'I told him to cover it with a tarpaulin, then call Harry – PC McGowan. I said I'd call our employers.'

'What was their response?'

'An answering machine. I left a message about the damage, and the expected visitors.'

Throughout the interview, Greg had been conscious of the detective taking notes. He was wondering whether Colin's version of events would match his own when Snyder changed tack again.

Looking up, he suddenly said, 'Were you resident in Blackrig when Ailsa Cummings went missing?'

'You think it's Ailsa?' Greg said, trying to sound shocked.

When Snyder simply repeated the question, Greg said, 'Yes, I was living in Blackrig when she disappeared.'

'You knew her personally, then?'

'It's not a big village, so yes.'

'A girlfriend?'

He almost blurted out that she was too young for him, but caught himself in time. 'I knew Ailsa, that's all.'

'Were you DNA tested back then?'

'All the men in the village gave a DNA sample, me included.'

Snyder nodded. 'So, who do you think damaged the hot tub?'

'I've no idea,' Greg said, hoping the lie wasn't too obvious to such a seasoned detective.

He was spared any more switching of topics by a call to Snyder's mobile. The detective listened, said 'right' and rang off.

Thanking Greg for his help, he then dismissed him, adding, 'I'll need to speak to you again. I'll let you know when.'

He didn't say that it would be in reference to the murder inquiry and not the damaged hot tub, but then again he didn't have to.

Greg could feel the hairs on the back of his neck stir as he exited the incident van, and knew that Snyder's eyes were upon him. All he could hope was that the astute detective wasn't able to read his blackened soul.

As he passed the roped-off area around the forensic tent,

he noted the suited figures minutely examining the area and thought of all the ways he and Colin might have left their mark. As for Josh and his gang, they'd left plenty of forensic evidence with the piss and fingerprints they'd decorated their work with.

Beyond, in the woods, he could see the team fanned out among the trees. He'd been there too, alone, and in the company of Joanne. Left his own mark against the tree.

As head keeper, he could go wherever he pleased on the estate, but that didn't mean that his lies wouldn't follow him.

The most recent ones, and those he'd hoped he'd left in the past.

Joanne

Kath had been right. Forrigan couldn't be seen from the track to Beanach. It was tucked in a hollow, its back against an outcrop of grey rock, its front facing slightly east of Blackrig towards the neighbouring hills.

Traditionally stone-built, long and low, with two small attic windows, it had a walled garden out front. Glancing through the gate, Joanne saw beds of flowers surrounding an overgrown patch of grass, with a wooden seat looking out over the nearby hills.

A sunny sheltered spot, where even now she could hear the lazy buzz of bees among the flowers.

She wondered what she would have thought had her parents scooped her teenage self out of London only to deposit her on some remote hillside near a village the size of Blackrig.

She would have definitely run away. Of that she had little doubt.

Why then had Ailsa's parents brought her here? Kath hadn't spelled out the reason for the family's move, but Joanne had picked up a sense that something had gone wrong in Glasgow and they'd wanted to remove Ailsa from it. Had she been seeing a boy they didn't like? Or been mixing with a bad crowd?

Who hadn't at that age? She certainly had.

As an only child of aging parents, she'd always felt like a late mistake. One they regretted. The years between fifteen and seventeen, before she'd finally left for university, had been hell, for her and her parents. She still blamed them for it, or at least their inflexible view of the world and her place in it.

And once away, she'd never gone back for longer than a weekend. She suspected that suited them as much as it did her.

More recently, she'd begun to question whether they'd been right all along and that she was incapable of knowing bad from good in the people she allowed into her life, especially the males of the species.

But what of Ailsa? Would there be anything left at Forrigan to help her understand what the girl had been really like?

Peering in at one of the front windows, she could make out a kitchen that closely resembled the one at Beanach. Greg's place, she suspected, hadn't seen much change since he'd lived there as a small boy. She'd found it endearingly quaint on first view. The kitchen range, with a couple of chairs alongside. The big table that looked as though it had been fashioned at least a half-century before.

Forrigan, it appeared, wasn't that different.

Walking round, peering in at the windows, she had a sense that Ailsa's parents had simply left, just as Kath had suggested, not taking anything of their life here with them. Perhaps because the memory would be too painful.

Keen to enter now for a proper look, she finally discovered that the scullery window at the back might be opened with a little effort on her part, which she set about doing.

Scrambling inside, she dropped down from the draining board and entered the kitchen proper. Now behind thick stone walls, most outside sounds masked, she breathed in the stale air and sense of abandonment, aptly symbolized by the two mugs left on the table, as though Mr and Mrs Cummings, having eventually accepted that their daughter was never coming back, had simply risen and left themselves.

The feeling of Ailsa's late presence grew even stronger when, on climbing the narrow staircase, she discovered the girl's bedroom.

The made-up bed, her chosen photos remaining on the walls, her make-up on the small dressing table. A photograph of Ailsa, she assumed, pouting at the camera, with what looked like the carving of the green woman in the background.

Assuming the police had searched this room after her disappearance, then her parents had made certain to restore it afterwards.

Clearing out people's belongings after they'd died must be one of the hardest jobs ever, she thought, and the Cummings didn't even know if their daughter was alive or dead. Maybe, by not stripping the room, they'd been committed to believing that Ailsa was still alive somewhere.

A hope that was about to be shattered, it seemed.

Joanne thought of her old bedroom at home and how quickly her parents had removed all evidence of her from it. In all honesty, she'd been grateful for that, because, on the odd night she did stay there, she wasn't required to stare at memories of her teenage self again.

Studying the collage of photographs, she noted one in particular.

In it, a laughing Ailsa was standing on what looked like a nearby hill, the wind blowing strands of her blonde hair across her face, her hand reaching up to remove them.

This looked like the real Ailsa. Full of life, and perhaps even a little in love with whoever had taken the shot.

Unpinning the photo, and slipping it in her pocket, Joanne made for the stairs.

It was on reaching the bottom that she felt an unexpected wave of nausea break over her. Sitting down on the bottom step, she waited for it to subside. When it didn't do so, she found herself sprinting to the nearby bathroom, grateful it was on this level rather than upstairs.

As she kneeled to vomit, her first thought was that she'd caught the virus or a mutated version of it. Her second and more frightening thought was that she'd brought it from London to Blackrig, just like the folk who'd visited the Party House had done.

Wiping her mouth, she sat on the bathroom floor, her logical self fighting back.

The infection rate of the remaining virus was much lower than catching a cold. The double vaccination programme had covered over ninety per cent of the population. She'd even had a booster jab. So she couldn't be a pariah bringing death back to Blackrig.

So why the nausea?

She wasn't exactly a vegetarian, but she rarely ate meat or fish, and she'd been eating mostly venison since she'd arrived. Maybe her stomach had merely rebelled?

Even as she considered such an explanation, she knew it wasn't the reason.

Which left one possibility to consider.

Sitting with her back against the bowl, her face cold with sweat, she tried to focus on how she might check whether she was right or wrong.

Blackrig was miles from anywhere, with only one shop,

where Caroline ruled supreme. She hadn't seen much of a pharmacy in there anyway. She could ask Greg to take her to the nearest chemist. He would, of course, ask her why, and whether she was okay.

Alternatively, she could order what she needed online, which is what they'd all been doing during the long series of lockdowns.

She decided that was what she would do.

She then had another question to answer.

A flashback reminded her, in all its garish detail, of when she'd last had sex with *him*. She couldn't bear to use his name. Even think it. Sex she hadn't wanted. Then how she'd singled out Greg from the list of attendees at the Highland Game event, knowing she had only three weeks to escape before *he* arrived back from his business trip.

She'd chosen Blackrig and Greg to be her hiding place.

She laid her face against the cool bowl. She'd come here to feel safe. And she had for the most part. Until now.

Pulling up her knees, she placed her head between them.

She'd been lying for so long, the truth was something she no longer recognized.

She also suspected Greg might be doing the same. That's why they'd spent most of their time together having sex. As though that expunged everything that had gone before, for both of them.

Eventually rising, she climbed back out of the window, shutting it behind her. From her vantage point, she had a good view of the moorland above Blackrig. Thinking she spotted figures up there, she took a look through her spyglass, wondering if Greg might be among them, but found he wasn't. Although it definitely looked like a stalking party.

Then she caught a glimpse of what they might be after.

A magnificent stag, bristling with antlers, standing on the brow of the hill.

Of course. It was July, red stag stalking season. Despite writing articles for various country and game magazines, she'd never embraced the desire to kill deer, or any other animal for that matter.

Even as she thought this, she heard the report of the shot and watched as the stag bounded away only to swiftly stagger and crumple to the ground.

She turned from the kill and began to trek across the moorland in the direction of the Beanach track.

Greg

Knowing he had to get away from the Party House and the police presence, he'd come to watch the grazing garrons, hoping that would settle his nerves. He and Colin had brought down the three sturdy wee Highland ponies, together with their two new foals, from their winter grazing in preparation for the start of the red stag stalking season.

Releasing Cal and Sasha from the back of the Land Rover, he whistled to the ponies, encouraging them to come his way.

Colin had taken one of the seasoned garrons on the hill with the shooting party. Greg wandered among the remaining shaggy-haired ponies, rubbing their heads, whispering Gaelic endearments, all the time reminding himself that Stratton and his party would depart and life on the estate would go back to normal.

It was a comforting thought, if only it were true.

Stratton would leave soon, but the police weren't likely to, judging by how long they'd stayed in the vicinity when Ailsa disappeared.

Greg realized that despite the soothing nature of the grazing garrons, he was still rattled by his first meeting with DI Snyder. The way in which the detective had conducted the initial interview, the switches in topic throwing him off guard, had been impressive. Snyder was a pro and, Greg suspected, the man was well versed in sniffing out a lie.

And he had definitely lied.

What if he'd told the truth and revealed his nocturnal trip to the Party House? Said he'd witnessed the gang attack on the hot tub? No doubt he would then have been asked if he'd recognized any of the men involved and would have said no, because they were wearing balaclavas.

Snyder would then have immediately questioned him regarding the voices. Blackrig was a small village, where everyone knew everyone else. How could he not recognize if the voices were local?

No, Greg decided. It was better this way. At least he hadn't grassed on Josh. In fact, he'd almost cheered when he'd seen him attack the hot tub, because he hadn't had the guts to express his own anger in that way.

Even as he'd contemplated his alternative version of the interview, he was aware that he was ignoring the real horror of that night. The moment when he'd caught a glimpse of blonde hair and knew with sickening certainty that it had to be Ailsa.

At that point, he was startled by the echo of a gunshot coming from the hill. He waited, hoping it was a clean shot to the heart and Colin wouldn't have to finish the beast off. Stratton fancied himself good with a rifle. Greg didn't agree.

The second one came minutes later, suggesting Colin had indeed had to finish the job himself. They would load it on the garron now and bring it down via the pony path to the larder.

Stratton never bothered with the beast after he'd shot it. Colin would be the one to dress and tag it.

Greg contemplated heading for the estate larder, the round stone building with its wooden slatted windows that sat next to the bothy where Colin stayed. Colin would be full of the hill story and eager to offload it, no doubt.

Not wanting to hear any more about Stratton today, or share his own police tale, he decided to head home to Beanach instead.

He sent Colin a text message to that effect, and with a final affectionate pat for each of the ponies, he took himself down to his Land Rover.

He had a fresh salmon in his own outside larder that he was planning for tonight's meal, and he found himself looking forward to seeing Joanne again, aware he would have to make things up to her after his earlier anger in the woods.

As he reached the vehicle, the sky clouded over, but he knew by the smell and the forecast that it wasn't set to rain yet. The closeness of the air had brought out swarms of midges. In general the tiny biters weren't attracted to his blood, although he'd seen grown men so tortured while on a hunt that they were eventually forced to give up. A rifle was of no use against an army of midges determined to suck your blood.

He drove home with the window down, enjoying what little movement of air that brought, aware that tonight the folk at Ard Choille would have to do their partying inside rather than on the balcony if they wanted to avoid being eaten alive.

Drawing up in front of Beanach, he made for the larder where he already had hanging the deer carcass from the day of Joanne's arrival. Taking the salmon from the fridge, he headed to the kitchen.

Joanne had been in here and recently. He could still catch her scent on the air. Her laptop was on the table, lid down. He imagined her sitting there, the look she would wear when deep in concentration.

His desire to see her grew stronger as he trailed her scent through the cottage, eventually discovering her in the shower, her back to him, singing something unrecognizable and, he thought, probably out of tune.

He stood for a moment, admiring the view. Perhaps sensing him there, she turned and smiled.

'Would you like to join me?'

He didn't have to be asked twice.

Later, as they got dressed, he apologized.

'For what?' she said, looking puzzled.

'For my anger earlier.'

Even as she forgave him with a kiss, he knew that tomorrow, or the next day, this intimacy they were sharing would likely be shattered. The police investigation would see to that.

As for Joanne, he suspected she too had a secret, although he doubted very much that it could be worse than his own.

Back in the kitchen, he gutted the salmon and slipped it into the range. Shutting the oven door, he turned to find Joanne watching him.

'Food in twenty minutes or so,' he promised. 'Hope you like fresh salmon?'

'I do.'

'Then I suggest a whisky before we eat.' When she nodded her approval, he invited her to choose one from the selection on the sideboard.

'Talisker, please.'

Settling beside her on the couch, he knew he should try to explain his behaviour in the woods, but before he could begin, she told him she hadn't come straight back to Beanach as she'd said she planned to do.

He waited, a little uneasy because of the seriousness of her expression.

'I went to take a look at the carving trail you mentioned.' She paused. 'And I met Caroline. Just after you told *her* about the body.'

The accusation in her voice was obvious. He'd avoided the subject with her, yet called Caroline to discuss it.

She was awaiting his response, her face a mask.

'Caroline had to be told, before she heard it from anyone else,' he said, silently cursing the bad timing of their meeting. 'She was Ailsa's friend. She took her disappearance very hard,' he added for emphasis.

'So you *do* think that it's Ailsa?' she demanded.

'The detective they've sent here gave that impression,' he found himself saying in order to get back in her good books.

'You've spoken to him?'

He hadn't been intending to tell her about the interview, but massaging the truth had brought him to this point and he would have to answer.

'He wanted to know about Colin's discovery of the vandalized hot tub, then Harry spotting the human remains.'

'And Colin never saw the remains before that?'

God, she was as good at interrogation as the Glasgow detective he thought, as he shook his head. 'He hadn't when he called me.' And there it was, another lie.

He watched as she absorbed this before asking, 'When was the hot tub put in exactly?'

Fortunately, he'd prepared his answer to that question, aware it would appear in a subsequent police interview.

'I can't remember exactly. Sometime after Ailsa's disappearance. The owners sent up workmen from the south. Before that there was only a slabbed area for sitting out by the lochan.'

She nodded as though absorbing all of this, then came the question he'd been dreading.

'How well did you know Ailsa?'

'Not well. She was a fair bit younger than me.'

Even as he lied, he was recalling an image of Ailsa in the woods. The flashback shocked him with its intensity.

Gathering himself, he drank his whisky and went to pour another, turning away from Joanne until he might regain his composure.

'Right. I believe our salmon should be ready by now,' he said, keen to change the subject.

He could feel Joanne's eyes on him as he took the fish out of the oven and carried it to the table.

'There's salad and home-grown early potatoes to go with it, plus a nice white wine.' His trip to fetch the wine glasses from the fridge happened in what felt like a pregnant silence.

After this, she would likely tell him she had to get back to London. The thought distressed him and yet that would probably be for the best. At least until this was all over.

But would it ever be over?

Not if the police managed to uncover the truth of what had happened in those woods five years ago.

Greg

Leaving Beanach, he found the sky had cleared again with no prospect of rain, just as the forecast had predicted.

Most outsiders couldn't believe how parched the Highlands would swiftly become without frequent rainfall. With the summer holidays now upon them, campfires would be the main concern. There were notices up about only using camping stoves and not live fires, but folk still lit them, and it only needed a single spark to start a moorland or woodland blaze.

The call from Stratton had followed their meal. With no mention of Joanne wanting to go back to London, he'd eventually relaxed and begun to enjoy himself. A feeling that had swiftly departed when his mobile rang and he'd found Stratton's name on the screen.

He'd risen from the table and gone into the hall to take the call.

Stratton's voice was cheerful, but demanding none the less. Greg was to come up to Ard Choille, and he would brook no refusal. His party wanted to see their head keeper, especially since he'd deserted them for most of the day, leaving them with an 'apprentice'.

'Colin's a stalking ghillie,' Greg corrected him.

The sound that greeted this made it plain that Stratton hadn't been impressed.

Greg sought a way out. 'I've had alcohol with my meal.'

'Then walk here, man. It's not far. We'll see you in twenty minutes.'

Joanne looked up questioningly when he came back in.

'Work, I'm afraid. I'm wanted at Ard Choille. The boss insists.'

'To do what?' She looked annoyed.

'Probably wants to tell me about his kill today, and complain that I wasn't there.' As soon as he said this, he realized she probably thought he had been, so added, 'The police wanted me to stay on hand until they vacate the site.' He was almost beginning to believe that fairy story himself.

'I saw the hunting party from Forrigan,' she said, surprising him.

Why the hell had she been at Forrigan? He felt his anger rise again, but tried to keep his tone light. 'I thought you said you were in the woods?'

'Kath Webster asked me in for a cup of tea when I was walking back through the village. Kath, Malcolm's mother,' she added.

'I know who Kath is,' he said, aware of the coldness of his voice.

By her expression, she'd noted it too, but she continued anyway. 'She'd heard the news that it might be Ailsa. She told me Ailsa lived near Beanach, at Forrigan.' She paused there for a moment, then added, 'So I went for a look.'

He realized his distaste for this must be obvious as he strove to maintain what little hold he had on his anger.

'I'd better head for Ard Choille,' he said, abruptly changing the subject. 'Not sure how long I'll be. Stratton will be the one to decide that. Don't wait up for me, anyway.'

He briefly considered a goodbye kiss, then decided against it, knowing how false it would appear at that moment.

His shout of 'bye' as he left was met with silence.

Having reached the road, he turned up the track for Ard Choille, his mind in turmoil, moving between thoughts that Joanne was spying on him, to a simple acknowledgement that she was a writer and therefore always interested in a story.

And what was happening in Blackrig at this moment was definitely that, which meant Joanne wouldn't be the only outsider keen to get the lowdown on the body found buried in the grounds of a posh house on a remote Highland estate.

Just like five years ago, Blackrig and its inhabitants would be fair game. In fact, he need not have gone to London to try to attract visitors. The discovery of human remains had done his work for him.

Pacing out his anger through swift steps, he was soon at the gates of Ard Choille, which was lit up like some fairy-tale castle. Despite his anger at being there, he still took a moment to admire the realization of Lord Main's dream. One which, sadly, the old man had not lived long enough to fully enjoy.

God knows what he would have made of what Ard Choille had become, Greg thought, as he spied the accompanying image of the forensic tent by the green lochan, also lit up, indicating the forensic team hadn't yet completed their task.

He attempted to compose himself as he approached the house. He had no idea what use Stratton would have for him tonight, except that it would most probably include humiliation in some form or another. His best bet was to say as little as possible and not let himself get riled. He would play the dour Highlander. After all, that's what they thought he was.

His rap with the stag's head knocker brought an almost

instantaneous command to come on up. Crossing the entrance hall, he stood for a moment before climbing towards the noise of the chattering voices and laughter, his disquiet increasing with each step.

They would have been drinking, of course. He'd vowed not to drink with them, but listening to the approaching cacophony, he was fast changing his mind, because it might be the only way to endure the evening.

They were all dressed up and had obviously not long finished dinner. He'd passed the dining room on his way up. Whatever staff they'd brought here were very discreet. The most he'd seen of them was a couple of females disappearing into the kitchen.

Dinner over, they were getting stuck into the champagne again, but Greg suspected the sparkling eyes came from more than just alcohol.

Stratton came to welcome him, clapping him on the back as though he was one of them, which he obviously wasn't.

His one concession in coming here had been to wear the Blackrig tweed suit, his estate uniform, which established him as head keeper. When Lord Main had owned the estate, Greg had been proud to don the ancient tweed woven in the colours of moorland and green lochan.

Wearing it here now, he felt like a traitor to everything the old man had stood for.

'A whisky? Or do you prefer something powder-based?' Stratton offered with a smile.

'Whisky,' Greg said.

Having been handed a large malt, Greg took a mouthful and waited to be told why he'd really been summoned here.

'We want to know all about Ailsa Cummings,' Stratton

said. 'What she was really like and what happened the night she disappeared.'

Greg felt an icy cold grip him, despite the warmth left in his gut by the whisky. Whatever he'd expected to happen tonight, it hadn't been this.

'It's an official police investigation now,' he tried.

'Ah, so they do believe the body is Ailsa's,' Stratton crowed as the others murmured their interest at this.

Only one person in the room looked as uncomfortable as he felt. The woman called Naomi, who threw him a concerned glance.

When it was obvious Greg intended to stay silent on his request, Stratton came over and, putting his arm round Greg's shoulders, quietly reminded him of his previous visit to the Party House during lockdown.

'Which you've managed to keep a secret from the locals. With my help,' he whispered.

When Greg failed to respond to the threat, Stratton turned to the group. 'We demand you give us the whole story or we might just come along to your local shindig at the Blackrig Arms tomorrow night. The first gathering since the end of the pandemic should be fun, don't you think?'

Greg gritted his teeth, knowing there was only one way out of this, and that was for him to tell them a story. Or, more importantly, a lie, which he'd discovered recently he was very good at.

'Sorry, it's a private party tomorrow night, folks. Anyway, I'm happy to tell you what I remember from five years ago.'

'Excellent,' Stratton said with a self-satisfied smile.

As all eyes moved to rest on Greg, eager for the story, Stratton topped up his whisky glass.

'To wet your whistle.'

Naomi had chosen a seat close to him and Greg was suddenly assailed by her scent and the proximity of her body.

'I'm sorry about this,' she whispered, her eyes showing her concern.

He nodded his thanks, pleased that he had at least one supporter among what felt like a baying mob.

He closed his eyes and, on reopening them, focused his gaze on the magnificent stag's head on the opposite wall. Then he began to tell his tale.

Joanne

'Lucy?' Joanne said tentatively.

'Who else would it be?' Lucy laughed.

Sitting brooding about the awkward exchange she'd had with Greg earlier, she'd answered her mobile on automatic, hoping it would be Greg, before registering Lucy's name on the screen.

'Are you free to talk?' Lucy said.

'Yes. Greg's out, checking on his guests.'

At least that's where he'd said he was going. Then again, maybe he was meeting Caroline to bring her up to date like he'd done earlier in the day.

'So all's well at your Highland retreat?' Lucy said cautiously, seemingly sensing her mood.

'I did get a call,' Joanne said to change the topic. 'From a number I didn't recognize. I didn't answer.'

'And you think it could have been . . . *him*?' Lucy instantly said.

'I don't see how.' Joanne attempted nonchalance. 'Only you and Greg are aware of this number. It was more than likely a spam call,' she added to convince herself and hopefully Lucy.

Silence followed, before Lucy, obviously trying to be cheery, came back with, 'So how *is* your gamekeeper? Or should I just call him Mellors?'

Despite her fear about the phone call, Joanne found herself smiling.

'As long as you don't refer to him as John Thomas.'

'Okay, Lady Jane.'

They both laughed.

'That English degree has stood us in good stead,' Joanne said. 'Especially the banned books part.'

'So all *is* well between you and Greg?' Lucy tried again.

Joanne wasn't sure. What she had learned was that Greg had a temper, bubbling away under the apparently calm surface. It had become apparent again this evening when she'd jibed him about telling Caroline that he thought the body was Ailsa's. Becoming even more obvious when she'd revealed her visit to Forrigan. He'd definitely had difficulty controlling it then.

Why had he been so angry at her for going there? Had there been something between him and the missing girl? When she'd asked him about Ailsa, he'd brushed it off. Said she was much younger than him. Since when did men care if a woman was younger than them?

Lucy's voice interrupted her colliding thoughts. 'Come on. There's definitely something you're not telling me,' she scolded.

True, but what to say exactly? Lucy was a dear friend who'd always been there for her through her good and ill choices.

'Something bad has happened on the estate,' she finally said. 'Greg's having to deal with it.'

'What exactly?'

She took a deep breath. Maybe the story would never reach the metropolis. But assuming it did . . . 'They discovered the body of a girl near the main estate house. She went missing from the village five years ago.'

'My God!'

'The police are here, preparing to interview everyone who lived on the estate back then. Including Greg.'

'He knew her?'

'Everyone knows everyone else here, so yes. According to Greg, it was a terrible time back then and it's shaping up to be the same again.'

'You could come back and stay with me?' Lucy offered.

'I'm safer here,' Joanne said. 'Plus it's a big story and I'm right at the heart of it.'

'You're going to write about it?' Lucy asked in a hushed voice. 'Is that wise?'

'I'm not sure yet,' she said truthfully. 'And, Lucy,' she continued, 'you can't tell anyone about this. We're a long way from the centre of the media universe, and a cold case in remote Scotland might not get traction in London. But . . .'

'Of course,' Lucy said. 'My lips are sealed.' She hesitated. 'You will be careful?' She didn't add 'this time' but that's what she meant.

When she'd finished the call, Joanne got up and purpose-fully poured herself another dram.

She hadn't been completely honest with Lucy, but then she hadn't told Greg the truth either.

And now there was another secret between them.

Sitting alone, wrapped in Greg's dressing gown, she real-ized how much she wanted him to return. The room was so different from her London flat. No passing traffic or sounds of people coming and going from the building. No TV to switch on. No radio. When she'd asked how he spent his evenings when he was here alone, he'd joked, 'Who says I'm always alone? I do get visitors from time to time.'

When she'd looked as though she might ask who, he'd added with a smile, 'You for instance.'

Finally hearing the sound of steps on the gravel outside, she opened a randomly selected book from her mobile's Kindle selection and pretended to be reading, her heart raising its beat.

'You're still up?' he said on seeing her there.

'I was reading,' she lied.

She suspected by the smell of whisky that he'd been drinking, but then so had she.

'Want some more?' He indicated her glass.

She nodded, thinking how tired and sad he looked. The sudden rush of feeling for him surprised her because, for the first time, it wasn't sexual.

'Are you okay?' she found herself saying.

He'd been studying his glass and now looked up to search her face.

'I fucking hate Stratton and his bastard friends.'

The cold anger with which he said this unnerved her, and she wondered again what Greg was truly capable of. But the look on his face as he drank down the whisky and came to kneel before her changed her fear to desire.

Greg

Greg took another mouthful of the strong coffee, hoping the caffeine would hit soon.

He'd slipped out of bed just after dawn, leaving Joanne sleeping. He liked waking up to find her beside him, the scent of her on the bedclothes.

Her presence at Beanach, he acknowledged, was both a delight and a problem.

Stratton's continuing threats had unnerved him. And being up at the Party House with easy access to cocaine had simply reminded him of what he'd got up to the last time.

What had happened with Joanne after he got back to Beanach was a bit of a blur, mainly because of his seething anger at Stratton's demands, plus the amount of whisky he'd consumed in order to concede to them.

They'd definitely made love, here in the kitchen and again in bed. Flashes of it were replaying even now as he drank his coffee.

Had his anger caused him to be rough with her? Too demanding?

Surely he would have stopped if she'd complained? Even having to ask himself that question bothered him.

Before he left for Ard Choille, he took through a mug of coffee and sat it beside her, hoping she might see it as a peace offering, or even a mark of contrition, when she woke up.

During the short drive, he vowed to try and spend some time with Joanne when they might talk properly. Get to know one another more than just physically. The weather was forecast to continue dry and warm. He could take her to his favourite spot on the far side of An Lochan Uaine. Have a picnic there, even swim.

The thought lightened his mood a little, although that disappeared when he saw a freaked-out Colin waiting for him just inside the gate.

'I was going to call you. Harry says they're about to remove the body.'

'Good,' Greg said. 'Then things can get back to normal, around here at least.'

'The ghouls are out.' Colin motioned to the Party House.

Greg glanced in that direction, swearing under his breath. He already knew what was planned for when the police departed. Stratton had told him after Greg had finished his fabricated story last night.

'We're all wanting our photos taken up there,' Stratton had declared. 'It's not often you get to holiday at a murder site. Plus it'll provide publicity for the estate.'

Greg's horror at that moment had threatened to engulf him. Stratton, it seemed, not content with ruining his relationship with the locals, had plans to advertise Ard Choille as a murder house.

'They're taking it to Glasgow,' Colin was telling him. 'Harry isn't giving much away, but they definitely think it's the Cummings girl. He even hinted at the possibility of forensic evidence from her attacker.'

'What evidence?' Greg said, his stomach flipping over.

Colin shrugged. 'He wouldn't say. Harry's really worried

by all this. He wasn't our local bobby back then, but he knows the guy who was.'

'Derek McNeil,' Greg said. 'He retired early, not long after it happened.'

'They're interviewing everyone who was here then, in the village hall, and swabbing the males. Harry says they'll make contact with those who've left.'

So, it was all happening again. The questions, the fear, the swabs. Greg felt sick at the thought.

'It won't affect you,' he reminded Colin. 'You weren't here five years ago.'

'Thank Christ,' Colin declared.

They'd dismantled the forensic tent, exposing a gaping hole and the broken pieces of concrete and hot tub that lay close by. Harry approached to tell them that the area should remain off limits for now.

'Can we put the tarpaulin back?' Greg said.

Harry nodded. 'And nothing's to be disturbed in case they need to come back. Crime scene tape should remain in place. Tell your guests to stay away.'

He would tell them, but Greg knew they would be up there as soon as the police left and he wouldn't be able to stop them. Not and keep his job. He felt a stab of anger at that.

As the last police car headed off, Colin fetched the tarpaulin from his vehicle, but before they could put it in place, sure enough, Stratton was there asking them to wait until they took their photographs.

'We want individual shots with our head gamekeeper.'

'I don't think that would be appropriate,' Greg said. 'I, like everyone in the village, am now a potential suspect.'

He thought he might have got away with trying to sound official, but his hope was short-lived.

'I insist we have one taken together,' Stratton was saying. 'The others don't need to have you in theirs.' He turned to Colin. 'You'll take it and make sure you get the grave in.'

Never more than in that moment did Greg wish he could bury Aidan Stratton in that gaping hole in the ground.

'We won't be requiring either of you today,' Stratton informed him when the photographs had all been taken. 'We have other plans.'

Greg badly wanted to ask them what those plans were but knew it wasn't his place to do so. He could only hope they didn't involve going into the village.

As the group left, Naomi, who hadn't had her picture taken, mouthed a silent sorry in his direction.

Securing the tarpaulin, Greg told Colin he would be taking a couple of hours off.

Colin made a suggestive sound. 'How is it going with the lovely Joanne?'

Greg found himself uncomfortable discussing anything to do with Joanne, and especially not in response to Colin's innuendos, so he ignored the question.

'Stratton's been known to change his mind on the spur of the moment. Make sure everything's ready in case he does decide to go out shooting. And stay at the Bothy. I'll call you when I'm back.'

As he made for the Land Rover, he could hear laughter coming from the balcony of Ard Choille.

It sounded like today's party had already begun.

Joanne

Not expecting Greg to come home until dinner time, and engrossed in what she was writing, Joanne hadn't noticed the return of the Land Rover.

When the door suddenly flew open and Greg appeared, a grin on his face, she tried to look pleased to see him.

'Writing a piece about your holiday in the Highlands?' he asked jokingly.

'Something for *The Field* on the beauty of this area, carrying on from my piece about the Game Fair,' Joanne lied, praying he wouldn't come over for a look.

Thankfully, he didn't.

'Good, then what I plan for you this morning will help,' he told her.

Nonplussed by this, she carefully closed the lid on her laptop.

'What's that exactly?'

'I'm going to take you to my favourite spots on the estate, one in particular.' Seeing her bemused expression, he added, 'Not the tree. Somewhere you've never been before.'

'You don't have to be at the Party House?'

'The police have left and the guests apparently have plans that don't require my assistance. For a couple of hours at least.'

He indicated where a shaft of bright sunlight was streaming

in through the window. 'When the sun's out in Scotland, the Scots act as though it's the last time they're ever likely to see it. So, go and get ready while I pack us a picnic.'

She could hear him bustling about in the kitchen as she got dressed and realized that, for the first time since the body's discovery, he sounded happy. She wondered if they spent time together like this whether she might learn more about him.

Did she even want that to happen?

If he opened up, he would expect her to do so too, and that worried her. After all, she was writing about Blackrig and the disappearance of Ailsa Cummings behind his back. Plus she couldn't tell him the real reason she'd come here in the first place.

Taking a deep breath to compose herself, she went through. 'All ready, then?'

When she nodded, he said, 'Right, off we go on our adventure.'

'It's not going to be a nasty uncomfortable one, I hope?' she joked back.

'I have netted hats and repellent, both of which are indispensable when in midgie country,' he said.

'So I'm going to be eaten alive?'

'Luckily, there's a breeze, so the only creature eating you alive might be me.'

She felt a sort of lightness of heart as they set off. If this could be called a date, it was the first proper one they'd had. He was silent for a while as he negotiated the Land Rover onto a rough track that led them to a tiny cottage and stable with a stone-built larder alongside.

'The Bothy, where Colin lives, the stable for the garrons and, of course, the larder for the kill. We walk from here.'

They began to climb the steep hill by the pony path that wound its way up to the west of the Party House grounds.

Eventually he said, 'I was born here. My father was game-keeper to Lord Main, who owned the estate back then. The main man, as my dad affectionately called him, was a bit eccentric, but everyone liked him. He cared about this piece of land and the folk who lived here.'

He paused there and she saw a shadow cross his face.

'I always wanted to follow in my dad's footsteps. I love the work and this place.' He turned and smiled at her. 'Even if the midges do drive us mad at times. It was a great place to grow up. Magical even. You don't realize that until you go away, like I did, and then come back.' He fell silent briefly, before adding, 'I'll never go away again.'

'Lord Main, did he build the Party House?'

He nodded. 'It was his dream to create a place so close to nature, it became one with it. Sadly, he didn't get much time to enjoy Ard Choille before he died. I can't imagine what he would say if he could see what it was used for now.' He shook his head.

'So who really owns it?' she asked.

'Global Investment Holdings, whoever they are. I tried finding out once. A tortuous business. All I do know is that they have a lot of money in the Cayman Islands and I doubt they pay much tax, if any. Their CEO is here. And I've escaped the bastard today.'

He stopped and, pointing ahead, told her to take a look. 'The view changes all the time, depending on the light. Sometimes you can't believe you're in the same place, looking at the same mountains.'

She watched as the sun, high in the sky now, cast shadows on the neighbouring hills of brown and green and grey rock.

'Come mid-August, all of this will be purple.' He smiled. 'Folk come thinking the heather blooms all the year round and are disappointed. They forget to look at all the other colours of the landscape and the sky.'

He stopped again, pointing out a herd of deer moving across a nearby hill, their russet coats burnished by the sun. After they'd moved on, he said, 'We go this way,' and turned into a narrower track heading through the thick heather towards a jumble of huge rocks.

'What now?' she said, laughing.

'Wait and see.'

He halted her a little way from the rocks, then approached them himself, only to suddenly disappear.

Following him, she realized he'd entered a crevice-like cave fashioned from the boulders. Inside, sunlight was spilling through a small opening, giving a view of the hill beyond.

When Greg pointed to a ledge where a bottle of malt whisky and two metal cups stood, she threw him a questioning look.

'Our hideout for the ghillies, while they wait for the shooting party to bag something, which can take a while.'

He poured a couple of drams and handed her one.

'Sláinte,' he toasted her.

She drank hers down, enjoying the warmth of its descent.

'It's also a refuge from the rain and the midges.' He pointed to where a fire had been. 'It's a natural chimney in the rock, so all mod cons.'

When they emerged later, he surprised her by taking her hand on the way back down the path to the Bothy. His hand encompassing hers felt more intimate than all the couplings that had gone before.

'And now the best place of all,' he promised as, picking up the Land Rover again, they drove downwards.

Ten minutes later, she caught sight of where he was undoubtedly taking her.

'An Lochan Uaine,' he told her. 'The green lochan.'

The closer they got, the more magical the clear green water became.

'I thought this was the loch near the Party House,' she said.

His face darkened. 'It is, but we're approaching from the far side. You won't see that damn place from where we're heading. When the estate was sold, Global Investment Holdings stopped locals from accessing the swimming spot near the house. All of us kids learned to swim from the beach. It's where families came in the summer,' he said. 'Folk were angry. People have right of way in Scotland. You should be able to walk anywhere. The new owners didn't care about that. They cut off access and built a sauna and a hot tub right beside the lochan for their guests.' He pulled up at the water's edge. 'So, I come to this end of the loch instead, where you can't see the house at all.'

They got out of the vehicle and stood gazing across the clear emerald water.

'Why is it this colour?' she said, intrigued.

'Scientists say it's because of minerals in the water – or alternatively,' he said with an endearing smile, 'it's because the fairies wash their clothes in it.'

'With Fairy Liquid?' she teased.

'Exactly.'

He began to strip.

'You're not going in?' she said, a little horrified.

'Of course I am. Come on,' he urged, running down the beach and throwing himself into the water.

She didn't know why she obeyed. Maybe it was the second

nip of whisky they'd had in the cave, or because the whole day seemed unreal.

Her heart almost stopped as she met the frighteningly cold water.

'Exhilarating, isn't it?' he shouted at her.

'More like fucking freezing,' she said, thrashing about, hoping to start her heart again.

Taking pity on her, he swept her up in his arms and carried her out.

'You're a southern softie,' he pronounced, rubbing her briskly in a blanket-sized towel until the blood began to flow through her limbs again. 'First up, hot coffee laced with whisky to get you warm again, then we eat.'

Dressed again and warm outside and in, she watched as he deftly served up the food, realizing this was the most relaxed she'd felt in a very long time.

'Okay now?' he checked.

'Better than okay,' she admitted.

'Then my job here is complete.'

Gazing out across the lochan, she saw that Greg had been right when he'd told her the Party House and grounds weren't visible from here. Maybe that was why he was so relaxed.

She mentioned the green man and woman in the woods and how this place reminded her of the green of that little glade.

'Are the carvings linked to fairy tales like the green lochan?'

His face clouded over momentarily before he said, in a light-hearted manner, 'Locals call it the fairy glen, although I don't think anyone's reported seeing fairies there. But it is the oldest part of the woods. The Scots Pines there are ancient and, tucked in the hollow, it has a magical feel. A bit like here.'

In the small silence that followed, he suddenly asked her why she'd really come to Blackrig.

He'd never posed such a direct question before, and she wondered if he suspected something.

She feigned a hurt surprise. 'You invited me,' she reminded him. 'Don't you remember?'

'I do.' He smiled. 'But I never thought for a moment you would take me up on it.'

'And why's that?' she said quietly.

'I just thought the time we spent together in London couldn't be repeated.' His penetrating look both unnerved and excited her. 'Turns out I was wrong.' Rolling over, he pinned her below him. 'Tell me if you want me to stop,' he said, staring into her face. 'Always tell me.'

Afterwards, they lay on the sand, gazing up at the sky.

'When will you leave?' he asked.

'Do you want me to?'

'The investigation is only just beginning.' He sounded haunted. 'Things will get very bad here.'

She put her hand on his. 'I'd like to stay a little longer, if you're okay with that?'

'If you're sure you can cope with the police presence.' He looked as though he might say more, then didn't.

She had every intention of staying, of course. More than one editor she'd tentatively approached had been interested in the inside story of the murder at Blackrig.

The radio in the Land Rover sounded and, cursing, he went to answer.

She tried to hear what was being said, but he had turned away from her. When he'd finished, he told her to dress, that he had to get back.

'Why? What's happened?'

'There's somewhere I need to be. I'll take you back to Beanach,' he said, his face like thunder as he quickly loaded their things into the vehicle.

As they retraced their journey, she said nothing, feeling the waves of his anger beat against her. How swiftly he'd changed from the man on the beach to the one beside her now, she thought.

What would happen if he ever found out the truth of what she was doing, or the real reason why she'd come here?

Barely giving her time to get out at Beanach, he roared away without even a goodbye.

Greg

Glancing in the rear-view mirror, he saw Joanne watching him drive off.

Even from a distance, he could read the consternation on her face. What the fuck would she be thinking? Jeez, he'd gone from a funny, affectionate lover to a raving loony in seconds.

Shaking with anger at himself, he gripped the wheel tighter. He should never have let his guard down, pretending that shite wasn't happening, that they hadn't found Ailsa's body . . . if it did prove to be her.

God, he was doing it again. Trying to fool even himself. Of course it was Ailsa. He'd known it from the moment he'd seen the blonde hair in the light of his head torch.

But how the hell had she got there?

He forced himself to think back to that night, aware that he should have talked to Caroline sooner. Got their story straight again, before the police started their interviews.

He tried to recall what exactly he'd said last time, because no doubt they would have the records of all those interviews from five years ago as the case had never been closed.

Did they still have the DNA records of every man in Blackrig? Or was it not the case that, if you weren't convicted of a crime, they had to remove your profile from the DNA database in Scotland?

He realized that it didn't matter, because they would simply do the tests again. And fingerprints, of course.

Colin had said that Harry thought they'd got trace evidence of her attacker from the remains. And five years, he reminded himself, was a long time in the world of forensics. God knows what they could do now.

Arriving at the village hall, he joined a line of vehicles parked outside, most of which he recognized. Across the road, the village car park was busy too, with holidaymakers' cars and a couple of campervans.

The Scottish schools had broken up at the end of June; the English wouldn't until the third week in July. So he had to assume for the moment that the tourist traffic was mainly from other parts of Scotland.

No doubt more folk would come, if or when the discovery of the body made it into the mainstream media. With no TV or radio at Beanach, maybe the news was already out there and he just hadn't heard it.

It was too late now to check online. He would have to do that later.

He suddenly recalled walking in unexpectedly on Joanne earlier, when she'd been at her laptop. She'd undoubtedly been surprised, maybe even displeased to see him, but had managed to cover it. Might she have been checking online to see if the discovery of the body had already made the news?

As he parked, he chastised himself for doubting her again. After all, he'd been the one to screw up today, not Joanne.

The double front doors of the hall being firmly closed, he made for the back entrance. A uniform he didn't know was at the door and checked his name off a list.

Glancing into the main hall, he saw the rows of seats set

out just as they'd been on the night of the council meeting to discuss the Party House reopening. This time, however, the seats were occupied by males only, all local.

Some concerned faces glanced out at him and he wondered if he was meant to join them, before the police officer motioned him into the smaller of the two back rooms.

'DI Snyder wants to see you right away.'

Why me? he thought, his stomach turning over.

The wee back room was normally used for meetings between Malcolm and folk who wanted to discuss problems that the community council might help with. He'd had a few meetings in here with Malcolm himself, which generally ended up in the pub, where the problem was usually solved.

On entering that familiar place, he found Snyder and a woman detective, he assumed, seated together behind a table, a single seat for an interviewee in front.

They were talking about something, and Snyder was laughing at whatever the woman had last said. It was strange to hear Snyder laugh, he thought. Especially since the detective was, in his eyes at least, already the devil incarnate.

Suddenly spotting Greg standing hesitant in the doorway, Snyder resumed his police officer expression and beckoned him in.

'Mr Taylor. This is Detective Sergeant Reid.'

Now that she was in full rather than side view, Greg registered an attractive woman, more than likely younger than him, with cropped blonde hair and steady brown eyes. As she mutually studied him, his first thought was that if she was already a detective sergeant in her mid-twenties, she was good at her job. So double trouble now on the interviewing front.

Snyder's voice brought him back to the task in hand.

'First, I'd like to check a few details with you?'

Greg nodded, as though he had a choice in the matter.

'Your name is Greg Taylor. You are head keeper on the Blackrig Estate and currently live at Beanach, about a mile outside Blackrig?'

Greg nodded again. 'Yes.'

'I'd like you to repeat your story regarding the discovery of human remains in the grounds of Ard Choille.'

Expecting to have to talk about the night Ailsa had disappeared, Greg was slightly thrown by the request to tell that story again, before remembering he had it off pat. Plus there might still be time to talk to Caroline about their story of five years ago, before he was asked to give it.

Relaxing, he repeated what he'd said before, noting at the same time that the female officer was listening intently.

When he'd finished, she was the first to ask a question.

'I understand there was bad feeling in the village about Ard Choille? Can you explain why?'

She must know this already, he thought, so why did he have to repeat it?

He gritted his teeth and gave a potted version of the virus story.

Her face, he saw, visibly changed when he told the stark truth about the deaths of five of the village children, plus their district nurse. Then she said, 'And this bad feeling was evident at the meeting earlier in the village hall?'

'People were emotional, yes.'

'That must have been awkward for you, being an employee of the estate?'

Greg could feel it still, the growing animosity in the hall, the angry glances thrown his way. Nevertheless, he said, 'I'm only an employee. I have no control over when the owners open Ard Choille.'

She nodded, as though accepting that, before she posed the next question.

'What happened when the group of young men arrived?'

So, someone had already told her about that, he thought, wondering who, and what exactly had been said. He decided to keep his answer general.

'Everyone was angry. They just joined in that anger.' Which was true enough.

'I understand you and your apprentice left at that point?' she said.

Who the fuck had given them the full story? It wouldn't have been Malcolm, that was for certain. He would definitely have played it low key, not wishing to point the finger at anyone.

'We had stuff on, and we weren't doing any good there anyway.'

'What stuff?' Snyder immediately asked.

'We've had reports of poachers in the area.'

God, shut up, he thought. What if they asked Colin the same question and got a different answer?

'Plus,' he added, this time sticking to the truth, 'as estate employees, we were becoming a distraction.'

Snyder came in then. 'Do you have any idea who might have destroyed the hot tub?'

'No, I don't,' Greg said firmly.

Snyder seemed to accept that and, with a nod to his colleague, said, 'We'd like to talk to you now about Ailsa Cummings. How well you knew her and what you remember about the night she disappeared.'

And there it was. The words he'd been dreading.

'You believe the body you found is Ailsa?' he heard himself say.

'That's still to be confirmed.'

But Greg knew by the detective's demeanour that they were already certain.

He hesitated, reminding himself internally to say little and to not elaborate. 'It was five years ago,' he began. 'And I said it all in my last statement.'

'Nevertheless, we'd like to go over it with you again,' Snyder said. 'But first Detective Sergeant Reid would like to take a mouth swab, if that's acceptable to you, Mr Taylor?'

He'd been expecting this all along, just not at this precise moment. It seemed it was Snyder's forte to lead a suspect down one path, only to surprise and unnerve them by suddenly taking another.

It was obvious that he couldn't refuse such a request, although every fibre in his body wanted to.

'Of course,' he heard himself say.

He almost gagged as she poked the cotton bud into his mouth, all the while thinking that they had to have got DNA from Ailsa's body.

Which would be bad news for him.

Joanne

It was as though there were multiple Gregs. The smiling funny one on their trip out today and the frighteningly angry one in the Land Rover.

And what about the sensual one? She and Greg were well matched sexually. He was as rough as she wanted, but also tender. Was liking two out of the three versions enough to stick around, even for a good story?

She was still trying to work out why his mood had changed so rapidly.

His anger hadn't been directed at her. That she was sure about. It was all to do with the radio call. He'd told her last night how much he hated Stratton and what was going on at Ard Choille. Might the call have been from Stratton?

If so, surely he would have headed for the Party House rather than downhill towards the village?

At that moment an alternative scenario presented itself. What if the call was from Caroline? Something was definitely going on between the two of them. What that thing was, she had no idea, but it was strong enough that he'd chosen to tell Caroline that the body was likely Ailsa's. Something he hadn't wanted to confide in her.

Not for the first time did she consider what the obvious bond between them might be. Just old friends or former lovers? Or might it be something directly related to the dead girl?

According to newspaper reports, Ailsa had been seventeen when she'd disappeared from Blackrig. Greg would have been in his mid-twenties back then. When she'd asked if he'd known Ailsa, he'd responded by saying of course he had, because everyone knew everyone else in Blackrig. But he hadn't known the girl well, because she was younger than him.

Caroline had said that she and Greg had gone to school together, so presumably they were around the same age. Yet Greg had told her that Caroline had been a close friend of the teenage Ailsa. A woman in her mid-twenties best friends with a seventeen-year-old girl? Was that likely? Not in a city, but in a small village perhaps?

Then again, if Ailsa had been a real friend, shouldn't Caroline have been traumatized by the possibility that she'd been murdered and buried in the grounds of Ard Choille, rather than triumphant that Greg had contacted her, yet apparently his latest girlfriend didn't know?

The more she thought about it, the more convinced she became that Greg wasn't being altogether straight with her on his relationship with Caroline, and maybe even Ailsa.

What was it Kath had said? *It'll be bad here again. Especially for Greg.*

Had that been a coded message about a possible involvement between Greg and the missing girl? Or was it because the body was found on the estate and Greg, being an employee of Global Investment Holdings, would be put in a difficult position?

Fetching the telescope from the house, she checked out the village in case there might be evidence there as to why he'd headed in that direction.

Seeing three police vehicles, plus a line of parked cars outside the village hall, Greg's Land Rover among them, she surmised that the reason for his rage was most likely to do with the investigation.

Had Greg been summoned to the hall? Was that what had so incensed him?

It was as likely an explanation as any other, she decided.

Having intended going back to work on her article, she now considered an alternative way to spend the afternoon.

Caroline's sudden appearance at the so-called fairy glen had stopped her plans to photograph the carvings there, to illustrate her Blackrig article. She would walk back and do that now, she decided. Plus she also wanted to check out the village cemetery for the graves of the children and the nurse who'd died during the pandemic, an essential aspect of the story of the Party House and the villagers' animosity towards it.

Setting off down the hill, she added a further possibility to her afternoon itinerary.

Kath Webster had seemed quite happy to chat to her earlier. Maybe her best bet was to call in at Kath's in the hope she might gain even more information about the comings and goings of the folk of Blackrig, including Caroline and Greg.

A small feeling of guilt nibbled away at her as she walked. Greg had welcomed her into his home and his life. Despite the fact he'd never imagined she would take him up on his offer to come here.

Yet here she was, digging into his present and his past. For what?

I have trust issues, she told herself. *Especially with men.*

But not all men are like *him*, she reminded herself.

Just as she reached the entrance to the woods, she spotted the post van climbing the hill towards her. Was it heading for the Party House or Beanach?

The answer presented itself as the post van drew up alongside her and the window rolled down.

'Joanne Addington?' a female voice asked.

She nodded. 'Yes.'

'I have a package for you. I can drop it at the house, or—'

'I'll happily take it here,' Joanne said. 'Save you the trip.'

The supplier had promised discretion, with no outward signs as to what the small parcel might contain. As it was passed out of the open window, she hoped the guarantee had been kept.

Trying to appear nonchalant, she slipped the package into her jacket pocket.

'Great weather for your stay,' the postie said. 'Have a nice holiday.'

Doing a swift three-point turn, the van then headed back towards the village.

Taking refuge in the woods, her heart pounding, Joanne waited until she was well out of sight of the road before she examined the package. It was impossible to tell what it contained, she decided, and luckily, since it hadn't been delivered to the house, she need not field any possible questions from Greg.

The next task would be to use it. She found herself recoiling at such a thought. Since the odd performance of her stomach in the house at Forrigan, she'd felt okay. Yet still the concern haunted her.

She would take a test and prove herself right.

But what if you're wrong?

She had weeks to sort that out, her inner voice replied. And the longer she stayed up here, the further she would be from *his* view.

The saddest part of all of this, she admitted to herself as she chose the path which led to the fairy glen, was that the longer she stayed, the bigger the web of lies would become.

Greg

Finally told he could go, a shaken Greg emerged to stand in full view of the forest path, which was the last place Ailsa had been seen alive. He wondered if the fire exit was being used as a memory jogger for the innocent or a way of triggering fear in the guilty.

DI Snyder, he now knew, did nothing without careful consideration.

So what had the detective thought of his performance? And what about his sidekick, DS Reid? Greg had been as uncomfortable under her gaze as he had with Snyder. His gut feeling was that DS Reid also had a keen nose for a liar.

And he'd definitely been one of those.

He made a call to Colin when he reached his vehicle. The speed with which it was answered didn't bode well.

'Where are you? I've been trying to get a hold of you.' Colin's voice rose in the way it did when he was more than a little freaked.

'I've just been interviewed at the hall,' Greg said as calmly as he could.

A horrified silence followed, before Colin said, 'About finding the body or five years ago?'

'Both,' Greg said. 'If, or when, they get round to talking to you, just stick with our story.'

'Okay.' Colin sounded doubtful.

'The murder inquiry takes precedence now and you weren't around when she disappeared, so relax,' Greg added for emphasis. 'Are you still at the Bothy?'

'I'm on the hill with Stratton and the other bloke. They decided to go hunting after all and he wasn't well pleased when you weren't available. I told him you were still organizing things with the police.'

Greg didn't openly congratulate him, but he hoped Colin could tell by his voice that he'd done well.

'How is it going?' he said.

'Okay. Stratton moans a lot.' There was a pause, then in a cheerier voice Colin said, 'Were you and Joanne up here at the hide?'

'We were,' Greg admitted. 'How'd you guess?'

'Someone's been at the whisky.'

'A giveaway,' Greg agreed. 'Can you continue to hold the fort? I'm going to have a word with Malcolm about the ceilidh tonight. Caroline and I had agreed to help in the bar.'

'Can Stratton sack me?' Colin suddenly asked.

'Over my dead body,' Greg assured him.

'That's what I'm afraid of,' Colin said grimly.

It was Greg's job to hire and fire his assistant ghillies, but Stratton might well decide to challenge him on that. If he did, that would be the last straw, he decided. If Colin went, so would he.

If you are still a free man, he reminded himself.

The front door to the pub stood open in the sunshine, the four outside tables occupied by visitors. Stepping into the dimmer interior, he found more tourists.

The sound of their chatter was both a pleasure and a sad reminder of the endless months of lockdown, when the hotel had been closed. Malcolm had dealt with the situation by keeping on his staff, cooking for those who were housebound or shielding, and doing up the main room in the pub.

He's done a good job too, Greg thought, as he made his way over to the bar, where Malcolm was pulling a pint for a customer.

Spotting him, Malcolm told Greg to head through to the kitchen. 'Help yourself to a coffee.' He turned to Karla. 'You can manage on your own for a bit?'

Karla smiled. 'No problem.' Originally from Denmark, she'd come over to work in Blackrig one summer before the pandemic and had decided to stay.

Greg poured two mugs of coffee from the machine and took a seat at the big kitchen table. During lockdown, he, among many others, had picked up the hot food deliveries Malcolm and Karla had prepared, and distributed them around the village and its surrounds.

Malcolm and his wife, Mairi, had been unstinting in their determination to help the village survive the pandemic. While Malcolm cooked, Mairi, as district nurse, had continued to carry out her duties, even delivering two babies during lockdown, before the new strain of the virus arrived to devastate the village and take her life along with the five children.

Something that should never have happened, he thought, feeling the familiar stab of guilt.

'So,' Malcolm said, with a nod of thanks for his mug of coffee, 'you okay for tonight?'

'I am,' Greg confirmed. 'Not sure about Caroline.' He skipped over the part where he hadn't spoken to her about it yet. 'Although it's going to be a squeeze having it here.'

'Police orders,' Malcolm said. He threw Greg a shrewd look. 'Have they interviewed you yet?'

'Just been there,' Greg confirmed. 'They're swabbing everyone again too and taking fingerprints.'

'Me, tomorrow morning,' Malcolm said. 'Should have been today, but I told the inspector there was too much to do now that they've shifted us from the hall.' He was silent for a moment, before saying, 'Have you any idea who destroyed the hot tub?'

Greg remained silent, but something in his expression must have suggested that he did.

'You and me both,' Malcolm said with a shake of his head. 'We might not be pointing the finger, but someone will. The hall was pretty full that night and not everyone was against opening up again, seeing as we need visitors back in the village to survive.'

'Pointing fingers will bring trouble. Just like the last time,' Greg said.

'About more than just the hot tub,' Malcolm said. 'At the end of the day, folk don't care about that. Trashing it wasn't going to stop wealthy folk coming to Ard Choille.'

'Stratton was revelling in it, especially once they found the remains.' The tone of Greg's voice displayed his anger about that.

'You've got a lot to deal with there, son.' Malcolm patted his arm in support.

When Greg had helped out at the hotel as a young teenager, Malcolm had always called him 'son'. As Greg had grown into an adult that had stopped, except in times of trouble, like now.

'Anyway, the police will be focused on what happened to that poor lassie.' A deep silence fell at Malcolm's words, with only the hiss of the coffee machine to break it. 'I take it you were questioned about the night she disappeared?'

Greg nodded. 'Same questions. Same answers.'

'She was a mixed-up kid. No doubt about that,' Malcolm said with a shake of his head. 'I honestly thought one of her old gang had come for her and taken her back to Glasgow. I wish I'd been right about that. Assuming the body is confirmed as Ailsa.'

When Greg didn't respond, he changed the subject. 'How long until the Party House folk leave?'

'They're supposed to be here for a week. At least, that's what they said at the beginning, before all the excitement happened. With Stratton, that could change on a whim. Add in a murder scene, who knows? Maybe he'll organize sight-seeing tours,' Greg said with a grimace.

'I doubt DI Snyder would be happy about that,' Malcolm said. 'I assume you've met him?'

Greg nodded. 'He was the one who did the interview.'

'He was adamant about taking over the hall,' Malcolm told him. 'We could have cancelled the ceilidh, but we've waited a long time for this, so I decided we'd go ahead here. Space is restricted, so no "Strip the Willow", but we've got live music and Karla's already made the stovies. We'll use the paper plates and plastic forks from the hall as usual, so no giant washing-up. As for the bar, it's bound to be lively, so I'm glad you're still willing to help. Will your friend Joanne be coming?'

'She's not local.'

'We'll make an exception for you.' Malcolm smiled. 'The folk at Ard Choille do know it's locals only?'

'They've been told,' Greg said firmly.

Malcolm nodded. 'Good. There'll be a private party sign out front for any visitors still around later. Plus we have our police guests on hand if anything goes wrong.'

'They're staying here?' Greg said.

'DI Snyder and DS Reid are in the hotel. The rest are next door at the Rowans with my mother.'

'Keeping it in the family?' Greg joked.

'At their request. Apparently they didn't want to be spread too thin.'

'So they know about the last time?'

'Looks like it.'

The intrusion of the police after Ailsa's disappearance had created more than just gossip and flying accusations. It had also caused some folk to show their annoyance by sabotaging police vehicles in B&B accommodation outside the village.

'So they're staying with the chair of the community council for safety's sake?'

'I may live to regret it.' Malcolm smiled back. 'At the next election or even before.'

They were both making light of the current situation, while knowing it was anything but a laughing matter.

Greg rose. 'Right, I'll go check in with Caroline before I head back.'

'You two all right working together?' Malcolm didn't need to add, 'in view of Joanne being around'.

'We'll be fine,' Greg said, aware that wasn't entirely true. 'I'll see you later.'

He'd been right to call Caroline immediately about the body, he thought as he headed along Main Street. Although excusing himself to Joanne by telling her that Caroline and Ailsa had been best friends had been a lie. One that it would be easy enough for Caroline to expose. And expose it she would if she thought it would help get rid of Joanne.

The most important thing was to do whatever was required

to keep Caroline onside, he reminded himself. However awkward that might prove to be.

Reaching the shop, he found a visitor reading the prominent sign that had so bemused Joanne on her arrival in the village.

'Is this for real?' he asked Greg.

'No mask. No entry. By order of the management,' Greg said with an apologetic smile.

'I don't have a mask,' the man said.

'Here.' Greg pointed to the supply box. 'Keep it in case you come back again.'

He waited until the man had re-emerged before going inside himself. Caroline, doing a quick check and seeing he was alone, treated him to a wide smile, which Greg quickly met with one of his own.

'So we're on for tonight?' Caroline said.

'Looking forward to it. Just heading back to Beanach to eat and change.'

Caroline scrutinized him. 'Is *she* still up there?'

'Joanne's still here, yes.'

'When's she leaving?' she asked pointedly.

'Not sure yet.'

Caroline threw him a 'what the hell?' look. 'We had an agreement,' she said sharply. 'Have you forgotten that?'

'We *have* an agreement. I intend on sticking to it. Joanne's presence doesn't change that.'

'It could do,' she said, challenging him.

He tried to remain calm. 'We'll survive this investigation just like we did the last one, *if* – he emphasized – 'we stick to our original story.'

She eyed him warily. 'You've already been interviewed?'

He thought it had been more of an interrogation than an interview, but didn't voice that. 'I have.'

'And you stuck to the story?'

'As close as I remembered it.'

Her face collapsed a little at that, and he saw fear enter her eyes. 'I'm not sure I can do this again.'

He went behind the counter and drew her into his arms. 'It'll be okay,' he said, knowing he'd told her that once before, and it hadn't been.

She looked up at him. 'I'm trusting you to make that true . . . this time,' she said, the veiled threat obvious.

He released her. 'I have to get going,' he said abruptly.

'I take it *she's* not coming tonight.' It was more an order than an enquiry.

He could explain that Malcolm had said that Joanne was welcome to come along, and that he'd already issued an invitation to her himself. However, he chose not to, saying, 'No, she's not,' instead.

Exiting with the lie still on his lips, he knew he would now have to try to dissuade Joanne from showing up at the ceilidh. Make some excuse about it being safer, what with tempers running high in the village.

Joanne wasn't one to be told what to do. He was aware of that, but if he chose his words carefully, then it might just work.

Joanne

Despite the presence of the package in her pocket, Joanne felt better for just being among the pines, their heady scent enveloping her.

She was worrying for nothing, she told herself. She'd come to Blackrig to be safe, and safe she was. She would stay for as long as she continued to feel that way. And the longer she remained away from London, the more hope she had that *he* would give up on her.

But he *doesn't give up*, she reminded herself.

From the first moment they'd met, Richard had been on a mission to capture her. At first it had been magical. He did everything right, especially sex. Their coupling had become her drug of choice, sweeping away any concerns she might have had about him as time went on.

He used it still, no longer to pleasure her but as punishment. His drug of choice was now her pain and humiliation.

You began the same way with Greg. You selected him. Seduced him. You did everything you thought he might want. And it had worked.

It was the first time she'd allowed herself to acknowledge the similarities. 'But I am not like Richard,' she muttered under her breath. 'I have no wish to control Greg.'

Richard, on the other hand, would do everything he could to find and resume his control over her. And he had both the power and the connections to make that happen.

She slipped her hand in her pocket to grasp the package. If he imagined for a moment that she might be pregnant . . .

That thought caused her to stop and take a steadying breath.

Even worse . . . if he ever thought that she might be pregnant with another man's child . . .

Richard had defended a man once who'd killed his wife and two young children because he believed she'd been unfaithful to him. The case haunted her still because of its ferocity. The man's weapon had been petrol, which he'd poured down their throats before setting them alight.

She'd had endless nightmares about it. Not because Richard was doing his job as a defence lawyer, but because he'd told her that, in his opinion, the man had been driven to it by his wife's infidelity.

So the woman's death and those of her children had been her fault, according to him.

Which is why you'll stay hidden here for as long as possible, she told herself as she descended the path into the fairy glen.

Its sudden and enveloping stillness seemed to calm her and she took a long, deep breath of the lush air. Here the scent of moss and water replaced the sharpness of pine.

She knew at once that she'd done the right thing in returning here to take photographs. Each carving was unique and beautiful, and she decided she must ask Greg who had created them, for she thought each had had a different artist.

Working her way initially through the woodland creatures, she kept the Queen and King until the last. The gentle rays of a late-afternoon sun filtering down through the overhead branches seemed to render them real, as though they might rise up from the mossy ground and stride out through what were undoubtedly their woods.

The figure of the green woman had been fashioned larger than that of the man. *Here I am,* she seemed to say. *You cannot create this abundance of life without me.*

Eventually she tore herself away from the fairy glen. Leaving a place of life for one of death didn't appeal, yet she felt herself drawn to the cemetery as though by an invisible thread.

It too was tucked in a hollow and her first image from above was of tended walkways and carefully mown grass among the gravestones, some ancient and weathered, others glossy in their newness, some fronted by bright flower gardens.

Entering by the turnstile gate, she stood for a moment, listening to the birdsong from the encircling trees. What a lovely place to end your time on this earth, she thought, but not if you were taken much too early, by a virus that swept through your community, regardless of your attempts to prevent it from entering.

She found the six graves in a far corner, surrounded by a white fence. Feeling like a voyeur, she hesitated before eventually pushing open the little gate and stepping inside the enclosure.

This is where the invisible thread had been pulling her. Until now, the tragedy of Blackrig had merely been an intriguing story. With this, it had become all too real.

The graves were in four rows, the granite headstones each carved with the name and age of the victim.

Closest to her were the infants. She read the inscriptions out loud: 'Tracey Scott aged eight months. Ben MacKenzie aged fourteen months.'

Then came the primary-aged children: 'Jenny Huntly aged six years and Rory McAlister aged seven years.'

Sandy Fraser, the only teenager, followed. Sandy had been sixteen years old when he'd died.

And finally, Malcolm's wife, Mairi Webster, fifty-one years.

A plaque explained that they'd all died over a short period during the previous winter. Joanne found herself in tears as she read the inscription.

No wonder locals didn't want the Party House to reopen. For them it would always be a symbol of their loss and the fact that justice had never been done over their children's deaths.

According to Kath, the visitors had come despite lockdown, already aware they were infected. If that was true, it was unforgivable, and the owners of Ard Choille should be held accountable for what she saw as corporate manslaughter.

Maybe if she told the true story in full, they might be.

Checking she was still alone, she began taking her photographs. She would write about this place in her tale of Blackrig. Seeing the graves had made her realize how terrible it had really been. It would no doubt do the same for her readers.

Before she departed the cemetery, she went in search of Greg's family plot, recognizing on the gravestone the story he'd told her of the death of his mother in his childhood, followed by his father when Greg was a teenager.

So he'd been telling her the truth.

She, of course, hadn't shared with him any of her own true story. In fact, she had no intention of ever doing so.

How would Greg react if he found out why she was really here and what she was actually writing about? Would he become like the version she'd seen earlier in the Land Rover? Would he end their relationship and send her packing?

Did she care if he did? After all, they hardly knew one another. And there was no doubt he had his own secrets, one of which included Caroline.

Back in the woods now, she chose the path that led to the village hall, intent on checking in with Kath Webster, if she was about. Kath had been pretty open with her thoughts on their first meeting, although Joanne had the feeling she was being scrutinized, as well as being informed.

If anyone was going to reveal the real story of Ailsa Cummings and her time in the village, then she was pinning her hopes on Kath.

Greg

As he approached the Beanach turn-off, his mobile rang. Seeing Colin's name on the screen, he switched to loud-speaker.

'You anywhere nearby, boss?' a hopeful voice said.

'Coming up the hill, just short of Beanach.'

'Can you meet me before the Party House gates?'

'Why, what's up?' Greg said warily.

'I'll tell you when I see you,' was the short reply.

Gaining the brow of the hill, he spotted Colin's jeep parked in the shade of a tree, his two dogs eagerly lapping at bowls of water he'd set down for them.

'What is it?' he said on approach.

'Stratton wants you at the house.'

'Any idea why?'

'Arrangements for tomorrow. He wants you to be the one to go out with them this time and definitely not me.'

It was what Greg had been expecting. His story of helping the police 'with their arrangements' was obviously wearing thin.

'Did they get a stag?'

'Not this time, which is why he's so pissed off. He also picked up a tick,' Colin said. 'Which was somehow my fault. If I'd had anything to do with it, it would have latched onto his prick rather than his leg.'

'Any word yet when they're leaving?'

'Sadly, none.' Colin sounded on the verge of despair.

'I'll stand you a couple of drinks tonight at the ceilidh,' Greg promised. 'And you can have tomorrow morning off to deal with any hangover. I take it you are coming?'

'Is there food?' Colin said, his cheery self returning.

'Karla's stovies,' Greg told him, aware that Karla herself was likely a bigger draw than her famous stovies.

'Okay, boss, I'll see you there.'

Greg left the Land Rover and walked the last section of road. Entering the gate, he found the women down at the beach on sun loungers, the view of the tarpaulin that covered the grave site apparently not spoiling their sunbathing.

He had hoped to pass by unnoticed, but had no such luck. A chorus of voices urged him over, their tone suggesting they were already on the champagne.

A quick head count found his only ally, Naomi, missing.

'Ladies,' he said with a small bow. 'Enjoying the sunshine and the lack of midges?'

'We were contemplating a swim, but if it's very cold we might require a lifeguard. Colin told us you often swim in the green loch.' Poppy eyed him. 'Is that true?'

'I learned to swim here as a boy, like most of the locals.' He almost added, *we're not permitted access now*, but didn't see the point. They were guests and could do nothing about that even if they wanted to.

'If you go in now, I'll join you,' Viola said with a smile.

'No trunks with me.' As soon as he said it, he realized his mistake.

'Even better,' Poppy offered, and they all laughed.

Greg decided an exit was required. 'Sorry, I'm called to

Ard Choille,' he said. 'Mr Stratton wants to organize things for tomorrow.' He didn't wait for a response to his apology but headed swiftly down the drive without looking back.

Stratton and the other men were out on the balcony and shouted at him to come on up.

'A pre-dinner drink, Taylor?' Stratton offered when Greg appeared.

'I'm still working,' Greg said.

'I'm the boss and I say you can share one with us.'

'Thanks, but no.' Greg tried a placatory smile. 'I'll be driving later.'

It was clear from his expression that Stratton didn't like being denied. Greg was pleased about that.

'You could always walk to the ceilidh. I hear it's been switched to the hotel because of the murder investigation.'

Greg remained silent, aware Stratton was trying to rile him.

'We thought we might drop in. As an owner of the estate, it's important to show support. Seeing as it's the first get-together since the pandemic ended.'

Greg's horror at that must have been obvious, because Stratton added, in a seemingly surprised tone, 'You don't think that's a good idea?'

Aware he was being played, Greg forced himself to remain calm.

'The village is just opening to tourists and there are still concerns about that. Might be better to have a party here instead,' he suggested.

It was the opening Stratton had been looking for.

'If you were to agree to come to such a party, then I'm sure the ladies would be content with that. Maybe bring young Colin along too. Kilts compulsory, of course.'

Greg was having none of it. 'As part of the hall committee,' he lied, 'I'm duty bound to help at the ceilidh.'

Stratton gave one of the smiles that didn't reach his eyes and nodded, as though that was the end of the matter.

'Now, about tomorrow. We'd like an earlier start and the ladies are coming along too. We want a kill this time.'

Greg made the arrangements, his mind racing. Had Stratton just been playing with him again? Or did he actually plan to come down to the village? If so, it was a truly bad idea in the present circumstances, but he had no way to stop them.

He reminded himself that the police were staying at the hotel if trouble broke out, and he could give fair warning to Malcolm on the possibility that the Party House visit might happen, despite his attempts to prevent it.

Arriving at Beanach, he found himself looking forward to seeing Joanne and was surprised and disappointed to discover the house empty. Spotting her laptop open on the kitchen table, he considered taking a look to see what she'd been working on.

It would be an invasion of privacy, he told himself, and she would most likely have it password protected anyway. Nevertheless . . .

As expected, his movement of the mouse brought up the screensaver, together with a request for a password. It was at that moment he recognized that the screensaver image was of the ancient pine tree where they'd made love when she first arrived.

She must have taken the picture the day he'd found her in the woods near the Party House. *And I was angry with her when I thought she'd been spying on us.*

The fact that she'd chosen this image as a reminder of

what had happened stirred him and he wanted her here with him again.

She can't be that far away, he thought. *If I can spot her, I could go and meet her and hopefully make it up to her*. The thought drove him back outside to scan the road from Blackrig and check out the woods.

When he saw no sign of her, he decided to climb the hill behind the house, where the all-round view provided a wider perspective, including the area of the Party House.

Despite trying not to focus on his current bête noire, he nevertheless found his eye drawn to the brightly coloured female figures by the lochside. Still no doubt enjoying the early evening sun.

As he watched, a figure appeared beside them. Adjusting the telescope, he saw that it was Aidan Stratton, but he was approaching the nearby trees, not the women.

At that moment a figure came from the woods to meet him. Shielded by Stratton, Greg couldn't make out if the person was male or female. Colin sprang to mind, but having released him from duty before his own visit to Ard Choille, Greg couldn't imagine Colin going back there of his own free will.

As Stratton stepped aside to gesture to the lochside ladies, he realized the figure was that of a woman. But who?

Intuition told him who it was before he could adjust the lens enough to see for himself.

'What the hell?' Greg said out loud. Why the fuck was Joanne there and talking to that bastard?

Immediately an ugly thought reared its head. She already knew Stratton. After all, she'd written pieces for *The Field* magazine, which was why she was at the event where they'd met. If that was true, she definitely hadn't mentioned it when he'd revealed Stratton's name and connection with the Party House.

Why was she back at Ard Choille anyway? Was this meeting with Stratton merely an accident or – *my God* – prearranged?

Totally thrown by this interpretation of what he was watching, Greg found himself wondering why Joanne had really chosen to visit him here in Blackrig, and at this precise moment in time.

Perhaps because she'd known that Stratton and his party were going to be at Ard Choille?

Then the biggest and most obvious answer to all such questions presented itself.

Joanne had set him up for all of this. Toyed with him to get the invite here, which he'd blurted out in a post-coital moment.

Employed by Stratton, she'd come here to write a piece about the estate, the village and the Party House. Maybe even about him, the head keeper.

His mind racing, he realized that would explain her interest and her questions about the estate, about himself, about the Party House and, of course, the disappearance of Ailsa. My God, the discovery of Ailsa's body must have seemed like a gift. No wonder Stratton was so intent on staying.

Rage grew to swamp him again. How could he face her after this?

He couldn't. Not immediately anyway. He would go back to the village and eat at the pub to avoid her. If she called his mobile, he would say things got rushed and he'd had to go and help Malcolm.

But what about when she turned up at the ceilidh?

Maybe by then he would have decided what to say or do, if anything.

Joanne

Finally escaping the insufferable Aidan, she headed back to Beanach, cursing herself for getting close enough to be seen.

How could she have been so stupid? So careless?

When Kath hadn't been home, she'd decided to take the path through the woods to the Party House to take photographs of the covered grave for her article. She'd been careful about the women clustered at the lochside, but they'd all been too busy drinking, talking and laughing to notice her.

Then Aidan had appeared from nowhere and called out her name. She'd initially contemplated fleeing into the woods, but realized he would more than likely follow.

By the time he approached, she'd decided to reveal herself properly and was already formulating her story. Was it safe to say she was staying at Greg's or should she say she was staying in the village?

God, what if he told *him* where she was? Were they even in touch? Her heart had taken off like a rocket at that point as she'd tried to assume a surprised and slightly embarrassed expression.

'Well I never, Maya, what are you doing here?' had been his response to her emergence from the trees.

His use of her writing name had helped make up her mind. There was no way she could reveal she was staying at Greg's after that.

'Having a few days walking in the Highlands now that we're allowed to travel here again,' had been her response.

'So why *here* exactly?' Aidan had been wearing a look which was both friendly and menacing at the same time. So much so that a shiver had gone down her spine.

She'd shrugged, then given him a partially honest answer. 'The village had a rough time during the pandemic. I wanted to see how it was now.'

'So why are you skulking in *my* woods?'

'I heard about the body being unearthed and came for a look,' was her honest response.

He'd looked animated by that. 'Yes, it has been rather fun having a murder mystery on our doorstep.'

She'd hoped to make her getaway then, but that was not to be, as he'd insisted she come and meet the women, who were all staring in her direction.

'Ladies, this is Maya Villan, the writer,' he'd announced.

One immediately trilled at that. 'OH MY GOD, I love your blog, but you never post a photograph so I had no idea what you looked like.'

'Why are you here?' they demanded in chorus.

'To hear all about our murder mystery,' Aidan informed them.

Realizing there was nothing to do but sit it out, she'd gladly accepted the proffered glass of champagne and resigned herself.

Once the women had regaled her with their version of the story, which had sounded more like a Hercule Poirot country house mystery, she'd eventually said she had to be getting back.

'I can run you down to the village if you like?' Aidan promptly offered.

She'd refused, of course, and not just because she was aware he too had been drinking.

'Where exactly are you staying in the village?'

Kath's house, the Rowans, had immediately sprung to mind, knowing she could ask Kath to back her up with the story of the odious Mr Stratton, who she was trying to avoid.

'Well, we're having a dinner party here tonight if you'd like to join us. We brought our own chef, so I can promise you it'll be delicious.'

She'd managed to stay non-committal on that and had eventually got away.

Reliving it all now, she went to the whisky bottle and helped herself to a large one. Greg would surely be home soon to shower and change before the ceilidh. She contemplated telling him what had just happened. Revealing that she knew the horrible man at the Party House, although she hadn't mentioned it before now.

I don't really know him. We've just met socially, she would say.

And what of her alias? Should she tell Greg about her alter ego, Maya Villan?

Showering often helped her to see things clearly when she was working on an article or when she had to make a decision. If Greg was to come back when she was in the shower, he might join her. That would make a confession easier.

Once under the spray, however, other thoughts came to mind. She found herself reliving her visit to the cemetery and that white picket fence encasing those gravestones. Contemplating how the selfishness of the rich had brought death to those children. If they'd killed them in any other way, they would have been charged with murder. During the AIDS epidemic, people were charged for knowingly infecting someone.

Those who'd come here when everywhere was in lockdown knew the restrictions. Were aware that the new variant attacked infants and children and that it was rife in London.

And yet still they'd come. And got away with it.

Even as she considered how she might frame her story of Blackrig, she acknowledged that Aidan Stratton was a powerful man, with a great deal of influence among the landed gentry and even those in government.

If he took umbrage at what she wrote, he could damage her career. She thought about Greg. If Stratton discovered she'd been staying here while researching and writing it, Greg's job might also be on the line.

An hour later, she was beginning to wish Greg would appear so that she could just tell him about Aidan. She would, of course, have to admit that she'd gone to the Party House to see the grave.

Maybe she shouldn't have done that, but she'd been curious. She would admit that. What else she might say, she wasn't sure. It would, she realized, be dependent on Greg's reaction.

Wanting him home now, she called his mobile, hoping he would be in an area with a signal. When he answered, she found her heart thumping again.

'When are you coming back?'

The silence that followed unnerved her and she wondered if somehow he already knew about her brush with Aidan.

'Sorry, I got held up and now Malcolm needs me to help set up for the ceilidh. There's stuff in the fridge if you're hungry. Or . . .' He hesitated. 'I could come up for you?'

She tried to read his tone but couldn't. Did he want her to come down there or not?

It was really for locals. A private party. But he'd said earlier it would be okay. Maybe Caroline had told him not to bring her and that's why he was being so weird?

'No need to come for me,' she told him. 'I might take a walk down later. It's a lovely evening,' she added, glancing out at a clear sky.

'Okay, I'll see you then.'

She heard Caroline's voice calling to him as he hung up, suggesting she may have been listening in to their conversation and that was why he'd sounded so lukewarm.

Fuck it! Why worry about any of it, she told herself. Aidan, Greg, Caroline. She'd be gone from Blackrig soon enough, and even quicker should Richard discover from Aidan that she was here.

Greg

Caroline was looking at him, a concerned expression on her face.

'Everything okay?'

Since she'd obviously been eavesdropping on his conversation with Joanne, he'd been expecting a re-enactment of the scene earlier in the shop.

'Everything's fine,' he said cautiously.

'Okay. Let's get bottling and you can tell me exactly what happened at your police interview, so we're on the same page when it's my turn.'

'All right,' he said, wondering how long Caroline's new persona would last.

In fact, her friendly demeanour persisted the whole time they were stocking up the bar together. When he told her exactly how the interview had been played by DI Snyder and DS Reid, she'd smiled.

'Ah, the female touch. So she's good?'

'She is,' he admitted. 'They make a good team.'

'So do we,' she said, touching his arm.

He wanted to say, *We did make a good team once, but that's in the past*, but didn't because in that moment he remembered how good they had been together. Before Ailsa, before the virus, before the deaths.

Malcolm appeared. 'You two ready?' he said with a swift look from one to the other.

'Fully stocked up and raring to go,' Caroline assured him.

'Right, the band's ready too.' He gave the young folk on the stage a thumbs-up. 'Once we open the doors and get enough of a crowd, I'll say a few words. Then it's party time.'

When Greg had told Malcolm how Stratton had suggested he might well turn up at the ceilidh, since he was a local, Malcolm had been circumspect about it. 'We'll deal with that if or when it happens. One thing's certain. They won't get to spoil our evening. We've waited too long for this.'

Sending Caroline through to Karla in the kitchen to check if she needed any help, Malcolm asked if Joanne was coming.

'She said she'd maybe take a walk down later,' Greg told him.

In truth, he was almost hoping she wouldn't since that would likely keep Caroline sweet. Then again, if she was here and Stratton did arrive, he might be able to deduce whether they were acquainted or not. Unless, of course, they were intent on keeping that a secret.

As the place began to fill up, he tried to put that thought out of his mind. Folk were subdued at first. That much was obvious. Bar the recent community council meeting, which had turned into what was commonly known as a stramash, the folk of Blackrig hadn't had a gathering like this for a very long time.

As the drink flowed and the band played, people began to relax, which, as Greg registered, was a joy to behold.

Once he was certain that everyone likely to come was there, Malcolm said a few words to the assembled group along the lines of how dealing with the pandemic had only been possible because they'd all worked together and supported one another.

He remembered those who they'd lost, including his wife, Mairi. There were a few mutterings about the Party House, but it was clear from those who shooshed them that tonight was for celebration and not recriminations.

Greg began to enjoy himself, thinking this might go okay, provided the subject of the police investigation didn't come up. It seemed that everyone was avoiding it, in particular the men, like him, who'd been interviewed that day.

It appeared they all wanted to forget about it, for tonight at least. As did Greg. Last time they'd all been at one another's throats and there was still plenty of time for that to happen again. *But*, Greg mouthed a silent prayer, *let it not be this night*.

He'd stayed clear of the drink just in case anything should kick off, although he'd noticed that Caroline had had a few. As the music started up again, he had just decided that he might have one to celebrate getting this far without trouble, when he noticed a face observing him from the link door between the bar and the hotel lounge.

It seemed DI Snyder was keeping an eye on the proceedings. Or perhaps on him in particular. Was it because of his interview earlier or had his DNA swab found a match?

He tried to tell himself that it was much too soon for the tests to be processed, and Snyder was merely checking the room, not just him, as Malcolm said he would.

A call from Caroline took him into the cellar, where she was trying to change a beer barrel.

'I should be the one doing that,' he told her.

'You were too busy studying that detective.' She gave him a smile. 'Ease up, soldier, I've got your back. I promise.'

He laughed. This was how it used to be between them. He found himself sorry that he'd messed up so badly.

Perhaps sensing this, she reached up and kissed him. For a brief moment he responded, just as he would have done in times gone by, before withdrawing and apologizing.

A flash of anger in her eyes told him the apology had been a mistake.

'Caroline,' he tried.

'Don't Caroline me.' She studied him. 'So, I've to lie to the detective even though you feel nothing for me any more?'

'That's not true,' he began.

'What's not true? That I have to lie or that you feel nothing?'

'We've not been together for a while now. It was the lockdown. You know that.'

'Well, we weren't *all* obeying lockdown all of the time. Were we, Greg?'

The barb hit home. Before he could respond, he heard Malcolm shouting for him.

'We'll talk properly at another time, I promise,' Greg said.

For a moment her gaze softened. 'You've made promises in the past,' she said quietly. 'The problem is you don't know how to keep them.'

Coming out of the cellar, Greg was even more discomforted to discover Joanne standing at the bar.

'Here you go,' Malcolm said, handing her a large glass of white wine. 'On the house, Joanne. Or maybe I'll take it out of Greg's wages,' he joked.

'It seems to be going well,' Joanne said, filling the awkward silence that followed Malcolm's attempts at levity.

Greg finally found his voice, although all he could think

about was what had just gone down with Caroline in the cellar. 'It is. They've already emptied one beer barrel.'

Caroline, who'd followed him out, gave Joanne the briefest nod of acknowledgement, then informed Greg she was going to the kitchen to help with the stovies.

'What are stovies?' Joanne said, obviously mystified.

Malcolm laughed. 'I'll leave it to Greg to explain.'

'A Scottish delicacy,' Greg told her.

'You mean like haggis?'

'Different, but equally tasty.' He met her eyes for the first time since his emergence from the cellar.

Joanne seemed to gather herself before saying, 'I need to tell you something.'

That was music to his ears. 'Okay. D'you want to go outside for a bit? It's noisy in here.'

Telling Malcolm they were going out for some air, he led Joanne through the crowd, many of whom smiled at her as she passed.

'They like you,' Greg said as they emerged into the night air.

'I'm glad I didn't make trouble for you by coming here tonight.'

'You're no trouble,' he said. 'But we do need to talk. I saw—'

At that moment, a big black 4x4 came along Main Street and drew up opposite them.

'What the fuck,' Greg said as he realized who was inside.

'Hey, Taylor,' Stratton called over on exiting the vehicle. 'And Maya. What a surprise. You didn't mention you knew my head keeper when we met earlier today?'

As Greg felt Joanne quickly free her hand from his own, his main thought was: who the fuck was Maya?

Greg

Ignoring Stratton's shout, Greg pulled Joanne into the shadows, then down the track that led to the back of the hotel.

'I need to explain about what Stratton said,' she began.

'Later,' he said, trying to keep a hold of his simmering anger that what he'd seen from the hill hadn't been a mirage.

The truth was, he was desperate for an explanation or even a confession, but this wasn't the moment. Not with what was about to go down inside the pub.

Besides, he'd just kissed Caroline in the cellar. Was he planning to immediately confess to that? Re-entering via the kitchen door, they found Caroline and Karla busy dishing up the stovies.

'Where the hell did you two go? We need your help to serve these,' Caroline said with an angry glance at Joanne.

'Explain what's happening,' Greg told Joanne. 'I have to warn Malcolm.'

On entering the bar, he realized he was already too late.

Malcolm threw him a relieved look. 'Glad you're back. Look who just strode in,' he said worriedly. 'Stay here, I'll speak to them.'

The Party House group of five (no Naomi, Greg noted) was standing in the open doorway like an invading army, with Stratton leading the charge, the fabricated bonhomie of their earlier meetings on display.

The crowd, suddenly sensing the invasion, began to hush and stare at the incomers. The band stopped playing. Malcolm approached and politely explained that the bar wasn't accessible tonight because of a private function. He alerted them to the sign outside, explaining exactly that.

'It was to be in the village hall, but the police have taken that over, so it had to be moved here,' he said in a conciliatory voice. 'We'll be open tomorrow as normal.' He didn't add, 'come back and see us then' as he'd done with a few earlier visitors who'd strayed their way.

'We're happy to pay for entry or give a donation.' Aidan smiled like a man used to money buying anything and everything.

Annoyed murmurs began to move through the room like a mounting wave.

Malcolm, ever the peacemaker, thanked him, but repeated firmly that it was a private function and not open to the general public.

Spotting Greg behind the bar, Stratton called out to him. 'Come on, Taylor, tell them we're okay.'

As all eyes turned his way to see what his response might be, Greg knew what he must do.

'I'm sorry, Mr Stratton, as I explained earlier, this is a private function arranged by the community council for local residents only.'

That wasn't what Stratton expected or wanted to hear from his head keeper.

'Since I am one of the owners of the Blackrig Estate,' Stratton said coldly, 'I consider myself a local.'

The audacity of this statement didn't go down well with

his audience. As he began his walk to the bar, the crowd surged forward to block his route.

Shouts of 'Fuck off' and 'Bastard' peppered the air. Josh and his mates, who'd been standing near the stage, began to push through the crowd towards him.

'You murdered my wee sister, you fucking bastard,' Josh shouted as he flew at Stratton.

Greg was already out from behind the bar and on his way into the melee, Malcolm pushing through from the opposite direction.

Greg got there first to drag Josh off his boss and secure him, while Malcolm tried to help a shaken Stratton to his feet.

Shouts of 'Police, break it up' were quickly followed by the arrival of Snyder with two male officers, one of them Harry.

As the crowd parted to let them through, all went silent, except for laboured breathing from Stratton in particular.

'That man assaulted me. Arrest him,' Stratton demanded.

'Right, you and you' – Snyder pointed at Josh and Stratton – 'outside.' He nodded at Malcolm and Greg. 'You too. The rest stay in here.' His tone brooked no argument.

Greg did as asked, fully aware that his job with Global Investment Holdings might well have just ended. At that moment he didn't give a damn. He'd tried to warn Stratton, but the bastard just wouldn't listen.

Out now in the street, Snyder stood in silence for a moment before addressing Stratton. 'That was a private function, Mr Stratton. It says so clearly on the sign. Why did you force entry to it?'

Stratton was regaining his cool. Ignoring the question, he said, 'That man,' pointing at Josh, 'assaulted me, officer, in front of witnesses. I demand he be charged.'

Behind Greg, the group who'd managed to cram in the doorway breathed in as one.

Snyder's firm expression didn't alter. 'I repeat, why did you force entry to a private party, sir?'

Greg had been impressed with the detective when under his penetrating gaze. He was even more so now.

'As owner of the Blackrig Estate, I am entitled to enter,' Stratton declared.

Watching Snyder's expression, Greg thought he caught the fleeting glimpse of a wry smile at Stratton's statement, before the policeman said, 'I disagree. You are a visitor and should have left when asked by the proprietor.'

Stratton decided to resort to threats. 'If you don't arrest this man for assault, I will have to speak to your superior.'

Snyder gave a brief nod. 'You are free to do that, sir. Now, I'd like you and your group to leave these folk to get on with their private party.'

Eventually the group moved back to the vehicle and climbed in. As it took off in the direction of the Party House, Greg heard a huge cheer rise from the crowd inside the pub.

Malcolm clapped him on the shoulder. 'Well done removing Josh from the fray. If you'd got that punch in, boy,' he told Josh, 'you would have been charged with assault.'

Josh looked as though he might say something, but a glance from Snyder stopped him.

Back inside, Greg headed for the bar, receiving claps on the back as he passed with a nod and a half-smile.

It was over for Josh maybe, but not for him. Stratton wasn't one to let things go. He would pay for his insurrection in some fashion and more than likely with his job.

Snyder, entering behind Greg, followed him to the bar.

'I'd like us to talk again tomorrow morning, Mr Taylor. Come for an interview at nine o'clock.'

'I can't, Inspector. I have to take my employer, Mr Stratton, and his party out stalking. If I don't, I stand to lose my job. Especially after tonight,' he added.

Snyder seemed to think about that for a moment before sliding his card over the counter.

'Call me to arrange a time, Mr Taylor.'

Turning on his heel, the DI stopped on his way back to the hotel lounge and had a few quiet words with Josh. Whatever was said, Josh didn't like it.

'What did he say to you?' Greg asked when Josh came for a drink.

'He wants me for an interview tomorrow first thing.' Josh assumed a defiant air and ordered up a pint.

Greg slid it over, gratis. 'Thanks for doing what I've wanted to do for a very long time.'

As Caroline and Joanne appeared to finally start serving up the stovies, Greg asked Joanne if she'd tasted them.

'I persuaded her to,' Caroline said with a smile, 'and she declared them delicious.'

The two women looked at one another and laughed.

Greg found himself uneasy at this sudden and unexpected female buddies' routine. What was Caroline up to now?

As he concentrated on fulfilling the orders at the bar, plus accepting compliments for his handling of 'that bastard, Stratton', he couldn't stop asking himself, what the hell was going on between them?

Was Caroline befriending Joanne in order to fill her in on a few incidents in his past or even in the present, which would likely involve her, or even worse, Ailsa?

Thinking of Joanne and their morning together at the

lochan and then again tonight, when he'd seen her waiting for him at the bar, he resolved not to let that happen.

Joanne wasn't part of his past, but she might be a part of his future. If he had one.

Later, as they walked home together under a bright moon, she stopped him when he tried to explain about Caroline.

'I've something I have to tell you,' she said.

He listened in silence as she explained about secretly visiting the Party House to check out the grave site. How shocked and embarrassed she'd been at being spotted by Aidan, who she'd met once at a Field Sports event.

'I told him I was staying in the village, in case my being at Beanach might make things difficult for you.'

He wanted to ask her why she was photographing the grave and why Stratton had called her Maya, but knew, if he did, this moment between them would be broken.

And he didn't want that. Just as he didn't want her to demand he reveal everything he was hiding about Caroline.

He took her hand. 'Ever made love under a full moon?' he asked, glancing up at the sky.

'No,' she gave a little laugh, 'but I'd like to.'

Joanne

An early call woke her next morning. Judging by the empty bed and silence from the rest of the house, Greg had already left to meet with his stalking party.

Checking the screen, she found Lucy's name and swiftly answered.

'I promise, I was planning on calling you today,' she said, before Lucy could speak. When there was no immediate response to that, Joanne said, 'What's wrong?'

'*He* was here late last night,' Lucy said in a frightened tone.

'What? How did he get your address?'

'Who knows? Probably the police. He's got enough contacts in the Met.'

She was right, he did.

'What happened?'

'He asked in that calm measured manner of his if I knew where you were.'

Joanne could see him in her mind's eye doing exactly that. When they'd first met, she'd loved his low, melodious tones. Even in court, she thought he often won his cases because of that voice. A voice suffused with honesty and calm integrity. Whatever Richard said his client did or didn't do had to be true. Didn't it?

'I said I thought you were on a research trip for an article, but I didn't know where.' Lucy halted there for a moment as though to gain strength to continue. 'He asked for your new number. I declined, saying it was up to you to give out your number, not me.' Her voice faltered a little. 'He was trying to persuade me in that way he has. Luckily, Paul came to my rescue and politely but firmly sent him packing.'

Joanne was horrified. 'I'm so sorry. I never thought he'd turn up at your place. Thank God Paul was there.'

'He's decided to stay here for a while.' Lucy didn't add, 'in case Richard comes back', although it was implicit in her tone.

'He's determined to find you,' she went on. 'Don't put anything up online that might identify where you are.' Her voice suggested the warning was in earnest. 'Not if you don't want him to turn up there.'

'I was in two minds whether to do that anyway, for a variety of reasons,' Joanne said. 'I don't want to do anything behind Greg's back.'

'So it's more serious now?' Lucy said.

'I don't know what it is,' Joanne admitted. She considered mentioning the fact that Aidan Stratton was here and that he'd seen her, but decided not to worry Lucy any more than she was already.

'Stay safe, please,' Lucy said as she rang off. 'And for God's sake keep your head down. He'll give up eventually,' she added, more in hope than certainty.

If only that were true, Joanne thought later as she mulled over her conversation with Lucy with a mug of coffee.

On a positive note, if Richard had come looking for her number from Lucy then the couple of calls to her new mobile had likely been spam. So she could stop worrying about them at least.

But she would have to worry about Aidan Stratton. Richard and Aidan weren't actually friends – in fact, he'd once expressed his distaste for Aidan to her. However, they did move in similar circles and if they were to encounter one another, she was pretty sure Aidan would say where he'd last seen her.

She had to face up to it. Being spotted by Aidan had been a disaster. She chastised herself for failing to ask about the people staying at the Party House, just in case she might know anyone. Then she would have been more on her guard.

Still, there was nothing she could do about that now.

She thought back to last night and the time she'd spent with Caroline. Things had definitely changed between them during her spell in the kitchen. Once away from Greg, Caroline had been demonstratively chatty and friendly.

She'd been told by Caroline that Greg was a nice guy, who deserved to be happy. That he would need Joanne's support during the investigation. 'That is if you intend to stay?' Caroline had added.

It was a question Joanne didn't have an answer to, so she didn't offer one.

'He was pretty cut up when Ailsa Cummings went missing,' Caroline had continued.

'I thought *you* were her friend,' Joanne had blurted out at that point. She'd thought that Caroline was about to deny this, but eventually she'd nodded.

'Everyone was shattered, the men especially, because they were all under suspicion and everyone was blaming everyone else.' She'd continued, 'Greg couldn't stand it and went away for a while, but he loves this place, so I knew he'd come back.' She'd said this with a satisfied smile and Joanne had wondered why.

Had he come back because of Caroline? Or did she just think he had?

'Now it's all started again.' Caroline had forced a smile at that point, before finishing with, 'But not tonight. Tonight is about fun and stovies.'

'Are you going to tell me what they are?' Joanne had said, relieved to get off the topic of Greg and the investigation.

'Sit down and I'll give you a plate. Plus a malt whisky chaser to go alongside.'

Dragging her thoughts back to the present, Joanne opened her laptop. She'd told Lucy she wasn't sure about publishing her piece, but that didn't mean she was going to stop writing it. The story of Ailsa's disappearance and the subsequent discovery of a body, yet to be declared as the missing teenager, intrigued her. The fact that it was also seemingly linked to the Party House made it even more compelling.

She flipped through the photos she'd taken, finishing with the one of the covered grave site.

If it was confirmed as Ailsa's body, its discovery occurred almost five years after she'd disappeared. Had the Party House been built then? Had she been killed beside the loch or did the killer take her there later? Who had access to the beach area at that time?

Her mind swam with questions about when Ard Choille had been built and when the slabs at the lochside had been put down. Had the body been buried before the slabs were laid or had they been lifted in order to bury it?

Burying a body wouldn't be easy. Plus she now knew from her research that a buried body caused the surface vegetation to change and the ground to sink as the remains decayed, but surely the concrete slabs would cover that?

The women at the Party House had told her the body had

been wrapped in plastic, but they didn't know if the victim had been naked or clothed.

Might they find the DNA of her attacker on her body or her clothes? Perhaps the killer's fingerprints were on the plastic? If she'd been raped, would there still be DNA evidence of that?

Watching crime dramas had taught her some things, but she had no idea how accurate they were.

She contemplated whether she could talk to Greg about it, but something told her there was a line he wouldn't cross with respect to Ailsa's disappearance and death. Was that because he, like the other men, had been a suspect, and might be again?

Leaving aside the forensics, she now focused her search on the origins of Ard Choille, the results of which expanded what Greg had told her earlier.

It seemed the original estate owner, Lord Main, had been benign, if a little eccentric. He had begun the tree-house concept because of his love of trees and the desire to have a house that became one with the landscape. The work had progressed in a leisurely fashion along with his thoughts on it.

Locals continued to swim off the nearby beach. Workmen came and went, depending on Lord Main's whim, although the house itself had been completed prior to his death.

When this happened, his remaining and distant family fought each other over ownership, eventually selling the estate to a conglomerate who had different ideas for its management. They'd kept on a skeleton staff, including Greg, put in the sauna and hot tub at the lochside and begun advertising Ard Choille as a party house.

In her research she couldn't find an exact timeline for

when things like the hot tub were actually installed. No doubt Greg would know, but dare she ask him?

If they spent more time together, like yesterday morning at the green lochan, then maybe yes.

She resolved to be as open and supportive of him as possible. She definitely didn't want to leave. Especially now, when she knew that Richard was back in London and searching for her.

Shutting her laptop, she resolved to do what she'd been putting off since the post van had delivered the package to her at the edge of the woods.

If the test was negative, she could relax about that at least.

If it was – she couldn't bring herself to think the word 'positive', let alone say it – she had an even bigger problem to deal with.

Rising, she forced herself to walk through to the bathroom, package in hand, unsure, even now, if she wanted to know the truth.

Greg

The weather hadn't yet broken, and the night had been muggy and uncomfortably warm, even with the bedroom window open.

She lay on her front, her dark hair spread across the pillow, her breathing soft, her cheeks a little flushed.

Who was she really, this woman who, he suspected, had set out to seduce him. Not that he was complaining. It was just that she was even more of a mystery to him now than she had been on that first wild weekend they'd spent together in London.

They had made love under a full moon last night, and he hadn't asked her who she really was. Maya or Joanne or how many other personas? Last night he didn't care. Not about that, nor what else she might be keeping from him.

Neither did he want to be asked what he was keeping from her.

Quietly closing the bedroom door behind him, he made himself some breakfast and rang Colin. Colin had watched the stramash in the pub last night, but had wisely kept his head down. A few brief words with him afterwards had alerted Greg to how worried Colin was about his job.

Greg felt exactly the same, but hadn't said that; rather, he'd tried to reassure Colin that all would be well. He could only hope that was true.

Also, if he were to leave, he would rather it was on his own terms. He'd left Blackrig before when things were bad, but then found he couldn't stay away. Whether he lost his job or not, he wouldn't be leaving his home village again.

Stepping outside, he noted the midges were already out in force, clouds of them. He wondered if Stratton would change his mind about going out considering how bad it would likely be on the hill. And what about the women he'd indicated would be coming along?

Somehow Greg couldn't imagine the females he'd seen sunbathing by the green loch being keen on slathering themselves in midge cream and putting head nets on, except perhaps Naomi.

Reaching the gates of Ard Choille, he found Colin waiting for him there, his face a picture of misery.

Choosing to avoid the subject Colin was obviously worrying about, Greg said instead, 'How'd it go with Karla?'

Colin's ability to switch from distress to joy was one of the reasons Greg liked him so much.

'Are we talking about her stovies or her company?' he said, his eyes lighting up.

'Both,' Greg said.

'In a word, perfect,' Colin said in the tone of a smitten man.

'So you two are a thing, then?'

'I wish.' Colin looked slightly crestfallen. 'There's a lot of competition. On that topic, how the hell did you manage to score with the lovely Joanne? She's bound to have plenty admirers in London. Why come up here to stay with you?' he asked in obvious disbelief.

Greg wasn't sure of that himself, so he just smiled in what he hoped was a mysterious way.

Jokes over, he said, 'Okay. Are we ready?'

'I'll go ahead and walk the garron up and meet you at the hide,' Colin offered. 'Stratton can't sack me from a distance.'

'He's not going to sack either of us, but I'll test the waters, and meet you at the stables.'

Stratton must have been watching for him, because he emerged from the house on Greg's approach. Unable to read the man's expression from a distance, he had to wait until he got closer.

When he did, Greg discovered that Stratton's furious face of last night was nowhere to be seen. In fact, he looked positively sanguine.

'Ah, Taylor. Well timed. We're just about ready for off. Myself, Chalmers and two of the ladies will be coming along as well.'

'You'll all need to cover up well, plus cream and face nets,' Greg warned. 'It's very still, even on the hill.'

Stratton waved the advice away as though it was a given. 'About last night,' he said.

Greg waited, unsure what would come next.

'I believe my assailant, Josh Huntly, is likely to be charged with the vandalizing of the hot tub, although he definitely wasn't alone in that.' He gave Greg a meaningful look as though he thought he might know of an accomplice.

'What evidence do the police have that would lead them to that conclusion?' Greg asked warily.

'I'm not privy to such information,' Stratton said with a shrug, 'although I assume fingerprints or DNA were found on the tools they used.'

Having seemingly satisfied his desire to punish someone for last night, he now returned to today's event. Two of the women were apparently keen to come – Naomi had shot stag before, Poppy just wanted to watch – plus he and Brian Chalmers would make up the party.

He also said a few not so complimentary remarks regarding 'your apprentice', which fortunately Colin wasn't around to hear.

Relieved at least that both he and Colin still had jobs, Greg didn't correct him on the 'apprentice' title.

'Where is he anyway?' Stratton said, looking round as though Colin might pop up to order.

'He's at the Bothy getting the pony ready. We'll walk up and meet him.'

Stratton muttered something under his breath, which Greg suspected was an insult directed at Colin. Choosing to ignore it, he instead greeted the arrival of the remainder of the party with a quiet nod and, marshalling them, set off towards the Bothy.

In fact, the morning went well. A quick glance from Greg on his arrival at the stables had assured Colin he hadn't yet joined the army of the unemployed, which had been greeted with a delighted smile.

After which Greg had led the walk up the steep zigzagging pony path, followed by the guests, with Colin and the pony bringing up the rear.

Naomi, Greg was pleased to see, had openly chosen to walk just in front of Colin, and Greg could hear her voice as she chatted to him in a friendly way.

Best of all, a warm, dry breeze had met them on the hill, swiftly ridding them of the swarms of midges.

Naomi had shown her worth as a rifle and bagged a decent-sized stag. Stratton failed to do so, but did his best to claim Naomi's kill as his own. Apparently he'd 'helped direct her shot'.

When they stopped for lunch, Naomi chose to have hers with Greg.

Now midday, the sun was high in the sky, and you could hear the dry rustle of the heather in the wind.

'It's tinder dry up here,' Naomi said, shading her eyes to look down into the valley. 'The woods near Ard Choille and the village must be the same. That must be a concern?'

'Rain's on its way, I'm told,' Greg said. 'June's traditionally a dry month in Scotland. July not so much. It should break soon.' He halted there and, changing the subject, said, 'I didn't see you with the other women down at the beach yesterday?'

'I've been taking a walk along the shore for my swim. Out of sight, of course.'

Greg was taken aback. 'Where exactly?' he said, hoping she hadn't discovered his own favourite place, on the other side of the lochan.

'Not far. I think it's where there was once a small campsite. There's a jetty. I go in from there.'

Greg knew where she meant.

'No one camps there now?' she said.

He shook his head. 'Lord Main set it up as a wild camping site. He used to go down and chat to the folk there. That all stopped when . . .' He hesitated.

'Global Investment Holdings took over the estate,' she finished for him. 'Look, I'm really sorry they went down to the village last night. I tried to dissuade Aidan from doing that and refused to go. Aidan said he was beaten up by one of the village thugs?'

They were sitting behind the stone hide, away from the others, but Greg kept his voice low anyway.

'I pulled Josh off him before he got a blow in. Stratton

had been asked politely to leave. Malcolm, the community council chair, explained it was a private event. Stratton wouldn't listen. Josh jumped him. There were a lot of others there more than willing to do that.'

'Including you, I expect,' she said with an understanding look. When he didn't respond, she said softly, 'I know what happened here during the pandemic. I'm sorry.'

'We're all sorry, but sorry doesn't bring the kids or Malcolm's wife, Mairi, back.'

A moment's silence followed before Naomi changed the subject. 'I was surprised to hear that Maya Villan's here. I assume she must be staying in the village. Maybe at the hotel?'

'Maya Villan?' Greg said, realizing this was his chance to discover who that persona of Joanne's actually was.

'The writer,' Naomi said. 'She emerged from the woods near the loch. Aidan knows her and introduced her to the sunseekers. Poppy was very excited to meet her in person. She writes a fabulous blog, but there are no images of her on it. Perhaps she's planning a piece on Blackrig coming out of lockdown.' She was looking quizzically at him as though he should know. 'Have you met her?' she added.

'Maya Villan? No, can't say I have,' he said.

Naomi shrugged. 'No matter, I just like her writing. I'll be interested to hear if she blogs or publishes something about Blackrig. I'll watch out for it.'

So will I, Greg thought.

On the way back to Ard Choille, the warm wind picked up, buffeting them as they descended. Colin had gone ahead with the laden garron.

As they neared the Bothy, Greg spotted a thin plume of

smoke rising from Blackrig woods not far from the village hall. Who the hell would light a fire in the tinderbox that was currently the woods near the village?

The beeping of his pager followed almost immediately, alerting him to what he'd just seen.

'I have a call-out,' he quickly explained. 'The local fire service. Some idiot's lit a fire in the woods.' He glanced at Stratton. 'You can make your own way back, I assume? Colin will deal with your kill,' he told Naomi.

Not waiting for an answer, he took off at a run, shortening the distance to the Land Rover by avoiding the route via the Bothy.

Reaching the vehicle, he could already hear the whine of the siren. Fortunately the local fire engine serving Blackrig and the surrounding remote villages was housed in the village car park not far from the hall.

Muttering obscenities about idiots who came on holiday only to ignore the signs expressly forbidding them to light campfires in the woods, he roared through the Party House gates and sped down the single track road towards the village.

Greg

Why would anyone deliberately light a fire in the village woods, and apparently so close to the hall?

Most problems with fires were from wild camping by tourists. The woods round Blackrig consisted of fairly dense pine and were floored by thick blaeberry bushes. No one would consider trying to put up a tent in there.

So might it have been lit on purpose, rather than caused by accident? Maybe because of the police presence in the hall?

The last time they'd seen such a large contingent of police officers in the village, tempers had also flared. The result had been a few tyres let down, but nothing more serious than that. Hence DI Snyder's decision to house all his personnel in the heart of the village.

However, many locals were openly asking why, when the law could turn up for a single dead body, they hadn't been remotely interested in the rich folk who'd broken lockdown and caused six deaths during the pandemic.

Might the fire be a protest about that? If so, it was a pretty stupid and dangerous one, Greg decided.

On reaching the village, he quickly parked up and followed the track the fire truck had taken into the woods.

Folk were watching what was happening from the back of the village hall. Spotting the fire truck parked up, its hoses already in action, Greg threaded his way through the crowd to join his fellow firefighters.

The area was being drenched, the air filled with a fine spray like the rain they kept praying for. The acrid smell of burning was present but, thankfully, there was none of the dreaded sound of crackling flames. It looked as though they'd already been doused, although a large mound of pine needles, beneath a tall pine, was still smoking.

He found Malcolm there, alongside two local kids, Kirsty MacKenzie and Ivan McAlister.

'An attempt at setting a giant wood ant hill aflame,' Malcolm told him on approach. 'Using lighter fluid. These two found it and tried to smother it with their hoodies. So no need for you to kit up.'

'Apologies, I was just coming off the hill when I spotted the smoke.'

'No worries, although it could have been much worse.' Malcolm gestured to a nearby semi-cleared area. 'Plenty of dry kindling there, and,' he said, looking upwards at the swaying pine branches, 'those needles are tinder dry. We've had a lucky escape, thanks to this pair.'

Glancing at the two youngsters, Greg thought they looked embarrassed, and perhaps a little guilty.

'Any rain forecast?' Greg said.

'Rory, our eminent local weatherman, says it's on its way, although he fears we might end up the dry spot in the centre of the storm.'

Greg groaned. To smell the approaching rain and have it miss them would be tragic in possibly more ways than one.

'Okay, you two. Thanks to your quick thinking, the woods were saved,' Malcolm said. 'Go tell everyone.'

They left speedily as though they'd expected an interrogation rather than a dismissal.

Malcolm watched them go, then said, 'More than one kid in this village has tried to set fire to a giant ant hill in these woods. It's almost a rite of passage.'

'You think it was one of them?'

'I suspect so, although they tried to put it out pretty quickly and were frightened enough to call us.' He observed Greg. 'Are you thinking what I'm thinking?'

'That they both have family that died from the virus?' Greg said.

Malcolm nodded. 'There's anger that the police are here now, but not when we asked them to come, when the Party House was occupied during lockdown. If they had turned up, removed those folk and charged them . . .' He halted there. 'Things could get worse here before they get better,' he said in a sombre tone.

Greg nodded. 'I know.'

'Any word when your guests might leave?' Malcom said.

'The sooner the better,' Greg muttered.

'Well, if you need to get back to them, we're all right here.'

'Snyder wanted to talk to me this morning, then let me off when I explained I'd likely lose my job if I didn't turn up for work,' Greg told him. 'Since I'm here, I might as well try and see him now.'

'I did my thing this morning,' Malcolm said. 'Not sure whether the scene last night helped his opinion of us or not. He's pretty thorough though.'

And devious, Greg thought.

Pulling out his mobile and the detective's card, he made the call. It rang out three times, then Snyder answered.

'Detective Inspector Snyder? It's Greg Taylor here. I'm in the village now if you have time to see me?'

There was some background muttering, he thought, between Snyder and his female detective sergeant, then Snyder came back on. 'Are you nearby?'

'At the back door.' Greg explained about his call-out as a volunteer firefighter.

'You're a busy man,' Snyder said drily. 'I'll see you now. The same back room as before.'

The main hall was still set out with chairs. Glancing in, Greg spotted Josh alongside his mates, the ones, Greg suspected, who'd been there the night the hot tub had been demolished.

It looked like Stratton might be right that the police were likely to charge them. Did that mean the DNA tests they'd all taken had found a match? Or had it been fingerprints? He felt sick at the thought of how much evidence might have been found on the body itself.

Just then, Josh looked up and met his eye.

Greg gave him a friendly nod, hoping Josh would read it as a message of support. After the fracas last night in the pub, Josh's attitude towards him had changed, although Greg wasn't sure if it had been for better or worse. Worse would be if Josh somehow thought that Greg had shopped them about the vandalism to the hot tub. But that was stupid, Josh had no idea that he'd seen them that night. Unless one of them had caught sight of him?

Greg stopped himself from going down that particular path. After last night, surely Josh would realize he'd saved him from an assault charge? Although, Josh could be mad at him for doing exactly that. He'd had a chance to deck Stratton and Greg had protected the owner of the Party House to save his own job.

There was always more than one way to read a situation, and by the look on Josh's face at the moment, Greg's way didn't match his version.

A last thought surfaced as he stood, hesitant, outside the interview room door.

What if Josh should discover that both Stratton and Chalmers had been part of the group that had broken lock-down at Ard Choille? What if he found out that he, Greg, had partied there with them?

Greg

The body was hers. DI Snyder had confirmed this.

He'd known that all along, of course, but still his head buzzed with the words as though a wasp had found its way inside his brain.

That fact established, they were now back on the subject of the Party House.

It was strange, Greg thought, that the more often you tell a story, the more it changes, despite all your efforts. He'd tried to keep it simple, but Snyder had a way of pinning down details, exact details. Some of which he didn't know or had chosen to forget.

He'd already had a cup of tea, courtesy of Maggie Carmichael, who'd come in to man the hall kitchen. It appeared the officers weren't used to life without access to a drinks machine and had asked Malcolm if tea and coffee facilities might be made available.

The tea had been good and strong, exactly what Greg had needed, although at more than one point in the proceedings he would have preferred a dram. The first, when Snyder had told him that the body was Ailsa. The second was now, as he was questioned on his whereabouts when both the house and subsequent hot tub were being constructed.

'Lord Main began building the tree house about seven years or so ago, before Ailsa . . .' he began, before realizing that he couldn't bring himself to say either the word 'disappeared' or 'died'.

'I wasn't here during some of the time.' He hesitated. 'I went away to work on an estate in northern England. Came back when my father died. The house was almost finished by then. I took over my father's position as head keeper on Blackrig. Not long after that, Lord Main died and his family sold the estate. Locals stopped calling it Ard Choille after Global Investment Holdings rented it out as a party house.'

'What about the slabs down at the lochside? Were they there when Ailsa disappeared?'

And there was the question he'd been dreading.

He pretended to think for a bit. 'Lord Main planned a patio area down by the loch where village folk liked to swim, but I'm not sure exactly when the slabs were laid.'

This time he was lying, hoping it didn't show. He'd gone over this again and again in his head. The area had been prepared, a mix of soil and sand, which was why it had made such an easy grave. Much easier than digging one in the woods.

Snyder exchanged a quick glance with DS Reid.

'Were contractors still working on the house when Ailsa disappeared?'

'There were some changes made inside after Global Investment Holdings bought it.' Which was true enough. 'So it's possible workmen were about. Although there were holidaymakers here by then. In the hotel and B&Bs round about . . . and a few folk at the campsite.'

'Campsite?' DS Reid said, as though that was the first she'd heard of it.

'A spot set aside by Lord Main for wild camping along the shore from the swim area. I remember some of the campers were at the ceilidh. I was manning the bar that night with Caroline Campbell. The campsite was shut down when the new management took over. No money in it, they said.'

The interrogation was bringing those terrible times back again. Things he didn't want to remember.

He was aware that Snyder was observing him closely. Greg imagined the blackness of his soul was being examined. Would the detective uncover the real truth of what had happened that night? So many secrets, probably better left hidden.

The sound of an argument coming from the main hall stopped whatever Snyder had been about to ask next. Rising, he said, 'Thanks for coming in, Mr Taylor. We'll be in touch.'

Summarily dismissed, a relieved Greg followed them out, keen himself to find out what the noise coming from the big room was all about.

Glancing in at the open door, he saw a couple of uniforms holding Josh Huntly and Finn Campbell apart. Something had made Caroline's normally mild-mannered younger brother really angry with Josh. He wondered what that might be.

Finn wasn't one of Josh's gang, although Greg thought they were friendly enough, in a distant sort of a way. Hence, he was pretty certain Finn hadn't featured among the crew that had wrecked the hot tub that fateful night.

Of the two, Finn's face was definitely the most furious. If Greg had been asked who among the village lads might take a potshot at Josh Huntly, he would never have chosen Finn.

Yet here he was, being prevented by the police from landing one on Josh.

What on earth had provoked him to behave like that?

Catching Finn's eye, Greg shook his head, trying to get over the message that this wouldn't help anyone, least of all Finn.

Finn said something to the restraining officer and, moments later, was released.

It struck him that Finn, like most of the villagers, including himself, probably wished the body had never been found. What Josh had unearthed with his anger-filled assault on the hot tub had brought this horror down upon them all.

Joanne

It was sheer luck she'd gone to the window in the hope that she might see Greg's Land Rover heading up the drive.

She'd heard a vehicle on the gravel, but it definitely wasn't Greg, or the post van, but a mystery car instead.

Joanne immediately withdrew from the window and retreated into the kitchen. Since Stratton had spotted her with Greg outside the pub, she was in fear that he might arrive unexpectedly at Beanach to check if she was staying here rather than in the village, as she'd told him.

Her second and more frightening worry was that Stratton, having encountered her, would set about getting in touch with Richard to tell him the story of how he'd run into her in Blackrig, writing a piece about the virus village.

Her heart slamming in her chest, she quietly moved into the back porch and waited, cursing herself for not locking the front door (which Greg never did) and planning her escape on to the hill at the back if need be.

'Greg!' a female voice called. 'Joanne! It's me, Caroline.'

Realizing she would have to emerge, Joanne quickly prepared her excuse and, marshalling herself, re-entered the kitchen.

'Caroline. Sorry. I was out the back and didn't hear the car arrive.' Even as she said the words, she knew how dire her excuse was. Of course she would have heard the car approach if she'd been outside, even at the back. She should have said she'd been in the bathroom. At least that might have sounded probable.

Caroline made a face. 'I thought you were hiding from someone. Maybe that arse Aidan Stratton,' she joked.

'I wasn't sure, when I didn't recognize the vehicle,' Joanne was relieved to admit.

Caroline gave a nod, signifying her agreement. 'I missed Greg when he was at the village hall earlier and wanted a word with him,' she said.

'I haven't seen Greg all day. I thought he was out stalking.'

'I was told he was at the village hall being interviewed again about Ailsa,' Caroline said, throwing Joanne a worried look. 'The word is that the body they found is definitely Ailsa.'

When Joanne couldn't find the words to respond to this, Caroline said, 'Is it all right if I wait here for Greg? I need to speak to him about Finn.'

'Finn?'

'My younger brother. I heard he got into a fight in the hall today when he was waiting to be interviewed. Greg was there at the same time and I wanted to talk to him about it. See if he saw what happened.'

'Of course,' Joanne said. 'I could make us some tea while you're waiting?'

'Don't worry. I can do that,' Caroline immediately said. 'I know where everything is.'

Joanne, not sure whether to be grateful or annoyed, decided to say nothing. Caroline was obviously trying to claim ownership of Greg's kitchen, indicating how often she'd stayed here with him. Or perhaps even lived here.

Now the kitchen and every other room in the house, particularly the bedroom, took on a different hue.

Caroline, seemingly oblivious to Joanne's discomfort, produced a pretty tray (where had she found that?) with a teapot and two china cups and saucers, none of which Joanne had known existed.

Pouring for her, Caroline said, 'This is the Earl Grey I left in the cupboard. I hope you found it?'

Joanne decided it was time to fight back. 'Greg makes fresh coffee for us in the morning,' she said with a smile, 'and he cooks for us at night.'

Touché.

Caroline accepted this without dispute. 'Yeah, he's used to fending for himself and he is a good cook.'

There was a few minutes silence while they sipped and Joanne swithered between wishing Greg would come home, thereby reinstating her as the woman of the house, and hoping he wouldn't. Something told her he would not be impressed to discover the two of them sitting drinking tea in his kitchen.

Caroline eventually broke the silence.

'Now the police have confirmed the body as Ailsa's, you probably should be told more about her.' She waited as though for permission to go on.

The truth was, Joanne was dying to know more, but wasn't sure she should say so.

Caroline continued anyway. 'People felt safe here in Blackrig. Ailsa's disappearance changed all of that. I had just found out I was pregnant. Greg was so excited about being a dad, and then our world fell apart.' She looked down at her clasped hands as though remembering. 'I lost the baby, of course.' Her voice broke a little. 'All that worry and trouble. Greg was heartbroken. That's why he went away.'

Joanne, shocked by such a revelation, tried to cover this

by giving a brief nod, as though she already knew that part of the story.

Caroline carried on, mentioning how Ailsa had all the men in Blackrig running after her. 'And those, like Greg, who weren't chasing her, she made a point of chasing them,' she said. Her face grew grim. 'Truth was, she was a devil and caused a lot of distress to folk in the village. Her parents were nice people, but they could do nothing with her. They'd brought her here to get her away from a bad crowd in Glasgow, but she just brought the trouble with her. Some of her city boyfriends turned up here too, bringing drugs in to sell. She was taking a cut on that.'

The story rolled on, while Joanne sat mesmerized.

'She set the village against itself. Then she disappeared and that made it even worse. We all thought at first that she'd skipped it back to Glasgow, but when they couldn't find her there, her poor parents were devastated and everyone began to suspect one another. We found out through gossip or the police inquiry who'd she been seeing. Many of them married men.'

Joanne listened in silence, not sure why she was being told all of this. Was it designed to put doubt in her head about Greg or to make out he was the only one not caught up in the Ailsa story, because he was in love with Caroline and their coming baby?

Either way, it made her feel bad.

The sound of the approaching Land Rover stopped Caroline mid-story. Nothing was said as they both waited for the door to open and Greg to enter.

Joanne found herself fearful of what his reaction might be at finding them sitting there together, having no doubt been discussing him.

Glancing over at Caroline, she found her demeanour to be much more relaxed than her own.

Forewarned by the presence of the car, which he would obviously recognize as Caroline's, Greg's expression when he entered was not one of surprise.

His eyes moved from Joanne to Caroline and back again, clearly wondering what the hell was going on.

'Good, you're back.' Caroline broke the awkward silence. 'I heard Finn got in a fight with Josh at the hall and that you were there. I came to ask you if you know what they were fighting about.'

'You should ask Finn,' Greg said.

'I can't. He's gone off somewhere, which is why I came here,' she said in a worried tone. 'Oh my God, he wasn't part of the gang that smashed up the hot tub was he?'

'He wasn't,' Greg said firmly.

'How do you know that?' Caroline demanded.

Greg was silent for a moment and Joanne wondered if he would backtrack on what he'd just sounded so sure about.

'I think he was angry at Josh for doing that. That's probably what started it.'

Caroline contemplated this. 'He was freaked by the Party House folk trying to barge into the ceilidh last night. I don't want him to do anything stupid,' she said, looking to Greg as though he might help her with that.

He eventually succumbed to the pleading look.

'I could try and talk to him if you like, although Finn thinks I do the estate's bidding, which in a way I do.' He looked frustrated by that.

Caroline shook her head. 'It's okay. I'll speak to him myself when he cools down. I'd better get home in case he comes back.' She looked to Joanne. 'Thanks for the tea. It was nice talking to you.'

Joanne watched from the window as Greg walked Caroline to her car.

They spoke briefly, their faces close. At the final moment, Caroline reached up to kiss his cheek before getting into the car. Not able to see Greg's face, Joanne didn't know whether he was pleased by that or not.

She learned soon enough. His expression was thunderous when he came back in.

'She shouldn't have come here. She did it to make you feel uncomfortable. It was nothing to do with Finn.'

Joanne waited, knowing by his expression, that there was more to come.

'So,' he said, looking directly at her, 'why the hell didn't you tell me that your real name was Maya Villan?'

Joanne, as angry now as he obviously was, responded with her own question.

'Why the hell didn't you tell me that Caroline was pregnant with *your* baby when Ailsa Cummings went missing?'

Greg

So Caroline had told her about the baby. Something she'd promised not to do. He felt the pain again, the suffocating knowledge that the miscarriage had been his fault. If Caroline hadn't found out about Ailsa, it might never have happened. None of it would have happened.

He stared at Joanne, asking himself why he'd invited her to Blackrig. It was never going to work between them, even before Ailsa's body was discovered. And yet, looking at her standing there, eyes flashing at him, he wanted her more than ever. That's why Caroline had told her about the baby, because even now she could read him well enough to know the strength of his feelings for this woman, whatever her name was. And she wanted that to end. She wanted Joanne to leave. She wanted him all to herself. He would, he realized, never be free of Caroline. Just as he would never be free of Ailsa.

In an effort to collect himself, he turned away from her and went to pour himself a whisky.

Joanne's angry voice interrupted his tortured thoughts. 'Why not offer *me* a drink? Is it because I'm no longer welcome here?'

He poured her a whisky and handed it over, their fingers brushing one another. That simple touch softened his anger and, by the look on her face, it'd had a similar effect on her.

She stared at the amber liquid for a moment before setting down the glass, untasted.

'Maya Villan is my pen name. I use it on my blog. Joanne is my real name. It's not a crime to have a pen name,' she said quietly.

'It's not a crime to have a past either,' Greg said. 'Even if it contains regrettable actions.' He met her gaze. 'Isn't there something in your past you're not happy about?'

Her face clouded over, indicating that there probably was. She looked as though she might reveal it, then stopped.

'The dreary dramas of dead yesterdays,' she said instead, with a wry smile.

'Did you write that in your blog?' he said, his mood lightening at her expression.

She shook her head. 'No, I stole it from a book by someone else.'

When she laughed, he found himself joining in.

'To the dreary dramas of dead yesterdays.' He offered up his glass for a toast.

She clinked her glass against his and they sipped their whiskies in unison.

In the quiet aftermath, he tentatively asked if she'd like to eat out tonight. 'The hotel does excellent seafood. Garlic crab claws are a favourite of mine. I could call Malcolm and book us a table,' he said, brightening at the idea.

'You don't mind showing me off in public, then?' she said with an enticing smile.

'Only when I've had a good look at you first.'

She set down her glass and pulled him to her.

What followed rattled the table, sending what he recognized as Caroline's tea cups to crash and spill their remains across the flagstone floor.

Afterwards, he gathered her to him, pressing her face to his chest, wrapping his arms tightly around her.

Something had changed between them, he acknowledged. The game had moved on, but how long would – or could – they keep on playing it?

She knew now about Caroline, or at least some of it. If Caroline was willing to reveal the story of the miscarriage, might she not also reveal other truths about him?

From what she'd said out at the car, she hadn't done that. Wouldn't do it. She'd promised him. She had his back.

'So,' he heard Joanne say, 'shall I get dressed for dinner?' She was smiling up at him.

'Definitely. Malcolm doesn't serve women who aren't wearing their knickers, regardless of how beautiful they are.'

'And how would he know I wasn't wearing them?' she joked back. 'We could keep it a secret.'

Among all the other secrets, he thought as she went off to get ready. Pushing that thought to the back of his mind, he called Malcolm.

'Sure thing. I'll give you the romantic corner,' he said. 'I'd also welcome a quick word with you when you get here.'

'What about?' Greg said.

'Not sure exactly, but I get the impression that DI Snyder and his sidekick are about to make an arrest. Something's going on, anyway.'

'Josh?' Greg said.

'I'm assuming so, but if they managed to get fingerprints off the weapons they used, it could be more than just Josh.'

'Jeez. Folk are not going to be happy about that,' Greg said.

'Maybe Stratton could be persuaded to drop any charges brought about for the demolition of the hot tub. After all, by wrecking it, they uncovered a bigger crime.'

'True.' Greg pondered whether he might consider suggesting that to Stratton. Maybe try and sell it as a way of easing tensions between the owners of Ard Choille and the village. 'I could approach him about it,' he said tentatively.

'Good,' Malcolm said. 'I could come with you, as chair of the community council. We don't need to talk about it further tonight. Let's see what happens, and if it does involve Josh and his gang, we'll see if we can persuade Mr Stratton together.'

Showered and dressed, Greg awaited Joanne's reappearance. The conversation with Malcolm had made him uneasy. If Malcolm had sensed excitement among his police house guests, then it looked like something was about to go down.

Whatever it was, it was bound to cause a ruckus. Locals would not take it well if Josh and his mates were charged. It would just look like the police punishing them, rather than the estate owners, yet again.

'Wow,' he said as Joanne appeared before him. 'Dressed to kill' was the phrase that sprang to mind, although he didn't say it.

Instead he said, 'You look beautiful.'

'Thank you,' she said graciously. She eyed him up and down. 'I wondered when I would get to see the kilt again.'

'I was supposed to put it on for the ceilidh but, as you know, things got a bit messy beforehand.'

'Well, I'm glad you chose to wear it now. Are we walking down?'

'I'll drive down and, depending on what we consume, we can always walk back.'

'I'll drive us back,' she offered. 'I don't mind not drinking.'

'Okay,' he said cautiously. 'If you're sure?' He realized that although she'd asked for a whisky earlier, she hadn't taken more than a sip. 'Malcolm does stock decent wine, in case you think we only drink whisky in Blackrig.'

She smiled in acknowledgement of that, then said, 'I'm quite hungry after all that exercise earlier. Can we go?'

The atmosphere in the car as they headed into the village was so good, he allowed himself to relax. Maybe it would work out between them after all. If dealing with Caroline hadn't fazed her, then it just might.

Malcolm, spotting the Land Rover from the dining room window, came to welcome them.

'Good evening, kilted Highlander and beautiful lady, your table awaits.' As he ushered them to a corner at the window, shimmering in candlelight, he told them that all the guests had been fed, so they had the place to themselves.

'A bit more civilized than the last time you were here,' he told Joanne as he helped her get seated.

'Hope there's food left?' Greg joked.

'We always cook from fresh, as well you know. Besides, Mum's on duty in the kitchen tonight, and she taught me all I know.'

'Tell Kath "hi" from me,' Joanne said. 'We had tea together the other day.'

'She told me all about it. You might have a fan there,' he added. 'I know what Greg'll choose,' he told Joanne as he handed them the menus. 'As for you, madam, I recommend the garlic crab claws provided you don't mind getting your fingers covered in garlic butter.'

Joanne looked to Greg. 'That's what you're having, right?'

'Always.'

'Okay, I'll have them too. We can get messy together.'

Malcolm raised a suggestive eyebrow at Joanne and she laughed.

Greg and Joanne settled into easy chit-chat. He felt again that the earlier row and what had followed had cleared the air between them. He'd been both relieved and impressed by the way she'd dealt with Caroline.

Although furious at his former lover, he couldn't make an enemy of her, particularly in the current situation. Plus he didn't want to hurt her more than he had done already.

'You okay?' Joanne's voice broke into his thoughts.

'I was just imagining life once Stratton and his crew leave.'

'Will that be soon?' She looked eager for a 'yes'.

'He can't stay on forever.'

'What about me?'

'I'm hoping you'll stay a little longer, either as Joanne or Maya,' he told her.

'I intend to,' she said.

'Good. Then will you be writing about Blackrig?'

She looked surprised by the question. 'You wouldn't mind?'

He shook his head. 'I'd rather you wrote about us than some of the bastards who covered the story of what happened during the pandemic,' he told her.

She was silent for a moment. Then said, 'And Ailsa's story?'

'That story has no ending as yet,' he said. 'I'd leave it alone for now, especially if you want to be accepted here.'

He'd tried to keep his tone even, but he could see that being told what she could or couldn't write hadn't gone down well with Joanne. He wondered if Caroline had included any of her thoughts on Ailsa during their conversation earlier, but couldn't bring himself to ask.

As he pondered whether he should say any more on the subject, Malcolm appeared, his expression one of shock. Greg immediately asked him what was wrong.

'DI Snyder wants a word with you. Now. He's in the hall.'

'Is it about Josh?'

Malcolm shook his head. 'He wouldn't say.'

Greg rose and, excusing himself to Joanne, went through to find not only DI Snyder, but DS Reid as well. He knew what they were about to say from their expressions alone.

'Greg Taylor, I am arresting you under Section 1 of the Criminal Justice (Scotland) Act 2016 for the rape and murder of Ailsa Cummings.'

Joanne

'They've taken him to Inverness police station for questioning.'

Joanne stared blankly at Malcolm, trying to process what he was saying.

'Why?' she said stupidly. 'What's he done? Is it something to do with Stratton or the guy you think smashed up the hot tub?'

Malcolm had an answer for her, he just didn't want to say it.

'He's being questioned about the rape and murder of Ailsa Cummings.' Malcolm's expression when he said this was as incredulous as her own.

She rose, feeling the need to move, to do something. 'I have to go up there with him. I can take the Land Rover. I haven't been drinking.'

'He asked me to give you the keys. He wants you to go back to Beanach and wait for him there,' Malcolm told her.

'But . . . but I should go with him.'

Malcolm shook his head. 'There's nothing you could do up there. They wouldn't let you see him anyway.'

She fought back the nausea that filled her throat and accepted the keys, before remembering. 'We haven't settled our bill yet.'

Malcolm waved that away. 'Go home, lassie. We'll no

doubt know more in the morning.' Taking note of her pallor, he added, 'I could drive you if you're not feeling well?'

'No. It's okay. I'll manage.' Lifting her jacket, she forced herself to walk to the front door, feeling Malcolm's anxious eyes follow her.

Once outside, she took a deep breath of the night air, willing her stomach to stop churning. This couldn't be happening, she thought. How could they think that Greg would rape and murder someone? As she slid into the Land Rover, she caught the scent of him.

'Christ,' she whispered out loud. 'Don't think about it until you get home.'

Home. That was a strange word to use. Beanach wasn't her home. It was his home. She was a short-term visitor. That was all. She owed Greg nothing. She'd paid for her bed and food with sex. Deliberately stalked him to allow her to come here.

She had to stop on the way up the hill, pulling into the passing place near the Beanach turn-off. Escaping the vehicle just in time, she vomited up her meal.

The worst over, she resumed her journey, aware now that she could put off the pregnancy test no longer.

If it proves to be positive, what will you do?

It was as though a God-like voice had posed the question, so she spoke her answer to the heavens.

'Let's get this straight. I have to decide whether or not to keep the offspring of a misogynist bastard? Or a rapist and murderer?' Her laugh, she realized, was verging on the demonic. 'Out of the frying pan and into the fire.'

How amused Richard would be by that, for a few seconds at least, until he decided he might progress to murder himself.

The front door was unlocked as usual. Once inside, she

began a search for the key. Had Greg ever mentioned where it was? If he had, she had no memory of it.

The voice from the ether was there again to taunt her. *Who are you locking the door against anyway? The man you've been having sex with, who, now accused of the rape and murder of a teenage girl, is currently locked in a police cell in Inverness?*

It was ludicrous. He wouldn't come back tonight. But what if he did?

Scrabbling through the various kitchen drawers, she finally found what might be the front door key. It was rusty with disuse but she managed eventually to turn it in the lock. The back door was easier, the bolt sliding smoothly across.

She congratulated herself. No one would get in here tonight. She could sleep easy. *Ha fucking ha.*

Re-entering the kitchen, her eyes were drawn to the whisky bottle. Why on earth should she not have a drink? She had no intention of keeping a baby, if there even was one.

Yet something still stopped her from pouring herself a large glass.

No. She needed to think and for that she required a clear head. Crossing to her laptop, she set about checking the times of the Inverness–London trains.

She could book a place on the Caledonian Sleeper. Leave tomorrow night. But where would she stay in London? Richard was there and undoubtedly searching for her. Plus he had friends in the Met who would help him. If he declared her missing, they would take him at his word. After all, he was a respected defence lawyer.

She'd tried to cover her tracks, of course. Taken out plenty of cash and not used any of her cards to get here. Hiding in Blackrig had worked so far. She laughed at herself for even thinking that.

She'd come to stay in the middle of nowhere with a man she barely knew, who was now accused of rape and murder. How could she have been so stupid?

She thought of Lucy. Dare she tell her the latest episode in her journey from one level of hell to another?

Not tonight, anyway. Fear and nausea had exhausted her. Taking herself through to the bedroom where the signs of her earlier rush to get ready lay scattered about, she stretched out on the bed, still wearing the dress Greg had so admired.

Closing her eyes, she could see him as she'd walked into the room, his eyes shining with delight. They'd even joked about her wearing knickers. Her face flushed with embarrassment.

But remembering the way he'd looked at her made her stop and think.

Malcolm obviously didn't believe the charges they'd brought against Greg. Kath wouldn't either. They'd known him all his life. They'd known Ailsa too.

She doubted Caroline would believe it either and she had been his lover when Ailsa had gone missing.

So what had the police found that had led them to Greg? What evidence did they have to suggest he'd raped and murdered her?

It must have had something to do with the DNA samples they'd taken from all the males who'd been in Blackrig when Ailsa had gone missing, she realized. They must have found Greg's DNA somewhere on her body.

But was that enough to convict him?

She stopped there, her brain seizing up at the horror of it all.

The question she really had to ask herself was . . . did she believe Greg capable of such a crime?

She dozed fitfully, her dreams full of an image of Ailsa in the fairy glen, pouting at the camera – but who was taking the photograph?

She still hadn't got used to the early sunrise this far north. Greg didn't have curtains at any of the windows in Beanach . . . 'There's no one here to look in,' he used to say to her. 'Except the darkness,' had been her response.

'The dark can't hurt you,' he'd told her. 'Besides, we've just passed the longest day. It barely gets dark here at this time of year.'

It wasn't the early light that woke her next morning but the unfamiliar ring of the landline. Groggy with sleep, she went to answer, thinking it might be Malcolm who'd said he would call Beanach if he heard any news.

He sounds broken, she thought, when Greg's voice said her name.

'Joanne,' he repeated when she didn't immediately respond. 'Are you okay?'

She had no idea how to answer him. She couldn't tell him how frightened she'd been last night. How she'd planned to leave here and as quickly as possible.

'I'm okay. How are you?' she managed.

He was silent and she knew he must have heard from her voice how she really felt.

'What's happening?' she tried. 'Will they let you come home?' Home. That word again. His home, not hers.

'Not yet. I'm being interviewed shortly. Not sure what will happen after that.'

'I'm sorry,' she muttered, her voice almost a whisper.

'I didn't do what they're accusing me of,' he said, his voice steady.

At this point she should tell him she believed him. Last

night she'd feared him. Had thought of him alongside Richard, which was wrong. Hearing his voice brought back their last few hours together.

'Should I come up?' she found herself saying.

'No,' he said. 'I'll keep in touch. Let you know what happens next.' The voice that followed was thick with emotion. 'I'll understand if you want to go home. Malcolm will run you to the station. You could catch the night sleeper.'

Now that he'd made the suggestion, she realized her desire to leave had diminished.

'I'll wait until we know what's happening,' she managed.

A surprised silence for a moment, then, 'Okay, if you're sure,' he said tentatively. 'Colin will come round for the dogs. Malcolm says if it's too lonely for you up there, you can have a room at the hotel or with Kath.'

The kindness of those who chose to believe in Greg made her feel ashamed. 'I'll stay here for the moment.' She didn't say *in case you come back*, but that's what she meant.

Before she could work out the best way to end the conversation, a voice from the background caused him to abruptly end the call, and she was left staring at the silent receiver.

Greg

They'd spoken to him only briefly when he'd been brought in last night. After which he'd been placed in the cell. He'd slept fitfully, worried more about Joanne than himself.

He'd been waiting for them to arrest him and, now that it had happened, he no longer had to wonder when, or if, they might.

It was the unveiling of the truth that he now feared the most. Although he wondered if that might be for the best. Ailsa's disappearance had haunted them all for long enough. Undoubtedly, someone would have to pay for her death. The question was, would that someone be him?

As he understood it, they could hold him for twenty-four hours without charge. Everything would depend on the evidence they had, which had led them to believe him guilty. They obviously hadn't enough to charge him right away or they would have done it. So what he said in the coming interview would be important. Very important.

His alibi could save him, but only if Caroline stuck to her story, and the police believed his lie.

For what he and she were about to tell them was most definitely a lie.

Malcolm had promised to let Caroline know what had happened. If she came voluntarily to the police station, he could be out of there soon enough. But before that would be the interview with DI Snyder. Whatever fear he'd felt being interviewed in the village hall would be nothing to what he would experience here. Of that he was certain.

His thoughts turned to Joanne and how she must have felt last night. He imagined her return to Beanach, wondering if she'd been living with a rapist and a murderer. How frightened she must have been.

He'd fully expected to have no one answer when he called the landline. To discover she'd left for Inverness and the train back south. He'd already envisaged the various ways she might escape him.

Malcolm would have given her the Land Rover keys as requested, so she could have gone back to Beanach and immediately booked an early morning flight south to Luton, Gatwick or Heathrow. Been back in London in just a few hours.

But she hadn't gone for an early flight and she hadn't sounded as though she intended catching the sleeper.

So she might still be there when the police let him go. Although that all depended on Caroline.

They'd come for him shortly after the telephone call.

The room he was now in spoke of its intentions. It made him long for the wee back room at the village hall. If he'd felt intimidated there, he felt it a lot more strongly now. He'd been given tea, if you could call it that, in a paper cup. He felt a desire for the thick brown hot liquid suitably sweetened by Maggie, who knew how he liked it, served in a big white mug from the hall's kitchen cupboard.

He would also have welcomed her 'Here you go, Greg' as she'd plonked it down in front of him.

Back home, he'd been a local caught up in Blackrig's latest horror. Here, he was a man suspected of raping and murdering a seventeen-year-old girl.

The recording switched on, the declarations and introductions given, DI Snyder and DS Reid now observed him with notably blank expressions.

I have become someone else, he thought, *even in their eyes*. He knew he could remain silent, but had decided to answer their questions. Perhaps that way he might discover what evidence they had against him.

It was Snyder who took the lead. 'Mr Taylor. We would like you to tell us again about the night of Saturday 22 July 2017.'

Greg, feeling the tightening of his throat, made an attempt to swallow before answering.

'I've told you all that already.'

'We'd like you to tell us again.'

He nodded as though understanding why this should be required, then reminded himself not to embellish. Just simple facts, even though they weren't true.

'I was manning the bar in the village hall with my girlfriend, Caroline Campbell.'

Snyder raised his hand to stop him there. 'You and Caroline Campbell were living together at the time?'

'No,' Greg said. 'She was living with her brother, Finn, in the village. I was living at Beanach.'

He didn't add, *We were already arguing about that. She wanted me down in the village with her. I didn't want her up at Beanach with me.*

'You saw Ailsa that night?'

'Yes. I saw her come up to the bar a couple of times.'

Snyder's expression didn't change. 'What did she have to drink?'

Greg knew exactly what she liked to drink, but if he revealed that, what would that say about the remote relationship he'd been promoting?

'The bar in the hall only stocks bottled beer, the usual spirits, gin, vodka, whisky, plus some soft drinks. I don't know what she chose.'

'You didn't serve her?'

'No.'

That was the truth. He'd avoided Ailsa all night, catching the eye of everyone but her.

'So, your girlfriend Caroline served her?'

'She must have done.' Even as the words left his mouth, he knew what horror they might bring.

'Is that the only time you saw Ailsa?'

In truth, he couldn't remember what he'd said when the police had arrived after Ailsa's disappearance. So whatever he said now was unlikely to be the same. He decided to just go for it and hope for the best.

'It was hectic that night. A real Blackrig get-together. Loud, with plenty music and dancing. When it's like that it goes past in a blur, just constantly taking orders.' He paused, hoping he'd set the scene, while remembering these two were from Glasgow where no doubt they had a lot more experience of such nights than he did.

They were waiting silently for him to continue.

'I might have seen Ailsa leave. At least, she was over by the open fire exit at the back because a few of the local lads were shouting at her.'

'Who was shouting?' DS Reid said. 'And what were they shouting?'

'Offering to walk her home. That kind of thing.'

'Who was doing that?' Snyder said.

'I couldn't see them, just heard them.'

'So how did you know they were local?'

'Their accents. The visitors were mostly English, plus a few campers.'

'Was Josh Huntly among the group asking to take her home?'

He had been. In fact, he'd been the most persistent voice he'd heard, but Ailsa had swatted him away the way she'd done to all the others. None of this he said.

'So no outsiders pestering her? No one making a nuisance of themselves?'

'Ailsa didn't entertain arses,' he said, remembering how easily she got her way. He knew, of course, he shouldn't have said that, because it gave the impression he knew her far better than he'd admitted up to now. The trouble was the truth forced its way out sometimes.

'Ailsa didn't entertain arses,' DS Reid repeated. 'You knew her well enough to be aware of that.' It wasn't a question, but he answered as though it was.

'It was what people said about her.'

'Did she consider you an arse, Mr Taylor?'

'I don't think so. I hope not.'

They were steering him somewhere, because he suddenly felt like a deer being driven across the moor towards the place where it would inevitably be met with a bullet in the heart or the brain.

'How well did you know Ailsa Cummings?'

That same question repeated. He repeated his answer. 'Not well. She was in a different age group from me. With different friends.'

'So you weren't *a thing*?' Snyder said.

He tried to look affronted by such a suggestion. 'As I said, I was in a relationship with Caroline Campbell at the time.'

He almost blurted out about the baby, but stopped himself in time.

The silence that followed seemed unusually long. Like that moment on the hill when they waited for the hunter, known as 'the rifle', to begin pressing the trigger.

He almost heard a bang as the bullet he'd been waiting for met its target. Him.

'Then, Mr Taylor, can you explain to us why your semen was found on the *inside* of the knickers Ailsa Cummings was wearing the night she died?'

Greg

Greg remained outwardly silent while his head filled with the sounds and images of that night. Ailsa at the bar, trying to catch his attention. Caroline's eyes on him all the time.

His despair when he saw Ailsa finally leave. That last look she'd thrown him, both teasing and certain that he would come after her.

He'd heard Josh and his mates giving her a hard time as she'd exited. Offering to walk her home, when what they were really asking for was sex somewhere in the woods.

He knew she'd already tasted some of the gang. Josh, certainly, and more than once. A couple of the others. Finn watched in silence from afar. She'd danced with Finn on occasion, she'd told him, but nothing more than that. He was too quiet for her and – she'd screwed up her face – much too nice.

'Mr Taylor,' Snyder's voice broke through the fabric of his thoughts.

'I'm sorry?'

Snyder repeated the earlier question that had caused his world to shatter. He was now waiting for an answer.

He decided there was no point denying it. 'I had sex with Ailsa the night she went missing,' he said quietly.

'You told us you hardly knew the girl. She was too young for you. Yet you had sex with her. Or did you not, in fact, rape Ailsa Cummings?'

'No,' he found himself shouting. 'I did not rape her. It was consensual.'

'Unfortunately, Ailsa's no longer alive and therefore can't confirm that,' DS Reid said pointedly.

'We were in a relationship. Of sorts,' he said.

'Of sorts?' DS Reid said. 'What does that mean exactly?'

He thought back to that moment in the woods when he'd found her drawing the carvings. How they'd chatted about her going to art college in the autumn. How she'd engineered more meetings. Or he had. How eventually one of them had led to sex. Something he'd welcomed.

'We met by chance one day in the fairy glen, where the carving trail is,' he said quietly. 'She was drawing the figures. We chatted. We met occasionally there and later at my place. She was living at Forrigan, which isn't far away from Beanach.'

She had never knocked. Just walked in. The first time he'd been shocked, angry with her. What if Caroline had been there, he'd told her. So what, she'd said, before kissing him.

Life for Ailsa had to hold danger or it wasn't worth living.

'How long had this relationship *of sorts* been going on?' Snyder said.

'A couple of months.'

It had lasted exactly eighty-one days, from the moment they'd met in the woods until the night of the ceilidh when he'd ended it.

'Did anyone else know about this clandestine relationship?' DS Reid said.

He suspected Josh Huntly did, and was mightily annoyed by it, since he thought he'd been in there first, but he wasn't about to shop Josh.

'Well?' Snyder said.

He shook his head.

'Not your girlfriend, Caroline?' DS Reid asked.

Then he told the big lie. 'Not that I was aware of.'

He knew his answers weren't convincing anyone, least of all himself.

'How did she die?' he said, thinking they had never yet spoken of her death.

'We were hoping you would tell us that, Mr Taylor.'

'I had sex with her that night. I didn't kill her.' But a small voice said, *If you hadn't sent her away, Ailsa would likely still be alive.*

Snyder came back in. 'Why don't you tell us exactly what happened after Ailsa left the ceilidh.'

Greg nodded. 'When I didn't turn up in the woods, she came to Beanach looking for me. I told her that it had to end. She persisted. We made love. I was adamant it was for the last time. I told her that I loved Caroline and that she was expecting our child. She was very angry at that. She left. I never saw her again.'

'Why did Ms Campbell give a statement at the time of Ailsa's disappearance that she was with you that night after the ceilidh?'

'She was. She drove up after she'd been home to check on her brother Finn.'

'Was she aware that Ailsa had been there?'

'I told her that Ailsa had turned up and that I'd sent her away.'

'Does she know you had sex with Ailsa that night?'

That was something Caroline didn't know and, if she found out, would likely change everything.

Joanne

She'd lost track of her last period, so intent had she been on her plan to escape. Richard rarely went away on business, and usually when he did, she was *persuaded* to go with him. After all, as a writer, he said, she could work anywhere.

When he'd announced his solo trip, she'd remained silent and biddable. Perhaps that was why he'd seemed comfortable about leaving her behind. Either that or he'd found some other female to take with him.

She'd hoped he had because that might free her. In fact, she'd prayed for it, even though she had no deity to pray to.

Reading the NHS website, she had just learned that, using no contraception, typically eighty-five in one hundred women would get pregnant in a year. With condoms you could expect fifteen pregnancies; the combined pill, nine.

They didn't give a percentage for the muddled method of forgetting to take a pill, which was the one she'd been using.

She took herself into the bathroom, having made up her mind that should the test prove positive, she would immediately book an online appointment for a termination. But where? Stay in Scotland or go back to London?

That was a decision too far, one she might not have to make at all.

Testing for the virus had become so much a part of life that the thought of another test shouldn't have freaked her. After all, at the height of the pandemic, for many people a positive test meant real sickness, often leading to a horrible death.

A pregnancy test was something else entirely, she told herself. *Although*, a small voice reminded her, *a death might result from it too*. Either of the foetus or her, should Richard find out.

It was over in seconds, much like the nose and throat swabs. The wait to find out the truth, however, seemed interminably long. She had just read the result when she heard Caroline's voice call her name.

Looking wildly around, wondering where she might dispose of the evidence, she eventually stuffed it in the small cabinet holding Greg's shaving gear.

This time she couldn't hide out the back because Caroline would no doubt come looking for her.

'I'm here!' she shouted as she headed for the kitchen, where Caroline already stood, her face a picture of despair.

'You've heard?' she said.

'We were having dinner at the hotel when it happened.' Joanne paused. 'Also, Greg called me first thing this morning.'

'He did?' Caroline looked put out by that. 'What did he say?'

'That he didn't do it.'

'Of course he didn't.' Caroline threw her a disparaging look. 'I told you what that bitch was like. She was determined to get Greg, no matter how often he told her no. Plenty others didn't refuse. Josh Huntly for a start. Why didn't they pick him up?'

Joanne didn't know what to say, so she filled the awkward silence that followed Caroline's trashing of Josh by offering her tea.

'Please,' Caroline said, settling herself at the table. 'We need to talk.'

That ominous declaration filled Joanne with horror. What could Caroline possibly want to talk to her about?

'Can you use my china and teapot?' Caroline said. 'And the Earl Grey, of course.'

Joanne nodded absent-mindedly as she reached into the cupboard for the cups and saucers, only to recall they wouldn't be there, because they'd been broken the day before.

She turned, an apology on her lips, but before she could say anything, Caroline, with a quick examination of her face, said, 'You look really pale. Come and sit down. I'll make the tea.'

Deciding she really did need to sit down, Joanne sank on to a chair. 'I'm sorry. Your cups got knocked over and broken. I was going to try and replace them,' she managed.

There was a moment when it looked like Caroline might comment on that, before she said, 'Never mind. I have others I can bring up.'

All went silent as Caroline set about putting a tray together like the last time. Joanne could almost hear her brain working. As for herself, it wasn't her brain but her stomach that was churning over. The tea might well be the final straw.

She closed her eyes and took a few deep breaths. When she opened them again, Caroline was sitting opposite, observing her.

'I was with Greg the night Ailsa disappeared,' she said. 'I'm his alibi. I told him I have his back . . .'

Joanne tried to focus. Was there an inaudible 'unless' at the end of that sentence? She chose to pretend not.

'So they should let him out soon?'

Caroline sat back in the chair. 'I need to go up there, be interviewed and give my statement first.' She paused. 'Meanwhile, you need to leave here.'

Joanne's nauseated brain didn't catch on at first. All she could think about was whether she needed to head for the sink or the bathroom. The sink won.

The retching was loud and violent, the little amount of tea she'd managed to swallow mixed with bile and an earlier coffee. When it was over, she turned on the cold tap and splashed her face with water. Then carefully patted it dry with the tea towel, putting off the moment when she would need to turn and face Caroline.

Eventually she did. 'I had crab claws last night at the hotel. Shellfish sometimes upsets my stomach. Plus I didn't get much sleep after what happened.'

Caroline looked almost sympathetic.

'Look, this isn't your fight. You should go.'

Her tone was even, but Joanne knew she meant it. When she didn't respond, Caroline continued, 'Greg belongs here. You don't. You two had fun in London. Why not? We'd all been deprived during lockdown. He's a good lay, but he didn't expect you to turn up in Blackrig. That much was obvious. Which makes me wonder why you did. For more sex or for some other reason?'

Everything she was saying was true. Every word of it. Caroline was perceptive. Perhaps more than even Greg realized.

'I'm here because Greg invited me. As far as he's concerned, what happened between you two is over.'

Caroline nodded as though considering this.

'So he doesn't need me any more. Is that what you're saying?'

Joanne shivered as she interpreted both the look and that pronouncement. Was Caroline insinuating that if she didn't leave Blackrig, then she would no longer supply Greg's alibi for that night?

'Greg's your friend,' she said swiftly. 'Has been from your schooldays together. You told me that yourself. Of course he needs you. Now more than ever.'

Did Caroline look mollified by her announcement? Joanne wasn't sure.

Caroline rose. 'I need to get back to the shop.'

'You'll go to Inverness and give a statement, won't you?'

'And what about you, Maya Villan? When will you be leaving Blackrig?'

Stunned by the use of her pen name, Joanne was speechless.

'Oh yes. I know who you are. One of those women at the Party House came into the shop and kindly told us all about you. Is that why you're here, to get the lowdown on all of us and our troubles for your blog?'

'I think you'd better leave,' Joanne managed, her voice trembling.

'I think you should be the one to leave. And the sooner the better. For Greg's sake.'

Greg

Returned to his cell, Greg had set about revisiting everything he'd said in the interview, already wishing he'd answered differently or, even better, retained his right to remain silent. He'd stupidly thought if he appeared helpful and cooperative, things would be okay.

It had all fallen apart, of course, when they'd revealed they had the evidence to prove he'd had sex with Ailsa the night she'd disappeared.

When she'd arrived at Beanach, furious at him for not meeting her in the woods, he'd tried to reason with her. Remind her that he'd told her they were over and that he would not meet her again, ever.

Her reaction had both surprised and worried him. Her anger had changed to despair. She'd professed that the only way she'd managed to keep her word to her parents to stay clean, not run away again and concentrate on getting to art college in the autumn was the time she'd spent with him.

He'd drawn her into his arms at that point, but had he coerced her into having sex with him one final time or had she been the one to decide?

No matter how often he revisited that scene, he couldn't be sure. Or didn't want to be sure.

When she'd left Beanach, she hadn't looked back. He'd stood at the door watching her disappear into the darkness, thinking, wanting to call her back. Apologize. Take her in his arms again.

Of course, he hadn't done that, because he'd promised Caroline it was over. It had to be over because Caroline was pregnant with his child. The child whose life had also ended not long after that terrible night.

Having feared being implicated in Ailsa's death, now all he wanted was to discover the truth and clear his name. And that meant finding out what had happened after he'd last been with Ailsa.

Where had she gone after she left him at Beanach? She definitely hadn't gone home. Her parents had never seen her after she'd left home that night for the ceilidh. He'd last seen her on the Beanach track, which met the road that led either back to Blackrig or to the Party House, where her body had been found.

Whoever killed her had either met her or followed her from his place. They need not have stayed on the road. There were numerous paths through the woods near the Party House, including the one which led to the ancient pine, where he'd first taken Joanne, and from where she'd spied on him and made him so angry. Whichever route she'd taken, Ailsa had lost her life either before or after she reached the beach by the green lochan.

When she'd initially disappeared, he'd assumed by the way she'd spoken that night that she'd run away again, and had partially blamed himself. He had never, even for a moment, imagined her dead.

He thought of Josh, who'd been the other main recipient of her interest. She'd told him she liked Josh because he was fun and wild. Didn't take shite from anyone. Like herself. Had she told Josh about him? If Josh had followed her that night from the ceilidh and seen her go up to Beanach, might that have made him mad enough to kill her?

Even as he contemplated such a scenario, he knew it didn't make sense. If Josh had killed and buried Ailsa, why would he take his mates to the Party House to smash up the hot tub, knowing there was a chance the body might be exposed?

Then another thought occurred. What if Josh, knowing Greg had had sex with Ailsa that night, had simply set him up for her murder by destroying the hot tub and exposing her body?

Still, why do that now?

Greg knew the answer to that would involve the virus and the Party House, and the fact he'd done nothing to stop it being rented out again. Even going to London to assure that would happen.

It was at this point in his musings that he became aware that Josh was here in the building and close by too. As scuffling footsteps threaded their way along the corridor, he heard Josh's curses, peppered by an officer's orders to be quiet.

Then, 'I know what you did, Taylor, I fucking know what you did.'

Greg sat down abruptly on the bed. Josh knew he was in here and wanted his message heard. The venom in his voice was obvious, but what was it he knew? That he was implicated in Ailsa's murder? Or that he was responsible for bringing in the virus via the Party House?

As for Josh, was his arrest to do with vandalizing the hot tub or with Ailsa's death?

Joanne

After Caroline's departure, she'd gone through to the bedroom and lain down on the bed, willing her stomach to cease its churning. She'd had no time to digest the results of the pregnancy test before having to face Caroline. Now, she tried to dispense with her threats and focus on her own imminent problem.

She was pregnant.

She said it out loud for emphasis, as if the words released to the air might make her face the fact head on.

Richard had wanted her to get pregnant, so much so that she'd had to pretend not to be taking the pill, while hiding them. He no doubt saw a pregnancy as yet another leash to tie her to him. The child, after all, would be under his control, just like her.

She began taking deep breaths, willing her heart to slow and the surge of adrenaline to come to an end. When it eventually did, she rose and went to her laptop. She knew she should book an appointment, but . . .

There was plenty of time to decide where she would go for the termination. No one knew except her, and no one would know. First, she needed to be sure that Caroline would continue to give Greg an alibi, and for this she needed to engage an ally, such as Kath.

*

The fresh air revived her. It was still warm, with a few clouds about. None that looked like rain clouds, however. Checking via her mobile, she found the weather would stay like this for possibly a further week. Something she knew Greg would be concerned about. As he'd reminded her, you didn't have a Highland landscape like this without rain.

Colin had arrived not long after Caroline left. She'd already fed the dogs and spent a little time with them. Although they'd been pleased to see her, there was no doubt who they were really looking for.

Colin had been a combination of sheepish and frantic. He too had heard the news about Greg from Malcolm. Not for the first time, Joanne had found herself relieved that the arrest had been made at the hotel rather than at Beanach, otherwise she would have had the job of telling everyone.

'Greg called me this morning,' she'd told Colin. 'He sounded okay. He said you would look after the dogs.'

Colin had asked what she would do. Stay in Blackrig or go home?

'I'm not leaving,' she'd said with certainty.

He'd seemed pleased by that and didn't question whether it would be at Beanach or in the village.

'Any word of Stratton going?' she'd asked.

At that, Colin's face had clouded over. 'The women and some of the men are leaving soon. Stratton and Chalmers are staying on. Stratton looked quite pleased that Greg had been arrested.' He'd sworn under his breath at that point. 'I think he's hanging about to see if he's formally charged. The bastard hinted to me that I might be taking over. As if I would.'

'The police will let Greg go,' Joanne said. 'Caroline will testify that she was at Beanach with him that night, after the ceilidh.'

221

Whether she was sure of that or not, her announcement had cheered up Colin no end. So much so that it had lifted her spirits too.

Reaching the end of the drive now, she turned towards the village. If Kath wasn't at home, she'd check in with Malcolm at the hotel. Just thinking about talking this over with Kath and Malcolm lightened her load.

Surely they held enough sway with Caroline to make sure she kept her word to Greg to 'have his back', despite the fact that Caroline hated that she was still here?

Reaching the village, she noted that the police interviews were still being conducted as evidenced by the cars lined up around the hall. Surely that was a good sign and hopefully meant that they hadn't totally settled on Greg as the guilty party?

The car park held a few campervans, but the real influx would happen, according to Greg, when the English schools broke up in a couple of weeks.

As for the press, she couldn't identify anyone in particular who might be here for the murder story . . . *except me*, she thought.

That was until a couple of blokes suddenly emerged from a car, and strode swiftly in her direction.

'Come away in,' Kath said as she opened the door before Joanne had time to knock. 'The bloody press is here, which was bound to happen.'

Once inside the sitting room, she urged Joanne to take a seat, then gave her a studied look.

'You look a bit peely-wally. Are you okay?' she said.

'I didn't sleep very well with . . .' She stumbled to a halt, not wishing to say the words 'Greg' and 'arrest' in the same sentence.

'No wonder. But you've talked to him this morning? He wanted you to be the person he called.'

'I did,' Joanne said.

'You'll be wanting some tea, with a drop of sugar. Good for shock, and this has been a shock and no mistake,' Kath said before heading for the kitchen.

The familiar comfort and scent of the room eased her thoughts. Kath believed in Greg, as did Malcolm. *As do I*, she reminded herself.

Once the tea was served, together with fresh scones, which Joanne found she could eat, she explained why she'd come.

Kath shook her head at Joanne's recounting of Caroline's visit. When it came to the threat that Joanne should leave, she was openly angry.

'I'll have a word with her,' she said. 'And don't even think of leaving. You need to be here when they let Greg go.'

'But what if Caroline withdraws her alibi because of me?'

'Then I'll testify to the fact that she did that out of spite, because Greg's with you now and not her. We all remember her story from the last time.'

Joanne wasn't sure that would work, but didn't say so.

'What about you up there at Beanach, all on your own? You're welcome to stay here or there's a room for you at the Blackrig Arms, until they let him go.'

'I looked it up,' Joanne said. 'They can hold him for twenty-four hours, then they have to let him go if they don't have enough evidence to charge him.'

'So,' Kath glanced at the clock on the mantelpiece, 'he should be back by late tonight.'

'How will he get back?' Joanne asked.

'Malcolm will pick him up.'

Joanne wondered what would happen if they didn't release him. If they believed they had enough evidence to charge him and remanded him in prison somewhere, either in Inverness or maybe Glasgow until his trial.

Kath had been silent for a moment. Now she said, 'The police arrested Josh Huntly this morning and took him to Inverness.'

'Josh?' Joanne said in surprise. 'What for?'

'No one seems to know for sure.' She looked worried by that.

'Were Josh and Ailsa a thing?'

Kath shrugged. 'That I can't say for certain. She hung out with Josh and his gang on occasion. They were better company than her Glasgow camping chums.'

'Camping?'

'Up near the lochside. Lord Main allowed wild camping up there for a while. The new owners stopped it.'

'And Ailsa used to go up there?'

Kath nodded. 'There was bad feeling in Blackrig about the campers. Folk said they brought in drugs from Glasgow.' Her expression darkened. 'Some said that Ailsa sold the drugs to the local kids for profit.'

'You knew her. Did you believe that?'

'She told me she'd promised her parents to stay clean. She wanted to go to art college in the autumn. She never got there, though, did she?'

The contrast between Kath's judgement of Ailsa and Caroline's was stark.

'Caroline hated her. She told me the drugs story and that Ailsa chased Greg, but he wouldn't have anything to do with her.'

'Caroline thinks she owns Greg. She doesn't.' Kath rose.

'Now, I'm going along to see if I can catch her at the shop. Feel free to stay here . . .'

'I'd rather go—' She was about to say 'home' but swiftly changed it to 'back to Beanach'.

'Have you enough food up there?'

'Plenty,' Joanne assured her, although she wasn't sure whether she could eat it.

Greg

Snyder was observing him thoughtfully, as though there was something about him he just couldn't fathom.

You and me both, Greg thought.

This time he'd decided to say nothing. He also had a lawyer present, a Mr McGann, arranged by Malcolm. Greg was grateful to his old friend for doing that, although he would still have preferred to answer Snyder's questions rather than say 'no comment'.

He was also keen to find out why they'd picked up Josh, because Josh's voice in the corridor had sparked another memory from that night.

When Ailsa had arrived at his door, she'd been seriously out of breath, and he'd realized she must have been running. He'd assumed she'd been keen to get to Beanach to tell him exactly what she thought of him for standing her up, but later he'd noticed that her legs were scratched quite badly. When he'd asked about it, she'd brushed him off, saying she'd taken a short cut through the heather.

He remembered the cat calls at the door as she'd left. Might Josh and his gang have followed her? Maybe even given her a hard time?

Snyder's voice brought him back from his reverie. 'Mr Taylor, Ms Campbell has been in and given a statement. She says she was not at Beanach with you on the night in question.'

Before Greg could say anything, Mr McGann stopped him with, 'My client has no comment.'

Greg's mind was racing. Why had Caroline withdrawn her alibi?

This time it was DS Reid who gave him the reason. 'It seems Ms Campbell was unaware that you had sex with Ailsa Cummings on the night in question.'

It was just as he'd imagined. Once Caroline knew he was lying about that night, the game was a bogey, as they'd used to say as kids.

After this revelation, both Snyder and DS Reid left, and Mr McGann said his piece.

'Ms Campbell contradicting her previous statement is unfortunate. However, they have until eleven p.m. tonight to charge you or they will have to let you go.'

'But the evidence they have . . .'

'Proves you had sex with the deceased before she died. It does not prove that you killed her.'

'Do you know how Ailsa died?' Greg said.

McGann shook his head. 'And they won't reveal that. I take it you don't know how she died?'

'I didn't kill Ailsa. She was alive when she left my place.'

McGann seemed to accept this. 'Then have you any idea at all who might have had reason to kill her?'

Despite all his musings, he knew he didn't and said so. 'They brought in Josh Huntly. I heard him pass my cell. Any chance you could find out why?'

McGann nodded. 'Okay, and I'll try and find out what they plan to do with you.'

Back in his cell, he thought of Joanne. Would she still be at Beanach if they did release him? Or had she been afraid to tell him that she was leaving? He imagined arriving home and finding her gone. Somehow his sadness at that was more powerful than his thoughts of his release.

If they don't release you and instead charge you with the rape and murder of Ailsa Cummings, she'll be gone anyway.

As for Caroline. If they did release him, he had no need to pander to her demands any more. For that alone, he felt relieved. Although the truth would be out there. Caroline would make certain that everyone got to know that he was having an affair with Ailsa while she was carrying their child.

That, he was definitely guilty of.

Joanne

As she crowned the hill, the image of Beanach's grey stones sparkling in the sunlight lifted her spirits a little. It looked so sturdy and permanent, much like the hill that rose at its back. Regardless of what might happen in the world of humans, Beanach looked as though it intended to survive.

On her return walk, she'd mulled over everything Kath had said. Fitting together Kath's pieces of the Ailsa jigsaw, together with the earlier version that was Caroline's.

Joanne had suspected from the moment the body was discovered that Greg hadn't revealed his true relationship with the missing teenage girl. She had known this, but had chosen to ignore it.

Every time she'd tried to talk to him about Ailsa, he had shut her down. He would only discuss what he wished to talk about. Not what she chose.

Back in the kitchen, she put the kettle on, then sat down at her laptop. Regardless of what might happen next, she knew she needed to write down everything that had occurred up to now, together with each individual story she had heard.

She wrote it as a timeline. Who had said what and when. Then she jotted down who she thought had the means, the motive and the opportunity to kill Ailsa.

The main difficulty was that she hadn't been in Blackrig

at the time of Ailsa's disappearance and had only met a small number of people who'd known her.

Her most recent chat with Kath had been enlightening. By the end, she was still sure that Kath believed in Greg's innocence, but she was also convinced that there were things Kath hadn't said. And she wondered now what they were.

Kath had been keen to give her support, and obviously wanted her to stay in Blackrig, constantly assuring her that Greg would return. Although, without knowing what evidence the police had against him, no one could be sure of that.

She spent some time online trying to learn what evidence might be collected from a dead body, and wondering what they had that pointed to Greg.

Regardless of what Kath had said, being arrested for the rape and murder of a young woman meant the police definitely had something on him – but what?

She thought back to that first morning when she'd been left alone in the house. How she'd checked in the bedroom cupboards to try to get the measure of a man she didn't really know. How everything had seemed normal in his surroundings, commonplace even.

There had been the gold marriage band, of course. She remembered wondering if Greg had been married before and hadn't mentioned it. That hadn't concerned her at the time, as she'd been hiding Richard's existence, and still was.

Now she knew Greg had been in a relationship with Caroline. Long-term or so it seemed, with a miscarriage as part of it. Greg had indicated that the relationship was over, but as far as Caroline was concerned, it didn't appear to be.

She went back into the bedroom, the rumpled covers still testament to her troubled sleep, and, sitting on Greg's side of the bed, opened the drawer again. The ring was still there, but this time she didn't feel guilty about examining it.

Holding it up to the light, she could make out a well-worn inscription which led her to believe that it had been his father's wedding ring. The discovery made her sad, and a little annoyed with herself for looking through Greg's things again.

The last time she'd checked the drawer, a similar feeling had made her shut it after the ring's discovery. This time she lifted the drawer out and sat it on the bed.

It was funny how the minutiae of life inevitably ended up together somewhere like this. How, after enough time, they were forgotten about. She laid each item out on the bed, disentangling tie pins from an old watch, some leaflets about a game fair together with newspaper cuttings, which, when smoothed out, she found related to Ailsa's disappearance, as well as to the arrival of the deadly virus in Blackrig.

Last of all, caught in the seam at the back of the drawer, was a plain envelope. Freeing and opening it, she pulled out a photograph.

It was of a baby scan, the grey shape of a tiny infant obvious. On the back a name for the child that had never been born, Mac, and the words 'My son' in Greg's handwriting.

It was a discovery too far. Fumbling with the envelope, she tried to make her trembling hands put the picture back. That's when the other item inside slipped out to fall directly into her lap.

The fine gold chain unfurled itself, the name tag at its centre clear enough to read.

It said *Ailsa*.

Why did Greg have a necklace that surely belonged to Ailsa Cummings? And why was it in beside a picture of his unborn son?

The reason presented itself almost immediately, and suddenly the hold Caroline appeared to have over Greg seemed obvious.

Ailsa hadn't been a passing acquaintance, too young for Greg to even take note of. It seemed she may have been much more than that.

Joanne thought again of all the times Greg had lied to her about Ailsa. How often he'd given the impression that he barely knew her. Yet he'd kept a memento of her beside an ultrasound scan of his baby.

Eventually, pulling herself together, she retrieved her weekend case from the corner and began to pack. Whatever evidence the police had on Greg must have pointed to him knowing Ailsa a great deal better than he'd claimed.

Her imagination now working overtime, she conjured up her own version of the story. Ailsa hadn't been stalking Greg, like Caroline suggested. It had been the other way round. He'd become obsessed with the teenager and, when she'd rejected him, he'd raped and murdered her.

Even as she imagined this, she knew she was turning him into a version of Richard.

She also couldn't believe that Caroline, if she even suspected such a thing, would have continued to cover for him, including giving him an alibi for that night.

Bundling everything into the case, she went to the bathroom to fetch her toiletries, then remembered the pregnancy test.

Her hand shook as she retrieved it from among Greg's shaving things. Clasped in her hand, the blue message that life was already growing inside her freaked her even more now than it had before.

She couldn't have this baby, even though she'd briefly

toyed with the idea. A child inherited half its DNA from its father, and whether that father turned out to be Richard or Greg, it was bad news.

Stop it, she told herself. *You are the product of your parents, and yet you are nothing like them. In fact, for years you thought you might have been adopted.*

Arguing against herself was just wasting time. She shoved the test back in its plain delivery box and stuffed it in the waste bin, dumping the toiletries she wouldn't bother taking with her on top.

As she carried her case to the Land Rover, she spotted a car heading up the Beanach track. Recognizing it as Caroline's, she covered the pink suitcase with her jacket and went back inside the house. Despite having made her decision, she would not give Caroline the pleasure of knowing what that decision was.

Joanne

Was this the real Caroline? The one Greg had fallen in love with? The one he'd almost had a baby with?

She'd apologized for turning up like this without warning, but she'd just come back from Inverness, and . . .

She'd stumbled at that point, trying to choose the words to explain.

'I was wrong before for giving you the impression that I would withdraw my alibi for Greg. I didn't intend doing that.' She halted there, and the distress on her face made Joanne uneasy.

'At first I confirmed my story of that night to the police even though it wasn't the whole truth.'

Joanne wanted the whole truth, now more than ever, but she didn't want to blurt that out, fearing that Caroline might change her mind.

'It's all my fault. If I hadn't covered for him . . .' Caroline stopped there.

Although looking straight at Joanne, her eyes were reliving some action or vision from the past which horrified her.

They had moved into the kitchen and were sitting at the table as before, although no tea had been offered, because Caroline had immediately launched into her story.

'What is it?' Joanne said, reaching to cover Caroline's trembling hand with her own.

Caroline gathered herself. 'When I gave the police my statement, they told me they had evidence to prove Greg raped Ailsa that night. They found his semen on her clothes. That's why they arrested him.' Her expression was a mix of puzzlement and horror. 'And I had protected him. All this time I believed him when he said Ailsa was chasing him. Not that he was stalking her.

'He has a temper. If he doesn't get what he wants, he can get really angry.' She looked up at Joanne. 'Have you seen that yet? How he goes from funny kind guy to someone frightening?'

Joanne had, but didn't confirm it.

'Malcolm and Kath haven't seen that side of him. Wouldn't believe it if you told them. If you refuse Greg what he wants, he just takes it anyway.'

There were images being conjured by Caroline's words that Joanne wasn't comfortable with. Scenes with Greg that might well fit her story.

'Once he has you where he wants you, that's when things change. Maybe you two aren't there yet?'

Joanne tried to keep her face impassive. It was probably evident that she harboured doubts, but Caroline had gone back to arguing with herself.

'I'd just found out that I was pregnant when it happened, how could I refuse to give Greg an alibi? It was really busy at the bar that night. Ailsa kept coming up, trying to get him to talk to her, throwing me dirty looks. Greg brushed her off, so I knew he was telling the truth about her pestering him. Afterwards, I was really tired so went back to my place because I had to open up the shop early next morning.'

She continued. 'We all thought she'd gone up to the campsite to meet up with her druggie friends. Gone back to

Glasgow. We never thought she could be dead.' She sounded surprised at this, almost as if she'd just found out. 'Greg was worried that folk had seen her chasing him. When she went missing he asked me to say I was with him that night. How could I not?'

Joanne understood that perfectly. Had it been her, she may well have done the same. Even now, despite all the evidence against him, she was still arguing with herself about going or staying.

It seemed as though she'd chosen a man just like the one she'd run away from. Manipulative, hiding their true nature until they'd fooled you into thinking they were someone else. Everything Caroline was saying chimed with her own experience of Greg.

And yet . . . and yet.

She had been the one to choose him. She had singled him out. Seduced him. Tried to work out what he wanted and pandered to it. Because she wanted away from Richard. She wanted to be the one in control.

And she'd thought she had been the one in control, but how long had that lasted?

How much Greg must have enjoyed playing her along. Indulging her needs, her fantasises, like the tree with the leather straps.

What truth had there ever been between them?

They had been merely playing a game. She to seduce him so that she might escape Richard's clutches. Greg, a seemingly free man in London, responding to her advances, and yet he already had someone back in Blackrig. A history. A partner. A dead baby . . .

'When the police told me he'd been with Ailsa that night, I was so angry. I kept thinking that, back then, we had a son. We'd seen him on the scan. We'd decided to call him Mac. Then it was all over. Mac was dead.'

From almost talking to herself, she raised her eyes again.

'He went there, you know. To the Party House, when the helicopter brought them in. He went to tell them to go, or so he said. That's not what happened though. He partied with them. Took cocaine. Ran naked like the rest of them, had sex with some woman he called Marion. Greg brought the virus into Blackrig. He had nightmares about it. I heard him talking about it in his sleep. He thinks he killed those children and he probably did.'

Joanne's heart was racing as fast as her thoughts. Greg had carried so many secrets, but then so had she. She still did.

'They won't let him out,' Caroline was saying. 'But what if they do?' She looked terrified by the thought. 'What if the evidence they have isn't enough to charge him?'

Joanne watched as Caroline contemplated such an outcome, fear etched on her face.

'He wouldn't hurt you,' she found herself saying.

'I don't know any more.' Caroline looked at her. 'You shouldn't be here either. He'll be angry about . . . everything.'

Joanne was thinking exactly that.

'I'm leaving anyway,' she said. 'My case is in the Land Rover.'

'You're too late for the night train.'

'I'll fly south first thing,' Joanne said, knowing that's exactly what she should do.

'Then come and stay with me tonight and, if you don't change your mind, I'll take you to the airport in the morning.'

Greg

It was late, but still light. The small window on the outer wall of his cell made a portrait of an evening as yet unwilling to darken.

He watched as eventually sunset bruised the sky. Just after ten o'clock, he was aware there was precious little time left before he was either charged or let go.

He imagined himself in the Land Rover heading west into the sunset. Seeing Beanach again in its warm glow with Joanne there waiting for him.

A dream, not a reality. He wouldn't return to Beanach, not tonight anyway, and even if he did, Joanne would no longer be there, despite what she'd said on the phone. After all, he'd lied to her, either openly or by omission, too often. How could she believe anything he said ever again?

She would return to London and resume her life. No doubt she would write about Blackrig and him. Maya Villan, of course, would have the inside story of the thirty-year-old head gamekeeper at Blackrig Estate, who had been charged with the rape and murder of seventeen-year-old Ailsa Cummings.

But he wasn't responsible for her death. Or maybe he was? He had sex with her that night, and then sent her out to die. If he'd met her in the woods as she'd asked, she would still be alive.

The setting sun had moved from bruiser to fire raiser, setting the sky alight, before it too died and left behind only darkness.

He lay down on the hard surface which served as a bed, but dared not close his eyes, because every time he did, an image of strands of blonde hair, barely hiding Ailsa's dead face, presented itself.

If he succeeded in banishing that, then other images replaced it. Ailsa laughing at what she called his serious lack of fun, his obsession with worrying. She would play at tempting him when she had no need, because he was always tempted by her presence. Sometimes the image of her pouting mouth arrived as she prompted him to take her photograph, showing how much she enticed him. But, each time, the image was slowly transformed into that other one. The one where she was dead.

The sound of footsteps in the corridor brought him to his feet. There was a rattle as the lock was undone. The door swung open and the uniformed officer urged him out. Greg realized by the look on the officer's face that it would be better not to ask questions.

Following him along the corridor, he heard a scuffle, then Josh's voice rasped from one of the side cells as they passed.

'They've got you, you bastard.'

Any hope he might have allowed to trickle in now gone, he steeled himself for what was to come.

Snyder was alone, DS Reid having no doubt gone home. Detectives had a life too, he thought. He briefly imagined what DS Reid's might be, and saw only pleasant things. As for Snyder, he wasn't so sure. How many murder and rape cases had he investigated? How many crime scenes and post-mortems and morgues had filled his life?

How many times had he caught 'his man' and charged him? Such as was about to happen here.

He felt cold, both outside and in. The phrase 'as cold as the grave' presented itself before that image of a real grave was with him once again. He pulled himself together as he realized Snyder was about to speak.

'We're releasing you, Mr Taylor. However, we expect you not to leave the area and be aware you may be rearrested in the near future.'

The words entered his brain in jumbled form, and he had to reconstruct the sentence in order to absorb it.

'You mean I can go?' he said, surprised.

'For the moment, yes.'

Having convinced himself otherwise, he now found he was at a loss as to what should happen next. He thought of how late it was and how he might get home.

As though interpreting his thoughts, Snyder said, 'Mr Webster is waiting for you in the car park.'

'How did he know you would let me go?'

'He didn't.'

Exiting the building, Greg was suddenly reminded that he was in a city surrounded by street lights and, no doubt, cameras. Malcolm's car, headlights on, started up and moved towards him.

Greg opened the passenger door as though in a dream.

'Get in, lad,' Malcolm's welcome voice rang out. 'I'm taking you home.'

Greg

After greeting him, Malcolm had been silent, concentrating only on the driving and leaving Greg to his own thoughts. Living in Blackrig and its surrounds, you rarely encountered traffic lights, roundabouts or even two-way traffic, except at passing places. Malcolm didn't venture to the city very often, which was obvious by his level of concentration.

Once clear of habitation, he began to relax. After which he suggested Greg give Joanne a call and let her know he was on his way.

It was the last thing Greg wanted to do, being the part of his dream he knew wouldn't come true.

'Go on. Give her a call. The lassie will be delighted.'

Greg remained silent.

'What?' Malcolm threw him a puzzled look.

'I'm not expecting her to be there,' he eventually said.

'And why would that be?'

'Because I lied to her, and to you and Kath and the police. I said I didn't really know Ailsa, which wasn't true. We were having an affair behind Caroline's back. In fact, we had sex at Beanach the night she disappeared.'

Silence followed, before Malcolm eventually said, 'I take it they found that out with their forensics and that's why you were arrested?'

Greg nodded. 'She walked away from Beanach that night,

alive and well, although angry with me because I'd broken it off with her. Caroline had just found out she was pregnant and—'

'Did Caroline know about the affair?' Malcolm said.

'She thought Ailsa was chasing me. I promised to be more firm with the girl. Tell her to stay away because Caroline and I were having a baby.'

Malcolm swore under his breath. 'Caroline went to see Joanne. Told her if she didn't leave Blackrig, she would withdraw your alibi for that night. Joanne came down to the village and told Kath about it, but when Kath went to talk to Caroline, she wasn't there.'

'The police told her they'd found my semen,' he said. 'She withdrew her statement.'

'Yet they still let you go?' Malcolm sounded both relieved and puzzled.

'Mr McGann said that it proved I had sex with Ailsa, but not that I killed her.' He turned to Malcolm, his voice breaking. 'I didn't kill her, but by sending her away that night, I might as well have.'

'Ailsa, God help her, made plenty of enemies in Blackrig. Men – and women too. Now, give Joanne a call. She headed back up to Beanach after she'd spoken to Kath. She had no intention of leaving, she made that plain.'

He tried her mobile first. It rang out a few times then went to voicemail, where a robotic voice, nothing like Joanne's, asked him to leave a message. He didn't.

He then tried the landline. It too rang out unanswered.

Catching sight of Greg's worried expression, Malcolm said, 'Call Kath and check if Joanne's maybe waiting there for you.'

Kath's delight at the sound of his voice was evident.

'Where are you now?'

'About ten minutes away. Is Joanne there?'

'She was here earlier, but went back up to Beanach. At least, that's where she said she was going.'

'She's not answering the landline or her mobile.'

'She was looking very peaky when she was here. Hadn't had much sleep last night, she said. I hope she hasn't been taken ill. D'you want me to go up?'

'She's probably asleep and we'll be there soon ourselves, but thanks anyway,' Greg told her.

'It's good to have you home, son.'

His sense of foreboding grew as they entered the Beanach drive. When the house came into view there were no lights to be seen. *If she's asleep*, he told himself, *that wouldn't be odd*. Except it was.

Malcolm's silence beside him spoke volumes.

Cresting the hill, he could make out the Land Rover in the headlights. If the vehicle was still there . . .

What little hope that had afforded swiftly evaporated.

There was no one here. He knew that even as he opened the door and stepped inside the house.

He still called her name as he walked through the lower rooms and climbed the stairs. Switching on the bedroom light, he saw the rumpled bed, the drawer from his bedside table sitting on top.

Then the envelope. The one he couldn't throw away. The one that contained his last connection with the two people he'd lost. His child and Ailsa.

He stood with the envelope in his hands, knowing she'd found it and realized just how many lies he'd told her. Glancing in the corner, he saw that his fears were well-founded. The missing suitcase confirmed it.

She may have told Kath that she intended to stay, but then she'd discovered his little secret. That had been the final straw. Chances were she was already on the Caledonian Sleeper, heading for home and out of his life forever.

He couldn't blame her for that.

Greg

'She's gone.'

He was saying it as much to himself as to Malcolm.

'Her suitcase is missing. I suspect she headed for Inverness to catch the sleeper south, but how she would get there—' He stopped as a horrible thought occurred.

'The women from Ard Choille were supposed to be catching the train. Maybe Joanne got a lift from them?' If she had, he thought, then her tale of how much she hated Stratton may well have been a lie.

Malcolm digested that. 'What time does the sleeper leave exactly? Do you know?'

Having used it recently, he did. 'Monday to Friday eight forty-five. Gets into Euston just before eight tomorrow morning.' He wondered if she'd had time to get there. 'Any idea when Joanne left Kath's place?'

'No, but I can check.'

He realized that the timing didn't matter.

'Even if she didn't make tonight's train, she'll be away first thing tomorrow.'

'D'you want to go looking for her?' Malcolm said.

Greg shook his head. 'She's right to have gone. There's nothing for her here. Who wants to stay with a suspected rapist and murderer?'

'You're not that,' Malcolm said firmly.

'Not to you and Kath maybe, but Josh Huntly definitely thinks so.'

'Josh? How do you know what Josh thinks?'

'Because he told me so at the police station. They have him up there for questioning.'

'About what?'

That Greg didn't know. 'I presume the wrecking of the hot tub.'

Malcolm's face clouded over. 'Rumour was that he and Ailsa were a thing. Might he be a suspect too?'

'If he killed Ailsa, why did he encourage his gang to wreck the hot tub, exposing her grave? That would be the last thing he'd want.'

He'd already gone over the Josh scenario when alone in his cell. He didn't want to revisit it again now.

'Thanks for the lift back.'

'Well, if you need me for anything else, just let me know.'

Malcolm had looked as defeated as he felt, Greg thought, as he watched the car's headlights disappear down the track towards the village.

Standing in the kitchen, he found a terrible weariness had entered his bones, but would he – could he – sleep? He poured himself a whisky and sat down to think and plan for tomorrow. He would have to report to Stratton and face poor Colin. He didn't give a damn about Stratton but God knows what Colin thought of him.

Colin, whose biggest fear had been that his fingerprint might be found on the plastic, now had to face the fact he had a suspected rapist and murderer for a boss. He almost smiled at that.

Swallowing down his whisky, he decided he would take a shower before bed, hopefully ridding himself of the smell of his jail cell, but he was unprepared for the sight of the bathroom, all evidence of Joanne's presence having disappeared. Some of her toiletries she'd obviously taken away. Some she'd discarded in the wastebasket.

He stood transfixed at the thought that she had really gone. She was never coming back. Ever. Until that moment, he hadn't realized how he might really feel about that.

He recalled the morning he'd picked her up at the station and driven her west. How entranced she'd been by the journey and her arrival at Blackrig and then Beanach. He remembered how he'd begun to doubt the reason for her presence, how he'd thought she'd come here for a story, and not him.

Maybe he'd been right all along. Maybe she didn't feel about him the way he now discovered he felt about her.

As for Blackrig and Beanach. He would have to leave them behind too, even should they find the real killer. He was tainted by what he had and hadn't done. Caroline would make certain of that and who could blame her?

Plus he couldn't and wouldn't work for Stratton any longer.

Stepping under the shower brought back those moments he'd spent there with Joanne. Tender, exhilarating, she'd made him come alive again. After the virus. After Ailsa, after losing Mac. After destroying whatever Caroline and he had had together.

The shower definitely hadn't changed his mood; in fact, it had probably made it worse. He got out and towelled himself dry. As he swept up his bundle of dirty clothing, he inadvertently knocked over the wastebasket, sending Joanne's discards to scatter across the floor.

He bent to pick them up, assailed by the scent of Joanne they left behind, and his eye caught sight of an open package, which looked as though it had arrived by post. Examining it, he saw the label had her name and the Beanach address.

Intrigued, he looked inside and knew immediately what she'd had delivered, and why she hadn't mentioned it.

Staring at the result of the pregnancy test, he felt himself transported back in time to when Caroline had handed him a similar test. Back then he'd been more stunned than pleased, since things were already rocky between them.

Was this the reason she'd left? Had she gone to have an abortion, without even telling him about it? Her body. Her choice. Wasn't that the rule? Of course, it might not be his. Might she have returned to London to tell the real father?

He took the item that had changed his world yet again and laid it on the bed beside the other remnants of his past.

She hadn't wanted him to know she was pregnant. That much was obvious. So what should or could he do, if anything? The one thing he couldn't do, he realized, was to leave her to deal with it alone. If she didn't want his help, she could tell him that to his face.

He fetched his mobile and brought up her number. Noting how late it was, he sent a text instead. Then he lay down on the bed to wait out the remainder of the night without end.

Joanne

Caroline's mood seemed to brighten as they drove towards the village. The trauma she'd exhibited in the kitchen at Beanach had almost disappeared. It appeared that Joanne's decision to depart had lightened Caroline's load considerably.

Joanne's own thoughts still darted about, like moths courting a flame. She found herself measuring her trust in Greg against her trust in Caroline. Had what she'd said about Greg and the police even been true? Or had what just happened in the kitchen all been a ploy to get her to leave Beanach?

She was aware that living with Richard had changed her mindset from thoughtful to paranoid. That hadn't eased even when she'd escaped his clutches and come to Blackrig. Although she'd been outwardly responsive to Greg, she'd internally analysed his every word, thought and move.

As they entered the village, she contemplated asking to be dropped at Kath's house. After all, Kath had offered for her to stay there tonight, despite stating her belief that Greg would come home, but something stopped her.

As they drew up outside the stone-built two-storey house attached to the shop, Caroline said, 'I feel much better for having confided in you. I feel we're allies now and not enemies.'

Joanne said nothing to confirm or deny this. All she wanted to do was try and get some sleep, then have Caroline deposit her at the airport where she would catch any plane that might take her swiftly south.

Once inside, Caroline offered her tea. 'Or even something stronger,' she added with a smile.

'Thanks, but I'm really tired.'

She looked a little disappointed at that, but then said, 'You're right. We'll have to be up sharp. I'll give you a call at six. Come on, I'll show you to your room.'

Alone now, Joanne sank down on the bed, her head feeling suddenly light. She realized she hadn't eaten or drunk anything for what seemed like hours, and she should probably have accepted Caroline's offer of tea at least.

Checking out the small bathroom, she filled the toothbrush holder with water and drank it down, noting the absence of the peaty flavour of Beanach's supply. She recalled Greg explaining that he got his water from the hill.

'The same water they use to make whisky,' he'd told her with a grin.

That pleasant memory was swiftly followed by another and another as she replaced the black picture of Greg painted by Caroline with the shared moments of joy they'd had together.

She took out her mobile, intending to call Lucy to tell her she was coming back. It was then she noticed a text message. A babble of internal voices warned her not to read it. One solitary voice told her the opposite.

Am back at Beanach. Sad to find you gone. Can we talk? Please?

The police had let him go and he was home. 'Home', that word again. His home, not hers. She hesitated as her finger hovered over the call button. Didn't he deserve to tell her his side of the story?

It was then she heard the front door open and someone come in. A male voice, one she didn't recognize, was talking loudly at Caroline. Might it be her brother, Finn?

Joanne eased open the door and stepped quietly on to the landing.

'Why is she here?' the voice was demanding.

Caroline's low reply was inaudible, so Joanne stepped silently towards the stairs.

At that point Finn came back in with, 'They've let him go. He'll be back at Beanach by now.'

Again Caroline's soft reply defied her attempts to hear.

'Because he didn't fucking do it!' Finn was shouting. 'Now they've lifted Josh. Who knows who'll be next?' His words sounded more like a threat than a question.

More muttered placating sounds from Caroline. This time Joanne caught the gist of what she was saying about running her to the airport in the morning.

'Are you mad? You're not taking her anywhere.'

The words were followed by his footsteps on the stairs. Swiftly merging back into the shadows, Joanne slipped into her room and shut the door. Moments later, it was flung open and Finn's tall body filled the doorway.

'Where's your case? I'm taking you back to Beanach.'

Joanne mustered herself. 'I'm leaving Blackrig tomorrow morning. Caroline kindly offered to run me to the airport.'

'Caroline's taking you nowhere. Greg can run you to the airport. You're his house guest. Not ours. She had no business bringing you here.'

Suitcase in hand, he pointed to the door. 'Out, now,' he ordered.

The sheer fury on his face made her comply. He let her go first on the stairs and, feeling the weight of him right behind her, she kept wondering if he might suddenly choose to send her hurtling down.

Caroline was waiting at the front door, her expression set back to fearful.

'I'm sorry, Joanne,' she said. 'Please be careful up there. Greg—'

'Shut the fuck up!' Finn said, pushing her out of the way.

Having swiftly installed Joanne in the car she'd arrived in, he revved the engine and took off. Heading along Main Street, he met the corner onto the single track road with a screech of tyres. Gripping the edge of the seat, Joanne asked him to slow down, but her plea was ignored.

Glancing sideways, she saw his clenched jaw and caught a whiff of what he'd obviously been drinking. She might be worried about returning to Beanach, but she was even more concerned about getting there in one piece.

They met the dirt road to the house in much the same way, kicking up the dry dust to envelop them. As they crested the hill, she could see the lights of Beanach blazing out like a lighthouse in the darkness.

Drawing up with a slam of the brakes, he told her to get out.

Joanne did as ordered, as he deposited her case alongside her. There was, she realized, no way Greg would not be aware of her arrival, so any thought she may have had of walking back down to Kath's was now out of the question.

Finn's last call before he slammed the car door was to emphasize that she should never see nor speak to his sister again. Ever.

'Or,' he said ominously, 'it will be the worse for you. Do you fucking hear me?'

Joanne indicated that she did.

'And tell him to stay away from her too,' he said before roaring away.

Greg

He stood at the open door, waiting to see what she might say or do. His main worry was that she was afraid of him and that's why she'd left. He felt sick at the thought.

'Do you want to come inside or would you rather I drove you to Kath's or the hotel?' he eventually said.

His offer, he noted, seemed to lessen her anxiety a little, and she said, 'I'd like to come in, if that's all right with you.'

He came to fetch her suitcase and, standing to one side, let her walk in first. Everything, he knew, would hinge on what was now said between them. What she asked, and how he responded.

He motioned to the kettle. 'Can I make you tea or would you like something . . .' He was about to say 'stronger' but swapped it for 'something else'.

The look she gave him at that point seemed to come from her soul.

'You know,' she said. 'How?'

'I knocked over the waste bin getting out of the shower. The Amazon package fell out.' Honesty, he'd decided, had to be the best policy from now on.

Apparently reading his expression, she said, 'It's not your concern. I will deal with it.'

He gave a little nod, knowing now was not the time to say anything to the contrary. Filling the kettle, he put it on the hot plate of the range and set about fetching mugs, milk and sugar.

She sat in silence while he did this, as though marshalling her thoughts. Eventually she said, 'Caroline was here earlier. She was very upset. She told me she'd gone to Inverness to give you an alibi. Then the police told her . . .'

He halted her there because he couldn't bear the word rape to come out of her mouth.

'Then you know I lied about Ailsa and that we were having an affair. I broke it off because of the baby. She wanted me to meet her in the woods after the ceilidh. I didn't go. She turned up at Beanach. We made love for the last time and she left. I never saw her again.'

There was, he realized, a huge relief in telling her the truth, whatever happened now.

'I found her necklace and the scan of Mac,' she said quietly.

'So you'd already guessed?'

He imagined her feelings when she'd seen what was in the envelope. How many thoughts and questions must have tumbled through her head? Especially if she'd just discovered she was pregnant.

But you mustn't mention that now, he told himself. *Let her be the one to talk.*

'Caroline believes you did rape Ailsa. That you were chasing her and not the other way round. That when you didn't get what you wanted, you just took it.'

He wanted to tell her that Caroline would say anything to get her to leave Blackrig. To leave him, despite the fact she knew they would never be together again.

'She said that now she knew the truth, she was frightened for me,' she continued. 'I told her I was planning on leaving anyway. She offered to put me up for tonight and take me to the airport in the morning.'

He silently marvelled at Caroline's dedication. First threatening not to give him an alibi, then saying she had, then telling Joanne he was a rapist. No doubt she'd mentioned murder too. All this he thought, but didn't say.

'I'll take you to the airport tomorrow, or the train station. Anywhere you want to go.' Noting her weariness, he added, 'You need to sleep. Go on up. I'll take the couch.'

She seemed to muster herself then, although her face remained too pale for his comfort.

'You're all in. Let me help you.'

Ignoring his proffered hand, she rose wearily and made for the stairs. He stayed there, listening for the creaks as she climbed, thanking God that he'd put away the drawer and its scattered contents. Waiting until he heard the bedroom door close, he then collected his jacket and went outside.

He needed to think and the natural world, his world, was the best place to do it. Fetching his rifle from the shed, he set off towards the woods.

The stars were out, a milky moon too. The sultry warmth of the day had dissipated, but as soon as he entered the woods, the sharp smell of pine hit his nostrils. Darker among the trees, he stood for as long as it took his eyes to adjust to the place he knew so well.

Letting his feet choose their own path, he eventually found himself by the ancient tree where they'd replayed what he'd believed to be her fantasy. The dance they'd played out together, both in London and here in Blackrig, had been just that. A fantasy.

Why had he ever countenanced her coming here?

If he was ever to have another serious relationship, it

could not be here among the secrets and horrors of the past few years. He'd thought he might start anew. How wrong had he been?

He reached out to touch the tree, as though in silent homage, then walked on, aware that the path his feet had chosen would inevitably take him to the cursed Party House and its grounds.

Despite the mind-numbing anger as he caught sight of the covered grave, his eyes were still drawn to the pale silver edifice that was the face of Lord Main's dream, Ard Choille, together with the satin-green sheen of An Lochan Uaine.

Turning, he took the path that led along the shore to the old campsite. He now let his mind move to Finn and his obvious fury at finding Joanne with Caroline. He and Finn had got on well when he'd been officially seeing Caroline. A quiet lad, he'd never been part of Josh's gang, although as far as he was aware, there had been no real animosity between them until the fight he'd witnessed in the village hall. As for Ailsa, Finn had, he thought, admired her from afar, with no hope of reciprocation.

He was fairly certain Finn had had no idea that they'd been conducting an affair, although near the end, when Ailsa realized all was not well, she may have made a point of telling Finn about them, knowing it would reach Caroline's ears.

Yet the open animosity of tonight . . . the rage with which Finn had deposited Joanne at Beanach. His warning for them both to stay away from his sister or else suggested – what?

That he most likely wanted to protect Caroline from further trauma.

Reaching the jetty, Greg sat down to stare across the shining expanse of water. The far bank was lit up by the moon and, close to the water's edge, stood a magnificent stag, head held high, its antlers a warning of what it might be capable of when the rutting season came and it fought to the death for its choice of female.

It made him wonder how far he was prepared to go to keep Joanne.

Greg quietly raised his rifle and got the big male within his sights, his finger poised on the trigger.

He felt the swift beat of his heart as the magnificent head turned as though drawn by his intent gaze.

Both the shot and subsequent death would be a clean one, as long as he didn't hesitate.

Joanne

She lay listening, her eyes straining in the darkness, her ears attuned to every creak and sigh as the old house rearranged itself with the firm shutting of the front door.

He had gone out, but to where and for how long?

She willed herself to get up and go downstairs, so that she too might walk away from Beanach, from him, from Blackrig, from this place where she'd felt safe, and did no more.

But what if he'd locked the door, intent on keeping her there at least until the morning?

She dismissed that thought. She would have heard the turn of the key. Having struggled with it herself, she knew how hard it was to lock.

But not hard for him. She thought of his hands, large and blue-veined. The strength of his arms, the height, weight and build of him. All of which he'd used to pleasure her, never to hurt her.

Caroline had made him out to be a monster and she'd done that to make her leave. The irony was that she had planned to desert him anyway.

She got to her feet and went to the window. The outside light was still burning and she could make out his distant figure heading towards the woods. With a start, she realized he was carrying his rifle.

Why was that?

Her sensible self told her he was a gamekeeper and some-times went out at night to hunt. Her frantic self told her of other reasons, all of them unpleasant.

Seeing him leave, she realized, had made her instantly want him to return.

She thought of earlier as she'd hurled those accusations at him, most of them originating from Caroline. How sad and hurt and lost he'd looked. She, on the other hand, had felt that somehow she'd won.

Yet the only person who'd won this time round was Caroline, and maybe Richard, should she take her pregnant self back to London.

She recalled Greg's expression when she'd announced that the pregnancy was not his concern. He'd wanted to say something but, reading her mood, had chosen not to, although he could rightly assume he might be the father.

Of course, she had never mentioned Richard nor any previous relationship, yet had questioned him about his. She'd thrown Caroline and now Ailsa at him at every avail-able opportunity. Like tonight.

He'd told her his truth, yet she hadn't deigned to tell him hers.

What difference would it make now, anyway, since she'd already decided to go?

And yet, watching him walk away from Beanach, away from her, she desperately wanted him to turn and come back.

She went downstairs and set about making herself some-thing to eat, something for both of them, since he might be hungry on his return.

When he did return, she would be there waiting for him.

Ready to tell him her secret. That she'd chosen him from the delegates that weekend to escape a psychopathic former partner. A criminal lawyer with friends in high places. One of them being Aidan Stratton, who might even now have informed Richard where she was.

She'd been dozing when the crack of a rifle shot woke her. Panic immediately sent her flying to the door and outside. She began to run, heading in the direction Greg had gone, hearing her heart and feet beat furiously in time.

Sound carried far here on the hills, with no traffic noise and the air as still as this. He could be a mile away or close by, she had no way of knowing.

He could be alive or dead. The writer in her was already fashioning an image of him with the rifle between his knees, its point in his mouth, his brains scattered around.

Meeting the edge of the woods, she sought the path, but – unused to the darkness within – soon stumbled and fell, cracking twigs and announcing her presence to anyone or anything nearby.

A sudden meeting with a low branch sent her sprawling. Winded and defeated, she hauled herself up to her knees, knowing she could go no further. Tasting blood trickling down from where her forehead had met the branch, she felt a sharp pain which may have been a stitch in her side from running, or something else.

Something she'd wanted to happen, but now no longer did.

He found her there, minutes later.

Catching sight of a figure sitting slumped against a tree, he'd been seized by a terrible premonition that it might be her, trying to escape Beanach and him. His horror that it should have come to this propelled him onto his knees beside her.

'Joanne?' he said, gently lifting her head so that he might read her face and check her pulse.

Seeing the blood smeared across her eyes, he washed it gently away with the water from his flask.

'Joanne,' he tried again.

This time her eyes flickered open and, instead of the fear and suspicion he'd seen earlier, he saw only pleasure and relief.

'I heard the shot. I was worried that . . .' She didn't finish.

'A stag by An Lochan Uaine,' he told her. 'He got away.'

He didn't tell her he was glad about that. Killing the stag tonight in that setting, in the mood he'd been in, would have felt like an execution.

'Can you rise or would you rather I carried you?'

When she told him that she was too big to be carried, he said, 'The stag would have been a lot heavier than you.'

He sensed that something had changed again between them. That they were perhaps back where they had been that glorious day at the lochside.

On her feet now, she accepted his help this time and they trudged back together towards the guiding light that was Beanach.

Greg

He left her sleeping, knowing she would be there when he returned.

They'd spoken long into the night. Her story mostly. She'd been frank enough about how and why she'd 'accidentally' met him at the entrance to the dining room that morning in London. He'd listened as she'd explained her reasoning, her need to escape with only a narrow window of opportunity to do so.

Her greatest difficulty was when she'd spoken about Richard, and her reasons for running.

There had been a horrible story of a man he'd defended for murdering his wife and children. Some scattered, stumbled words about the method he'd used to do that, and Richard's thoughts on where the blame lay for the man's actions.

At that point his own fears since they'd discovered Ailsa's body seemed meaningless beside hers.

Eventually she'd been persuaded to go to bed. He'd tucked her in, then lain alongside, his arm cradling her. Once she was asleep, he'd taken himself down to the couch with a blanket and tried to rest in the few hours that remained before he had to face Stratton again.

He decided he would go early to the Bothy, rouse Colin and pick up his dogs, Cal and Sasha. That thought made him happy, despite the prospect of dealing with his boss.

Other thoughts had crowded his mind, denying him sleep.
Was Stratton aware that Joanne, or Maya as he knew her
by, had been living here with him? Or did he still believe what
she'd told him, that she was staying at Kath's guest house?

It wasn't beyond Stratton to ask about in the village. Find
out for sure where the journalist was staying. Even more so
if he'd thought after seeing them together outside the hotel
that they might be an item. Stirring things up for folk was
what gave the bastard a hard-on.

The easiest way would be for Stratton to ask Colin outright
if she was staying at Beanach. Colin didn't have the heart
or devious mind of a liar and would no doubt answer without
thought that there might be consequences.

Greg eventually managed a couple of hours' sleep before
his alarm buzzed to wake him. Rising, he made himself coffee
and – after checking on Joanne, who was still sleeping peace-
fully – headed out.

As he drove up the road towards Ard Choille, the two big
black 4x4s appeared. Drawing into a passing place, he
watched them go by, the smoked windows concealing the
occupants, although he made the assumption, as predicted,
that the women and two of the men were on their way to
the airport for the flight south. If so, then only Stratton and
his sidekick Chalmers would be at home. He found himself
relieved to be rid of Poppy, Jessica and Viola, although not
so much his one-time ally Naomi.

Arriving at the Bothy, he discovered Karla's wee red Mini
parked outside, and gave a silent cheer that things had turned
out well for Colin, despite the stramash at the ceilidh.

Loath to march in on his assistant without warning, he
went to fetch the dogs from the kennel, knowing their barks
of delight would either rouse Colin or else interrupt him.

The two Labradors were mightily pleased to see him and he took some time showing them that the feeling was mutual. When he rounded the Bothy with both dogs at heel, he found a slightly sheepish but obviously delighted Colin out front, and even more impressive, dressed and ready to go.

'They let you out.' He gave Greg a maniacal grin.

'They did, on orders that I don't go anywhere.'

'Word is they lifted Josh.' Colin looked worried by that.

'He was in a cell along from me,' Greg told him.

The word 'cell' didn't go down well with Colin. 'You don't think Josh did it?'

'I don't,' Greg said. 'If he had he would have been a massive fool to go and smash up her grave.'

'But what if he didn't know she was buried there?' Colin said, wide-eyed.

'Murderers usually bury or hide their victims' bodies,' Greg reminded him.

'Not always,' Colin informed him. 'I've been watching *True Crimes* and there was this one where the killer went back to hide the body and it had gone. Disappeared. Someone had taken it away and buried it someplace else.'

Greg thought back to his own reaction when he'd first viewed the body, his first thought being how had she got there. Might Colin have a point?

Judging it was time to change the subject, Colin said, 'D'you want me to go with you to see Stratton? He was mightily pleased you were locked up, I have to say,' he added angrily.

'Which means he'll be mightily miffed that they let me out.'

'Also, your Detective Snyder is back in the village, conducting interviews again. Rumour also has it that a guy turned up. Someone Ailsa knew from Glasgow. He was staying at the campsite the night she went missing. He says she visited him there, then said she was going home.'

If that was true, and Ailsa had been at the campsite after she left Beanach . . .

'So maybe that's why you're off the hook,' Colin said cheerily.

Greg didn't believe it would or could be that easy, but thanked Colin for bringing him up to date.

'Did Stratton mention Joanne at all when talking to you?' he asked.

Colin's cheerful look disappeared. 'Why?' he said worriedly.

'Did he ask if she was staying at Beanach?'

After a short and obviously anxious pause, 'He might have. Is that bad?'

Greg's heart raised its beat. 'What did you tell him?'

'I said I didn't think so. I didn't want to get you into trouble if it wasn't allowed.'

Greg could have hugged him. Instead he clapped him on the back. 'Good.'

Colin looked a little perturbed at such an open demonstration of praise.

'Right, I'll head down there now,' Greg told him.

'Remember,' Colin said, 'if he sacks you, I'm going too.'

Ard Choille already wore a deserted look. In the morning light, its silver birch shone just as brightly, but its balcony and walkways lay empty. No more clinking of glasses. No more brightly coloured butterflies inhabiting its branches. No more raucous laughter.

An Lochan Uaine still lay green and inviting, but no sunshades or loungers sat alongside. Only the ugly evidence of the covered grave.

Greg ordered the dogs to wait by the Land Rover and, steeling himself, approached the main door and once again banged the stag's head knocker. When there was no response, he opened the door and stepped inside, determined not to put off the moment of confrontation any longer.

'Mr Stratton,' he called up the open staircase. Eventually a voice he recognized as Chalmers bid him come up.

He passed a deserted dining room with no sounds of any remaining staff from the nearby kitchen. Had they gone too, he wondered?

Chalmers was in the balcony room with a pot of coffee.

'Take a seat,' he ordered, rather than offered. 'Aidan's on a phone call in the study.'

Greg had never really registered Chalmers. He was one of those men who, if you didn't know to the contrary, you would assume was Stratton's assistant. He'd always remained in the background, said little, although it had been obvious that Stratton deferred to him on occasion.

At this moment, Chalmers was studying him closely, perhaps revisiting his opinion of the estate's head gamekeeper. It made Greg wonder just how much of Chalmers's money was involved in Ard Choille and the estate in general.

'They released you? Do you know why?' he said.

'Because I didn't do anything wrong,' Greg said.

Chalmers accepted that with a little nod. 'Then we still have a head gamekeeper.' He said that as if it were his decision and not Stratton's.

This was the moment he should resign and take Colin with him, Greg thought. Walking up the drive, he'd imagined Stratton trying to sack him, and him getting in first with his resignation.

The way this was playing out wasn't at all what he'd anticipated.

A brief silence followed before Chalmers said, 'We will be here for another couple of days, but won't be needing either you or your apprentice. You can return to your normal duties for now.' At this he turned away.

'What about Mr Stratton?' Greg said.

'It's not necessary to wait for him. I've said what was required.'

And with that he was summarily dismissed.

Emerging from the house, he looked up to find Chalmers on the balcony watching his departure. Greg was reminded of the previous night when he'd had the stag in his sights, just before it had darted away. He had the feeling of being in Chalmers's sights, but luckily with no rifle in his hands.

For some reason he had been spared Stratton's wrath. He wondered why that should be. He also wondered why the two men were remaining there alone, without catering staff, and what business they were conducting in the emptiness of Ard Choille.

As he released the dogs with a whistle, they came bounding towards him.

Greg allowed himself a fraction of a smile as he climbed into the Land Rover. He'd been praying for Stratton's departure and not only did it look as though he was actually going, it would happen in a couple of days' time. Added to that, he need not see either man again before they left.

Greg

As he drove through the open gates, he felt a new sense of freedom. He would call Colin and give him the good news, tell him to use the day to do whatever he liked. He hoped Karla might play a part in that.

He now headed back to Beanach to check on Joanne and prepare them both some breakfast. If she was up for it, they might make the most of the continued good weather. There were other places he could take her, the waterfall being one, or she might prefer heading back to their spot at An Lochan Uaine.

As he crested the hill, he realized there was a car outside the house, and recognized it as Malcolm's. He'd been aware he'd need to call on Malcolm and tell him what had subsequently happened last night, so was pleased he didn't have to head to the village to do it in person.

Entering the kitchen, he found the two of them seated at the table, drinking what smelled like freshly brewed coffee.

Joanne looked up with a smile at his entry and he noted that she appeared a lot better than she had last night, when he'd helped her back from the woods.

'How'd it go with Stratton?' Malcolm said.

'Never saw him, but Chalmers gave me the impression all was well and I still had a job.' He could hardly believe what he was saying. 'Him and Stratton are around for a couple more days, but they won't be needing me or Colin.'

Malcolm looked as surprised as Greg felt.

'Colin says some Glasgow bloke from Ailsa's past has turned up saying she was at the campsite after she left here?'

'News travels fast in Blackrig,' Malcolm said. 'That's the good news. Unfortunately there's also bad news.'

'What?' Greg looked from Malcolm to a sombre Joanne and back again.

'They've arrested Finn,' Malcolm said.

'Finn?' he said, aghast. 'What for?'

'I managed to get an explanation of sorts from Harry, though he was loath to divulge it.' Malcolm halted there as he chose his words carefully. 'The police apparently retrieved his fingerprint from the plastic sheet the body was wrapped in.'

'But Finn wasn't with the gang that destroyed the hot tub,' he said without thinking.

Malcolm was staring at him, obviously perplexed. 'How do you know that?'

He could have fobbed Malcolm off, but with Joanne's eyes watching him closely, he knew he had to tell the truth about that night and his role in it.

'I was up there when it happened. I hid when the gang appeared. They wore balaclavas, but I recognized the voices. Finn's wasn't among them,' he said, beginning to realize how serious this was. If Finn wasn't there, how the hell did his fingerprints get on the plastic?

He wondered if Malcolm would ask why he'd visited the Party House, and whether he could bring himself to tell him that he was revisiting the scene of his crime. The one involving the virus.

When Malcolm remained silent, Greg said, 'Josh knows who was with him.'

'So you're both witnesses to Finn not being there.' Malcolm cursed in Gaelic and ran his fingers through his hair. 'The likelihood is the police know all this already.'

Joanne was reading their expressions. 'You think Finn killed Ailsa?' she said in a shocked voice.

Greg couldn't believe it. Or wouldn't believe it. The mild-mannered Finn he'd known since childhood, who had mysteriously turned into the furious man who'd deposited Joanne at Beanach's door last night. Telling her – no, threatening her – to never go near his sister again.

'He brought Joanne back here last night. He was—'

Joanne interrupted him. 'I told Malcolm what happened,' she said quietly.

'What can we do for Finn?' Greg said. 'There must be something.'

'If you or Josh tell the truth, it'll condemn him. If you tell a lie . . .' Malcolm came to a halt.

The enormity of what had just been said threatened to overwhelm Greg. He'd been hoping that the police would eventually come to the conclusion that Ailsa had been killed by someone from outside Blackrig. A lone camper, a tourist or even a workman from Ard Choille.

Not Finn. Never Finn.

'What about Caroline?' he said. 'How's she taking it?'

Malcolm looked uncomfortable. 'Saying it's nonsense and it should be you they're locking up. Telling everyone you had sex with Ailsa that night. That the police knew that, yet still they let you go.'

Greg glanced at Joanne, worried about what she was thinking. To show him, she reached for his hand.

'So what do we do about Finn?' he said again, as much to himself as to Malcolm.

'Nothing,' Malcolm said. 'We do nothing. They lifted you on a DNA sample and now Finn on a fingerprint, if what Harry let slip is true.' He paused there. 'A fingerprint on the plastic doesn't prove he killed her. Just like your DNA wasn't enough for them to charge you.'

It was, Greg felt, a hope, but a forlorn one none the less. Although he also hoped the police wouldn't rearrest him. They'd told him not to leave town, making him well aware they might be back again to knock at his door.

'I'll come down later,' he told Malcolm as he bid him farewell at the front door. 'There's something I want us to talk about.'

Malcolm nodded. 'I'm glad, son, that you're about to get that bastard Stratton off your back. And even more so that Joanne decided to stick around.'

When Greg re-entered the kitchen, he found Joanne frying bacon.

'I thought we'd eat together,' she told him. 'I'm starving, and seeing as you left early after only a cup of coffee, I expect you are too. Then we can talk.' She hesitated. 'There are other things I need to tell you.'

'Okay,' he said. 'But we'll keep the other things for later. Chalmers basically gave me the day off. I extended that to Colin. We can take a run out, enjoy the sunshine, because according to the forecast the weather's about to break.'

'Let's do that,' she told him with a tentative smile.

Greg

'So where are you taking me?' she said as they set off in the Land Rover.

'Are you up for a shortish walk? Rough, but at the end of it is a fine waterfall with a deep pool.'

'You're not going to make me swim again?' she said, sounding a little worried.

'Definitely not . . . unless you want to.'

'I won't want to,' she said firmly.

The interchange over, a silence fell between them. Greg made a point of concentrating on his driving, although he knew the track he was taking very well. He would have been happy to walk to the gorge, but finding her last night, pale and bloodied, and obviously in pain, he wouldn't have asked that of her.

There was, he acknowledged, an awkwardness between them since the previous night's revelations. Those moments that follow baring your soul that are sometimes filled with regret at having done so.

It couldn't have been easy for her to speak about Richard. Or the reasons she'd made a play for him in London, and then visited him here. Although he was glad that he now knew how and why it had all come about.

She'd indicated she'd wanted them to talk about something over breakfast and he was sorry he'd asked her to wait until later. Mainly because he now thought she'd maybe changed her mind in the interim, and would likely not mention it. Whatever it was.

He could prompt her, of course, but if he'd learned one thing about Joanne, it was that she didn't like to be persuaded.

The silence remained until they reached the place where he planned to leave the vehicle. As she climbed out, she seemed to emerge from her reverie to look around at what he knew was a view worth coming up here for. From this height, they could look four ways and get a real feel for where Blackrig lay among the surrounding hills.

'Look west, and you can just get a glimpse of the sea,' he said. 'We could go west sometime soon if you like, then you can try swimming in the sea, rather than a freezing cold loch.'

He immediately saw by her expression that he'd made an assumption too far.

Silence fell again. It was, he thought, as though last night's conversation had robbed them of further words.

He handed her his telescope and pointed. 'You can see Beanach and, a little to its left, Ard Choille and An Lochan Uaine.'

She dutifully took it and looked.

He realized his notion of showing her where Blackrig sat in the firmament that was Scotland had fallen flat. And was sorry for it.

'We can go back,' he said. 'If it's too much, after last night,' he added.

It was the first time either of them had mentioned last night, although they'd both probably thought of little else.

'How many weeks pregnant was Caroline when she lost the baby?' she suddenly asked.

He found himself at a loss, knowing whatever he said would only be an estimate. He decided to be honest about that.

'I don't know. Caroline didn't tell me right away about the pregnancy. Why she didn't . . .' He paused. 'Maybe she thought, like you, that it was only her concern.'

She nodded as though his answer had fitted what she thought.

'I will have to leave, and soon. I need to take care of this,' she said.

He felt for her hand. 'I want to—' he began.

She pulled her hand away. 'You want to what? Be a father this time round? Make up for messing up the first time?' Her question wasn't said in a cruel voice, just an honest one.

He couldn't answer that, because he didn't know.

'You're right. Only you can decide, but I'm here if you need me.'

A shadow played across her face, as though a sudden cloud had appeared in a cloudless sky and covered the sun.

'I'll make an appointment,' she said.

'Here in Scotland somewhere?' he asked.

'It'll be easier to go to London. I'll have to go sometime anyway.' She paused. 'I spoke to my friend Lucy this morning. Richard hasn't been back asking about me. She thinks he's given up. I can stay with her and her boyfriend initially.'

So she'd already decided about the pregnancy and about him. He looked up to find her eyes on him.

'It could just as well be Richard's and then it'll have a homicidal maniac for a father,' she said bluntly.

'You mean rather than a suspected rapist and murderer?' he tried, with a wry smile.

He watched as she decided to take his answer the way he'd meant it.

'Not to mention a mother who chose to have sex with both men, without thinking of the consequences,' she said.

'I thought it was more than just sex,' he said, realizing that was true.

That seemed to put her at a loss. 'I wish I could swear in Gaelic,' she said. 'Like Malcolm.'

'I'll teach you if you want.' Even as he answered he was following her gaze, which had become fixated on something.

'Isn't that smoke coming from the hill over there?' she said, pointing.

He retrieved the telescope and took a look. The smoke, he thought, was the least of their worries as, adjusting the lens, he spotted a bank of flames swiftly moving across the planted pines that circled the hill opposite.

'We have to go back,' he said. 'I'll drop you at Beanach.'

Before he drove off, he checked for a mobile signal. Noting it was poor, he radioed Colin, praying he wasn't too far away from his own radio.

'What's up, boss?' Colin said in a cheerful voice.

'There's a fire by—' He gave the location. 'Alert Malcolm and the crew. I'm up near the gorge with no mobile signal. The fire's currently moving westward.'

Colin okayed that and rang off.

'Can you check for a mobile signal as we head down?' he told Joanne. 'As soon as you get one, call Malcolm just to be sure.'

He'd taken care on the way up, aware that Joanne might still be hurting after her fall last night in the woods. Excusing himself for what would be a rough and speedy return journey, he told her to hold on.

This was what they'd feared. A dry spell that had gone on too long, leaving the heather-clad hillsides and woods tinder dry. As they descended, they came within smelling distance of the smoke blowing across the valley.

'That's all we need,' he said grimly. 'A wind to give it oxygen.'

'Is the village in danger?' Joanne said anxiously.

'We've had to evacuate once in the past. At the moment it looks to be heading away from Blackrig, but things can change very quickly.'

As he drew near the Beanach track, Joanne told him to let her off there and she'd walk up.

'You're sure?'

'Go,' she ordered, getting out and waving him away.

Joanne

Halfway up the drive she turned back, deciding that rather than wait at Beanach for news, she would walk down to Kath's. At least there she would know sooner rather than later what was happening about the progress of the fire, and no doubt Kath's opinion on the latest developments in the police investigation.

Also, the thought of the elderly woman's no-nonsense approach to pretty much everything made her wonder if she shouldn't confide in Kath about her own current dilemma.

She found herself sniffing the air periodically as she walked, looking for the whiff of smoke they'd encountered up on the hill earlier, but whatever way the wind was blowing, it wasn't sending it towards Blackrig . . . yet.

Before he'd left her at the crossroads, Greg had given her a brief resumé of the previous time the village had had to be evacuated. The fire had started in the woods south of Blackrig. Jumping the road, it had met a wood lorry, which on catching fire itself had contributed to its spread.

'How it started, it's difficult to know,' he'd said. 'A cigarette thrown from a car. The sun on broken glass at the roadside. A camper's fire. Probably similar reasons to how this fire began.'

'What about deliberate?' she'd said.

His face had grown fierce at this. 'They're the worst ones, because the people who start them are rarely caught and don't pay the price for the devastation they cause to wildlife and people.' When he'd said that, his jaw had tightened, and she'd realized she'd seen that expression before, when he'd spoken of the virus and the casual way it had been introduced to Blackrig.

She recalled Caroline's claim that Greg had been the one to blame for that. Something she hadn't repeated last night, when she'd told him Caroline's other accusations.

Preoccupied with her colliding thoughts, she didn't realize she'd passed the entry to the woods, which had been her planned route to Kath's house. Now she would have to walk down the Main Street, which meant passing the shop, and possibly Caroline.

Choosing to stay on the other side of the road, she took her courage in both hands and walked swiftly by – but not swiftly enough, it seemed.

She was only a few steps further on when she heard her name being called. She stopped on the second, more strident, shout and turned to find Caroline heading towards her.

Bracing herself for a torrent of abuse, she was surprised to see her concerned expression.

'I'm really sorry about Finn's reaction to you staying last night. It was so unlike him,' Caroline said.

Joanne waited, unsure how to respond.

'I'm sure you've heard already, but Finn's in Inverness giving a statement to the police about the night Ailsa went missing. Josh gave one, and now he's home. Finn will be home soon too.'

Her voice faltered a little on that, and Joanne felt a well of sympathy spring up.

'I'm sure he will,' she offered. 'And don't worry about last night.'

Caroline accepted this with a little nod of acknowledgement before saying, 'So you're not leaving, then?'

'I am, but just not today. The fire . . .' she began.

Caroline looked pleased to hear that and said brightly, 'Of course, poor Greg will be in the thick of it. Fire teams from all round have been called out. It'll be hectic until they manage to dampen it down, or' – she gazed skywards – 'the weather breaks. I'm helping with teas and coffees at the hall. If you want to come along, the tea van's parked outside, because the police are still using the place.'

'I'll maybe do that,' Joanne said, stunned at being asked.

They parted then, Joanne to cross the road to Kath's, Caroline striding purposefully towards the village hall.

Joanne realized with sadness that in every interchange she'd ever had with Caroline involving Greg, she could see her own relationship with Richard reflected back in some way. How many times had she hoped things would eventually go back to the way they'd been at the beginning of their relationship? Too many, regardless of Lucy's warnings.

Despite everything that had happened between Caroline and Greg – Ailsa, the miscarriage, now the madness that the murder had brought to Blackrig – Caroline still thought that she and Greg might get together again.

Provided I leave Blackrig, she said to herself.

Reaching Kath's house and finding an open door, Joanne stepped inside and called for her.

'Come away through,' Kath's voice came back. 'We're in the back garden.'

Wondering who Kath was with, Joanne did as instructed.

The two women were seated by a table on the lawn, enjoying a pot of tea.

'Ah, Joanne. Meet Megan Huntly, Josh's mum.' Kath waved at Joanne to join them. 'Take a seat. I'll fetch you a cup.'

'Kath's told me all about you,' the woman said, observing her intently.

Joanne had no idea how to follow that, because all she knew about Megan Huntly was that she'd lost a child to the virus, and that Josh, who she'd never met properly, had led the gang that had destroyed the hot tub, releasing the horror of Ailsa's death on the community.

Perhaps noting her discomfort, Megan said, 'They let Josh go. He's out fighting the fire with Greg and the others.'

'Is he a volunteer firefighter too?' Joanne said, relieved to have the fire as the main subject of their conversation.

'Not normally, but in emergencies, yes.'

'So it really is an emergency?' She hadn't thought of it in those terms up to now.

'We're a wee village, miles from anywhere, and surrounded by woods. We have a burn close by and the loch up by Ard Choille as water sources, but getting enough manpower and water anywhere near the fire is a problem.'

Kath, back by now and pouring Joanne's tea, added, 'Last time this happened, they were fighting it for three days.'

'Is there anything I can do to help?' Joanne said. 'Caroline says there's a tea and coffee van set up outside the hall.'

The two women exchanged looks. 'You've been talking to Caroline?' Kath said.

Joanne nodded. 'I met her on Main Street on the way here.'

'Then you'll know about Finn?' Megan said.

'Yes,' she admitted.

Kath shook her head. 'It's a bad business. All of it.'

Her declaration seemed to bring an end to the tea party, at least for Megan.

'Right,' she said, rising. 'I need to get back. Thanks for the tea, Kath, and,' she turned to Joanne, 'it was nice to meet you, Joanne.'

When Kath returned from showing her out, she immediately said, 'Megan knows Josh led the raid on the hot tub. She hates the Party House with a vengeance and she has good reason. I suspect she knows Finn wasn't with Josh when he did it. Whether Josh told the police that, we don't know.'

Kath refreshed her tea before continuing. 'Malcolm told me he advised Greg not to say anything about being there that night. I think he's right. Remember, we don't even know whether the fingerprint story is true. If folk in Blackrig don't know the whole story, they tend to fill in the blanks themselves, usually coloured by how it affects them personally. That's human nature.'

She stopped, as though thinking something through, before saying, 'Forensics can take a while, despite what you see on TV. They'll work out eventually how the lassie died, and no doubt they'll also find proof of who did it.' She looked to Joanne. 'And it won't be Greg. I'm certain of that.'

'You know about me deciding to leave?' Joanne said.

'I do. I also heard that Caroline featured in that decision.'

'She didn't really, I'd already made up my mind.'

'Can I ask why?' Kath said.

'To answer, I probably need to begin by telling you why I came to Blackrig in the first place.'

What she told Kath was true, although she'd softened the

edges. In this version, Richard had become a nuisance, rather than a threat. Her visit here a way of escaping his attentions, and getting herself back into a good place to write, and, of course, to get to know Greg a little better.

She realized by the end that this sanitized version was the one she'd been portraying both to herself and the world for the past eighteen months. Even in pouring her heart out that night to Greg, she hadn't been as honest as she might have been, although she had called Richard a homicidal maniac at one point.

Kath listened without interruption, her only reaction being to place her soft hand briefly on Joanne's when she stumbled or took time to take a breath.

Sitting in silence afterwards, with just the sound of the bees feasting on Kath's flower beds, Joanne briefly considered revealing the pregnancy. Something she hadn't even told Lucy. Caution, she decided, was the better bet. She knew Kath would keep her confidence, but the truth had a way of revealing itself, despite all attempts to stop that happening.

Just as it had done with Ailsa.

'Well, I'm glad to know your story,' Kath was saying. 'And I can assure you it will go no further. But . . .' She hesitated. 'I can't help but feel that fate brought you here to Blackrig, and to Greg. It seems to me that you two meeting has made life better for the both of you, despite what you've been up against.'

As Joanne rose to go, Kath added, 'And I wouldn't join Caroline on the tea van, I'd go back to Beanach and have something ready for Greg if or when he gets a break from firefighting.'

Joanne

Greg came home only to briefly eat, shower and sleep for a few hours during the two days following.

In between, he told her there were five fire appliances mobilized from the nearest villages with around fifty firefighters and forty workers from the neighbouring estates, working in shifts, all battling to bring the wildfire under control.

'Over four square kilometres of grassland, heather and woods is on fire,' he'd told her.

'What about Blackrig?' she'd asked.

'Okay for now, but be prepared to shift if necessary,' he'd said before lying down on the couch for the couple of hours' rest he allowed himself.

Studying his weary expression even in sleep, the creases of fire-smoked skin, the parched lips, she'd thought that now she perhaps had the measure of the man she'd chosen to be her refuge. It made her ashamed of how much she'd doubted him.

Sometimes Colin would appear with him and together they would go through the same routine, Colin taking the couch, while Greg, encouraged by her, would head gratefully to the bed for the small amount of time before she heard his alarm go off and they were up and away again.

She spent her day writing about the latest trauma to hit Blackrig and preparing food, so that there was always something hot and ready on the stove, whenever they should appear.

On one occasion, Josh arrived with Greg. This time it was only for food and copious amounts of water. She imagined that, despite their breathing apparatus, their throats must feel like the inside of a blackened chimney.

The two of them seemed easy in one another's company, but Joanne had no opportunity to ask what may have passed between them to ease the tension Greg had spoken of in the prison.

She took to walking up the hill at the back of the house to see if she might watch the firefight at a distance, but all the spyglass could show her were flying sparks like bonfire night and plumes of smoke dancing like wraiths above the charred land.

In her mind's eye, she imagined what might happen if the fire should turn and fasten its wrath on Blackrig, perhaps circling the hill on which Beanach stood or attacking the ancient pinewoods that bordered An Lochan Uaine.

An image of skeleton trees, one of them 'their' tree, as she thought of it, blackened in death beside the satin-green sheen of the fairy loch almost moved her to tears, until she reminded herself that her imagination had created the picture, and it had no basis in fact.

But it could happen, she told herself. *It could happen*.

She slept little herself. Always out, always checking. The longest day well past by now, she could count the difference in the daylight hours. Even as she watched the fire move inexorably across the landscape, so too did she search the neighbouring sky for any sign of clouds and approaching rain.

Whether it was her prayers to the Rain God or not, a light

spatter of drops arrived on the third day. Not enough to do the work of a firefighter but enough to give a small hope that the forecast of a break in the weather might come true after all.

For as long as the shower lasted, she stood outside, letting the rain patter her head and trickle down her face and body. She thought of the morning Greg had persuaded her to swim in An Lochan Uaine and how shocked and angry she'd been at the assault of cold water on her skin, how relieved she'd been to be carried out in his arms and wrapped in a warm, dry towel.

'Southern softie' he'd called her as he'd rubbed her briskly to make her warm again.

Standing there in front of Beanach, chilled again by rainwater, she felt nothing but relief, despite her shivering. Once the fire was finally put out, he would come home and they could talk again about the future.

Not wanting to leave Beanach in case Greg should return, however briefly, she'd kept in touch with Kath by phone. She'd learned that the police had freed Finn, with the instruction that he should not leave the area.

It seemed that whatever the evidence they had on Finn, as with Greg, wasn't sufficient to charge him with the rape or murder of Ailsa Cummings. The truth would come out, Kath had told her, although Joanne wasn't so sure of that.

The truth about Richard never had.

In retrospect, she believed she'd been just one of his many victims, who, like her, had never spoken of their abuse, both psychological and physical. If they had, likely his veil of respectability, his standing in the justice system, his cronies in the police force, had made sure he was never brought to task for it.

She fetched the spyglass, intending to climb the hill and check out what was happening on the fire ground. On his last brief visit home, Greg had mentioned small breakout fires away from the main conflagration, which they were controlling with beaters. There was also a helicopter taking water from An Lochan Uaine and dumping it on a stretch of forested area where conditions underfoot were horrendous, preventing access by the firefighters.

Standing at the front door, she took a quick look at Blackrig first, noting the area around the hall, firefighters and vehicles replacing the earlier numbers of police vehicles, before she climbed the hill behind the house.

Following the line of the fire scene, which at first glance appeared comfortably distant from the green lochan and Ard Choille, she then spotted what she assumed must be some of the smaller outbreaks Greg had spoken about, close to the near shore.

As she attempted to adjust the magnification for a clearer view, she heard a car on its way towards Beanach. Thinking it might well be Greg, who'd arrived via a variety of vehicles during the emergency, she pocketed the spyglass and quickly made for the back door, intent on pulling her latest food offering onto the hot plate for Greg and whoever else he'd brought with him.

The routine which normally followed was a shout as he and the others entered, then the scuffling as they removed their smoke-stained outer garments, before Greg himself appeared in the kitchen.

Puzzled when this didn't happen, she went to find out why.

The car had arrived but apparently no one had got out, or if they had, they were nowhere to be seen. Perplexed, Joanne looked about, then shouted Greg's name.

It was at that point she heard a sound coming from the shed where Greg kept his hunting and fishing equipment.

'Greg?' she tried again.

When no answer arrived, she went for a look.

The figure inside, dressed in stalking gear, staring at the selection of rifles, kept his back towards her.

'Can I help you?' she said, thinking this must have something to do with Ard Choille.

'I hope so,' a voice said, before turning.

She had never seen him dressed in anything other than his city outfit. Smart suit, shirt and tie. Either that or dressed for court in gown and wig.

You look like a different person, she thought stupidly.

He smiled. 'Joanne. Aidan informed me that I might find you in Blackrig, but he wasn't sure where. Luckily, the woman in the local shop, Caroline, was *very* keen to tell me exactly where you were.'

So Caroline had sent him here. *Her final attempt to get rid of me*, she thought.

'What do you want?'

He gave her that wry smile of his, suggesting a friendly joke between them, rather than him sizing her up before deciding on his mode of attack, either mental or physical.

She felt herself rooted to the spot, knowing that a move, any move, could well escalate whatever he had planned.

'Time to come home,' he said in a pleasant voice.

In her head she heard 'little girl' at the end – if not vocalized, then definitely in thought.

'This is my home now,' she heard herself say.

The smile, so carefully constructed, was wiped from his face by her words. She watched him marshal himself, still considering which way he might play this out.

'Greg will be here soon. I thought it was him arriving,' she said.

'Ah, the gamekeeper. Aidan told me all about him. How he raped and murdered some poor seventeen-year-old girl and buried her on Ard Choille land.'

She clenched her teeth to stop herself from responding.

'Just the sort I defend all the time. I'll leave my card, in case he should need it.' His eyes brightened at his own little joke. 'Shacked up with a gamekeeper.' He sighed. 'So how good is Mellors in the sack?'

She knew every word was being carefully chosen to try to anger her. He liked the scent of anger, but he loved the smell of fear even more. For him, it was an aphrodisiac. He relished these moments between the fear beginning and the sex that would undoubtedly follow.

She had a mental image of being thrust to the floor of the shed or up against the rifle rack, and the horror of it almost overwhelmed her.

Yet, if she could keep him talking, Greg might well arrive. That encouraging thought was quickly replaced by a much darker one.

What would *he* do if Greg did appear?

His eyes, having used up their friendly sparkle, had now grown cold.

'You know what you deserve for running away and hiding from me?' He adopted the look he used in court when he explained to the jury what was expected of them. A little dip of the head, then a straight look in the eye.

At this point she was supposed to plead, or become a vamp, encouraging him to move straight to sex.

When she did neither, he came determinedly towards her. Aware what would happen next, she turned and ordered her legs to walk. The time delay for her limbs to respond gave him the chance to catch her arm.

Swinging her round, he took aim at her stomach, a favourite punchbag of his.

'Don't,' she screamed, 'I'm pregnant.'

His fist halted as though in slow motion, while his left hand gripped her wrist even tighter.

'What did you say?' His voice dripped ice.

'I said I was pregnant.'

He dropped his fist.

'How pregnant?' he said, no doubt calculating the days since they'd last had sex or, alternatively, the last time he'd raped her.

She'd counted the number so often, she could tell him without hesitation.

He considered this new development. One he'd wanted, and she'd tried secretly to avoid. Obviously not hard enough.

He gave the smile he used for a jury who'd agreed with his arguments and announced a not-guilty verdict. 'That's wonderful.' He drew her into his arms, tilting her face so that he might kiss her long and penetratingly.

'So, now we go home,' he announced when his tongue had stopped its probing.

She had avoided his punches. Now how to prevent him taking her away?

'My things,' she said as he frogmarched her out of the shed.

'You've plenty at home. Plus you'll need new ones, now that you're pregnant.'

Outside, the scent of smoke was clearly discernible.

'The wildfire,' she said. 'It must have spread in this direction.'

As they crossed to the car, she could see the scattered outbreaks puncturing the woods around the green loch.

'I have to find out what's happening,' she said. 'Make sure they know it's jumped the loch.'

When he ignored her protests, she tried another tack. 'I have to let the dogs out. If the fire reaches Beanach . . .'

'Let your gamekeeper worry about that.'

Dragging her to the car, he shoved her into the passenger seat. Seconds later they were bumping their way down the dirt track, the smoke funnelling towards them through the glen. The wind had turned, she realized, and brought the fire with it.

Greg

His earlier fears had been well-founded. He knew these hills and glens, just as he knew the winds that visited them.

The westerlies were warm and often rain-filled, different from the snell blasts that occasionally came from the north and east. The westing wind had gone, a cooler east wind replacing it, changing the fire's course, driving it towards the green lochan, carrying showers of sparks across to ignite the ancient pines on the other side.

They'd been working in teams of beaters. Identifying breakouts and beating them to death, or that was how he saw it.

His group consisted of Josh, Finn, Fergus, their driver on the truck and himself. Finn had joined them as soon as the police had let him go. He was back to his subdued self. Nothing like how Joanne had described him when he'd deposited her back at Beanach.

As for Josh, he too had changed from the Mr Angry of the village hall, perhaps concentrating all his fury on the fire. Greg had even taken him back for food at Beanach earlier in the proceedings, when they'd believed the blaze to be under control.

How wrong they'd been about that.

You could dig firebreaks, blast water, even drop it from above, but you couldn't control moving air and the oxygen it pumped into keeping a wildfire alive and kicking.

Even now, should they manage to put it out on the surface, it had already set the underlying peat alight. They could smell the powerful scent of it smouldering as they worked.

The peat would burn on, likely for months. Huge holes would have to be excavated and water pumped into them to put it out. Even then, it might reignite, until autumn rain or a clothing of winter snow suffocated it at last.

He paused for a moment, wiping away the sweat from his dripping brow, thinking what a strange team they made. Three men who'd all been accused of being involved in the death of Ailsa Cummings. Perhaps not guilty, but not wholly innocent either.

Josh had pursued her and got what he wanted when it had suited Ailsa. Finn had watched from afar, coveting her, but had been spurned, or so it seemed.

As for himself? He'd believed himself immune at least for a while, but his fall from grace had been the worst one of all.

At this point in his thoughts, a shout from Fergus urged them together.

'The fire's jumped An Lochan Uaine. Orders are we're to head for Ard Choille.'

'It's got as far as the house?' Greg said.

'Not yet. We're to help do the same thing on the far bank.'

Trekking back over two-and-a-half kilometres of rough ground to the fire truck had taken its toll on all of them. It had also eaten up precious time.

Once on board, he tried his mobile, cursing the lack of a signal which was unlikely to improve much before Blackrig. On the third try, he finally got a ring tone from Joanne's phone. When she didn't immediately answer, he thought perhaps she was outside, checking with the telescope.

But I told her to keep her mobile with her at all times, he muttered inwardly.

He tried the landline, as he had done from the prison. Listening to it ring out, he knew in his heart that she wasn't at Beanach. So where was she?

He tried Kath next.

'We talked earlier on the phone,' she told him. 'She was watching the fire from the hill behind Beanach. What's wrong?'

'The fire's jumped An Lochan Uaine. We're headed back to Blackrig and from there to Ard Choille.'

'Is there anyone still in the Party House?' Kath said worriedly.

'Not as far as we know. Stratton was scheduled to leave yesterday.'

'D'you want me to go up to Beanach and check on Joanne?'

'Wait until we get up there with the fire engines. Then maybe keep trying her mobile. Tell her I want her to come down to the village. If she doesn't answer, head up there and get her and the dogs. I won't be back at Beanach for God knows how long.'

Ringing off, he tried to turn his attention to what would come next. There was open ground in front of Ard Choille, then the lochan itself. But behind were dense dry acres of birchwood. Christ, Ard Choille itself was built round a giant birch tree.

A house like Beanach, built of solid stone, would be harmed, but likely its walls would stay standing. Lord Main had built what amounted to a tinderbox, the perfect sustenance for a greedy fire.

Had Stratton and Chalmers left already? He hoped to God

they had. He hated Stratton and everything he stood for, but he didn't wish him dead.

Then there was Blackrig. If the fire claimed Ard Choille, its next port of call would be the woods that surrounded the village.

Kath hadn't mentioned the likelihood of an evacuation. With Malcolm on the hill with the other firefighters, his deputy on the community council would have to take the decision to move folk to the neighbouring village, six miles away. He hoped Joanne would be included in that and, having spoken to Kath, he now felt confident she would be.

He took a slug from his water bottle and thought of the morning he and Joanne had swum in the green loch together. He'd suspected then that what lay between them was special, despite how it had begun, and he now made himself a vow that he would do everything in his power to support her, even accompanying her to London, should she allow him to do so.

'Jesus Christ.' Fergus, a man not given to expletives, drew all their eyes to what lay before them.

In the distance, they could just see the tops of the tallest trees south of the green lochan whipping in the east wind, sending their sparks to ignite their neighbours both near and far.

'At least we'll have the loch water for our pumps,' Finn said hopefully from behind Greg.

'But only if we can get near the lochan,' came a reply, which Greg recognized as Josh's voice.

Back on the single-track road that climbed towards Ard Choille, Greg spotted a car at Beanach. So either Kath or someone else was there to pick up Joanne and his dogs.

He gave a sigh of relief at that. He would be happier knowing she was safely in Blackrig.

Joanne

Time is not a constant, she thought.

In the shed, her eyes glued on him, time had appeared to move at a snail's space, in direct opposition to her rapid breathing and racing thoughts.

Yet despite her speeding heart, she'd been too slow to flee, her limbs not reacting quickly enough to her silent command.

He'd taken his time driving up the hill to Beanach. Now, having captured her, he was driving like a maniac on the dirt track, the undercarriage scraping the raised centre, small stones rattling against the car to fly off in all directions.

She clasped the seat, her nails sinking into the upholstery, her stomach lurching up and down and threatening to arrive in her mouth.

'Please,' she managed. 'Slow down or I'll be sick.'

A quick glance sideways and an easing of the accelerator followed her plea, suggesting the sheen of sweat on her white face had warned him that what she'd said just might be true.

He slowed. Not for her benefit, she knew, but to protect the interior of his car.

'You're sure it's mine?' he said.

'I am.' She made herself sound certain, despite the fact she wasn't.

They had crested the hill and now had a view of the tarred

road below. A wind was whipping smoke down the valley and she could see that the outbreaks she'd spotted earlier from the hill were gaining ground, and rapidly.

'It'll be at Ard Choille soon. Aidan's not still there, is he?' she said in a horrified voice.

He didn't bother to answer.

Approaching the crossroads now, he turned left towards the village, just as two fire engines appeared, one behind the other, heading towards them.

She assumed he would draw in to let them pass, but it seemed he had no intention of doing so.

'They have right of way,' she screamed. 'Get into the passing place.'

He swore, but at the last minute swerved onto the verge as the first fire engine, siren now full on, showed its intention to keep coming.

Cursing it from behind his smoked-glass window, the siren drowning all sound, he didn't hear the click as she released her seat belt and opened the car door.

Then she was out and running. Dodging behind the first engine, then immediately into the woods, knowing that if she ran down the road, he would swiftly follow.

But here among the trees, she might just have a chance of losing him. And if she managed to follow the path to the big pine and beyond, she would emerge in the grounds of Ard Choille, where surely the fire engines were heading.

At first she heard nothing but the pounding of blood in her ears. She was reliving her last run through these woods. The darkness then had frightened her, causing her to stumble and hit her head. Now she craved the dark, knowing it would have helped her stay hidden from him.

Compelled to stop for a moment, she bent double, trying

to get her breath back and ease the stitch that gripped her side.

It was then she heard him, crashing his way through the undergrowth towards her.

How could she imagine he wouldn't catch up? She was his prey in here, just as she had been in London.

Forcing herself to stand up and get her bearings, she heard the rapid approach of someone or something from a different direction.

Frozen in her tracks, she watched as a big stag came leaping from the undergrowth, its eyes wild with terror, jumping and weaving, trying to escape the smell of smoke and the crackle of flames. Above it, birds rose in a cloud, echoing its fear, as they too fled the pockets of fire.

Was the stag running towards the lochan? Or away from it?

Disorientated, the wisps of smoke catching at her throat, she stood hesitant, with no longer any idea in which direction she should run.

Then she heard him shout her name.

Her cry of relief, when the noisy advance had turned out to be a stag, had alerted him to her location.

Now she knew which way to run. Anywhere as long as it was away from him.

As she took off, she heard him behind her. Telling her to stop because she was running towards the fire.

Was she? And what was worse? Running into the flames or being caught by Richard? She knew the answer to that question.

It was then she caught a glimpse of the lochan, the fire on the far side turning the green water a russet red.

She tried to up her speed, staggering like a drunk across

the rough ground. Now on her knees. Now up again. Feeling his presence close on her heels. Dreading his hand suddenly grabbing for her, as he'd done so often before.

Then she was free of the trees and tottering onto the rocky shoreline. So what now? Try to hide somewhere along the shore? Or in the water?

Greg had laughed at her when she'd found the waters of the loch too cold. Now the thought of walking into them seemed like a godsend. If she could submerge herself, even briefly, he might not see her, think perhaps she'd gone along the shore.

Despite longing for it, the shock of the cold water hit her like a sharp slap, causing her to gasp. Taking a breath, she forced herself to walk on out, tripping over hidden roots and boulders.

But she was already too late.

'Joanna, stop. Please. I won't hurt you. I'm sorry. So sorry. Please come back to the shore.'

She turned, despite herself. Time had slowed again in his presence. Her movements with it.

'I don't want to hurt you. Think of the baby.'

She saw that he was coming for her, yet she couldn't move. It was as though he'd frozen her in time.

He reached out a hand. 'We must get away from the fire. We'll walk along the shore to the big house. We'll get help there.'

Her voice suddenly broke free from her paralysed body.

'It's not yours,' she said. 'The baby isn't yours.'

'What?' he said, his expression quickly transforming from pleading concern to simmering hate. 'You bitch.' His lips curled round the words. 'You fucking bitch in heat. You'll die for that.'

Greg

'That looked like Joanne,' Josh shouted above the scream of the siren. 'She crossed between us and ran into the woods.'

Greg had made note of the black car suddenly appearing in front of them. He'd even cursed the driver's stupidity for not drawing into the passing place and briefly wondered if he was fleeing Ard Choille, whether, in fact, it might be Stratton behind the wheel. It would be just like Stratton to assume that he, and not the fire engine, should have right of way.

'Joanne?' he repeated stupidly.

Josh was behind him on the passenger side with a view to the woods.

'A bloke's just got out of the car and is following her,' he said, sounding bewildered and worried at the same time.

Who the bloke might be suddenly hit Greg with the force of a fist.

'It's that bastard,' he said, reaching for the door handle.

It had to be the Richard guy. She'd been afraid Stratton might tell him where she was, and it looked like she'd been right.

Sensing what was about to happen, Fergus slowed down enough for Greg to jump out of the cab. Then the fire engine, siren blaring, was on its way again into the ever-increasing smoke.

Standing for a moment to get his bearings, he realized he was close to the track he'd brought her to on the day she'd arrived at Blackrig. Could she be heading for the pine tree, and from there to Ard Choille or the lochan?

Why hadn't she headed for the village, he asked himself? The answer, of course, was obvious. She intended to try to lose the bastard among the trees.

You should have run in front of us. You should have shouted for help.

He launched himself into the woods, pounding the wider track that led to where he'd left the Land Rover on the first occasion, his heavy gear beating against him. He contemplated losing some of it, then realized he shouldn't because the route he thought she'd taken was likely heading towards the pockets of fire they'd been sent to extinguish.

Reaching the narrower section of path, he recognized the place he'd found her the night when she'd heard the rifle shot and come frantically looking for him.

If only she were sitting here now, dazed but safe.

He stood for a moment to listen. The siren sounds had gone, so the fire engines had reached their destination. The upper trees had stopped swaying, giving him hope that the wind had dropped or at least changed direction.

He'd been concerned she was running towards the fire and not away from it.

As for her follower . . . he'd heard no sounds as yet of his pursuit.

Continuing swiftly on, he began to call out her name. Now that the wind had dropped, his cries would carry. If she heard him, she would surely recognize his voice and realize he was coming for her.

He'd reached the big pine, but there was no sign that

anyone had been here. This was where he'd raged at her for spying on him at the Party House. How momentously stupid he had been in his fury. Despite that, she hadn't backed down, hadn't given up. *And she wouldn't now*, he thought.

He began to hope that the reason she wasn't responding to his shouts was because she'd already emerged near the fire engines and was now safely in the hands of his fellow firefighters.

That was until he heard a distant sound which closely resembled a scream.

Sensing it was coming from the direction of the lochan, possibly the old camp ground, he turned that way. The undergrowth of gorse was thick here among the wider spread of trees.

Gorse was one of the worst for fire, the old dead bushes perfect as household kindling. Dry as bone, its branches could alight in seconds. If any of the sparks crossing the lochan should meet this bank . . .

Eventually emerging from the trees, he found himself yards from the jetty where Naomi had come to swim. Shocked by the vision of the far shore burning, he didn't immediately see them.

For there were two figures in the water, one almost submerged.

What was happening took some moments to make itself plain. Even before it did, he was wading into the water, cursing his fire gear but knowing he couldn't attempt to remove it if he was going to reach her in time.

She re-emerged, spluttering from the water, her hands clawing at the man's jacket, his face, anywhere she could get a hold.

Too intent on what he was doing, the man was unprepared

for the sudden presence of Greg behind him. Grabbing his shoulders, Greg wrenched him off her.

Startled by the unexpected onslaught, he released his hold on Joanne and she sank swiftly below the surface of the water.

Greg swithered between letting go of the man to grab for Joanne and his desire to kill her assailant. Out of the corner of his eye, he saw there was someone else in the water, wading swiftly towards them.

As Joanne resurfaced, coughing and spluttering, Greg set about doing what he had always intended. To kill the bastard who had hurt her.

'Greg! Stop!' Two voices shouted.

Yet still his fist met that face, again and again, sinking it further into the water with every blow.

He heard Joanne's pleas, but still he could not stop.

Then Josh's hands were firmly on his shoulders, pulling him away. 'Enough, mate. Enough.'

Moments later, as he dragged a spluttering Richard to the surface again, he heard Josh's shouted warning that the gorse on the nearby bank was ablaze and they had to get out of there, fast.

The whooshing sound that followed his warning was repeated as the fire began to leap its way along the length of the dead bushes behind them.

Abandoning Richard, Greg went to Joanne, wrapping her in his arms, checking she was okay.

'We'll have to wade along the shore towards Ard Choille. Can you manage that or shall I carry you?'

'I'll manage,' she told him.

The choking smoke from the blazing gorse was already catching at their throats.

'Right,' Greg said, fixing his mask over her face. 'Now, hold on to me,' he ordered.

He began to wade through the shallows, stumbling over hidden rocks, holding her fast to him, never looking back to see what had happened to her attacker, but aware Josh would, despite his feelings towards Richard, be helping the bastard evade the fire.

As they at last reached the long length of golden sand by Ard Choille, Greg saw what his fellow firefighters were now faced with.

What they had feared had already happened. The birchwood behind the house was alight and the only thing saving what had become the hated Party House was a circle of firefighters dousing it in a continuous stream of water from An Lochan Uaine, the green fairy loch.

The Blackrig Wildfire

by Maya Villan

They fought to save Ard Choille. I wondered if they shouldn't let it burn because it had brought such pain to the village in so many ways. But they fought for it none the less. They'd loved the man who'd built it, you see. Lord Main, the main man they called him, they considered as one of their own.

He'd built Ard Choille so that it might be one with the trees, where he could watch the birds, and look over An Lochan Uaine, or the green fairy lochan, as I like to call it.

By the way, I still can't make the 'ch' sound, so say 'the green lockan'. Greg is working on that, but I fear such cultural sounds are acquired when young, and difficult, perhaps impossible, to acquire as you get older.

Anyway, they saved the house by hosing it continuously with water from the green loch as they bulldozed fire breaks all around it.

The far side of the loch was the worst hit. It was there they lost a fire engine and the firefighters had to flee to safety as an oxygen tank blew up.

From there the fire burned far up into the moorland. They say the peat is still smouldering underground in many places. They will need to dig holes and pump them full of water to douse these underground fires.

Although the firefighters and volunteers did their best,

they were eventually saved in their endeavours by the rain. It began to fall in sheets forty hours after the fire began.

It rained for days, heavily at first, then just steady and continuous. I watched from the hill behind Beanach as the blackened, roasted landscape greedily swallowed that water.

Then, in the evening, we watched as the rain beat the darkened windows of Beanach and slid like tears of joy down the glass.

Greg

When he rose in the early morning, the clear sky reminded him that the rain had indeed stopped. In its ferocity, he'd imagined it might rain for forty days and forty nights, so biblical were its proportions.

He and Colin had ventured out as soon as they felt it opportune to do so. Despite their proximity to Ard Choille, the Bothy, Colin's home, and the estate larder had avoided the fire.

Greg had been surprised at how hard the local crew had fought to save the hated Party House. Or perhaps by saving it, they'd hoped to bring it back from the dead in the eyes of the folk of Blackrig.

Of course, what happened to it now lay with Global Investment Holdings, not the local community.

He'd spoken only once by telephone with Chalmers since the fire, when he'd been given the impression that whoever was currently at the helm of the company, it certainly wasn't Stratton.

Why, he didn't know for certain, although thinking back to Chalmers's attitude at their last meeting, he wondered if Stratton's behaviour that night in the pub had demonstrated how bad relations were with the locals.

Regardless of why he had gone, Greg was relieved that he had. He wasn't expecting Chalmers to do a better job, he just thought he couldn't do worse.

Putting on the coffee machine, he went to feed the dogs before making his own breakfast.

Despite the freshness that met him as he stepped outside, he still found himself checking for the scent of burning. When you've been immersed in that smell for as long as the Blackrig crew had been, it was difficult to get rid of it from your nostrils.

He stood for a moment, breathing the hill air, aware that the summer scents would be different this year, especially in August. Much of the surrounding heather-clad hills had been reduced to ashes. The heather in those parts wouldn't, couldn't, bloom this year and he would miss the heady scent of it.

Glancing up at the bedroom window, he thought of Joanne and what her decision would be, now that she was no longer in fear of going back to London.

After the fight in the lochan, Richard Longman had been removed by the police and taken to Inverness police station, arrested for his attack on Joanne.

He might have been accompanying him had Josh not pulled him off the bastard when he did. He would be eternally grateful to Josh for doing that. As far as Josh was concerned, he had just been returning the favour of that night at the ceilidh. Or so he'd said.

He'd taken Joanne to Kath's after that, not wanting her to be alone at Beanach, and there she had stayed, writing up her blog report of the fire until it had finally been extinguished.

He, like Josh and Finn, had gone back to fighting it, with all their efforts focused on the Party House, which had become a symbol of survival, rather than one of death.

In the end, the battle had been won by the rain, but they

had been the army that kept the enemy at bay until the rain had arrived.

Heading back inside, he found Joanne up and busy at the stove.

He came up and, standing behind her, gently kissed the nape of her neck.

Things had been good between them since her tormentor had been removed from her life, although he knew she feared his influence as a defence lawyer might yet see him walk free.

That was something they wouldn't talk about, unless she chose to.

It wasn't the only thing bothering her. He had made it plain in their conversations after the fire that he wanted to support her in whatever decision she made regarding the pregnancy.

'I told Richard it was his to stop him hitting me in the stomach,' she'd eventually revealed. 'I said I was sure. I'm not sure, but he will likely demand a prenatal DNA test.'

'Can he legally do that?'

She'd shaken her head. 'I don't know, but he will do whatever it takes to find out.'

'And if he's not the father?' he'd said quietly.

'He won't want it, but he may fight for it anyway. He believes in retribution where I'm concerned.'

They sat down to eat, although he barely tasted his food, aware that some sort of decision was in the offing.

Should he tell her what he really wanted? That she should have the baby and stay here with him, regardless of who the father was? Or remember that she was the one who had to decide her future, not him?

Richard had not permitted that. He'd tried to manipulate

and control her. Anything he did or said, however mild, might remind her of that fact.

Plus he, Josh and Finn were still under suspicion with regard to Ailsa's death and thus he wasn't allowed to leave Blackrig, so couldn't go to London with her, should she decide to have the abortion.

She was looking at him, perhaps trying to read his thoughts.

'I think we should have the prenatal DNA test,' she said haltingly. 'If you wouldn't mind, that is?'

He wanted to sweep her up and hug her, but wasn't sure that would be welcome, so he simply said, 'No. I wouldn't mind. I wouldn't mind at all.'

'We have to wait until the seventh week of pregnancy,' she said.

'We can do that,' he answered with a nod.

He didn't want to ask her what she would do with the result. He was content for the moment to wait out the time. Perhaps by then they would have discovered Ailsa's killer, and he would be a free man again.

Although not one without shame.

The sound of a quad bike sent him outside once more, to find Josh on his way up the track towards him.

They hadn't spoken since the wildfire had been officially declared as over, although after the scene at the lochan, they'd had a heart-to-heart discussion about what had actually been going on there.

Josh's expression as he dismounted suggested something had happened that Greg needed to be told about, and in person.

'Josh,' Greg said. 'D'you want to come inside?'

'Is Joanne in there?'

'She is.'

'Then I think we should maybe talk in the shed?'

Puzzled now, and a little troubled, Greg nodded an okay and led Josh inside the shed, shutting the door behind them.

'The police have lifted Finn again. Caroline's going mad with worry.'

'Do we know why they've rearrested him?'

'I tried Harry, but he's not saying anything except they must have more evidence against him.'

Greg racked his brain for what that might be, but since they didn't truly know for sure what they'd had the first time round . . .

'There's no way Finn killed Ailsa,' Josh said. 'He can't kill anything. He won't come hunting with us. Not rabbits, deer. He won't even go fishing.'

Greg knew all this already, which was why he'd been so surprised by Joanne's story of Finn's fury the night he'd found her with Caroline.

'That time he was angry with you at the hall – what was that all about?' Greg said.

'He blamed me for causing all the horror by wrecking the hot tub. He was right about that.' Josh looked to Greg. 'I'm going to tell the police he was with us that night. So, if there is a fingerprint, then that's the reason it's there. I want you to back me up.'

'What?' Greg said stupidly.

'You were there that night. I saw you as we ran off. I thought maybe I was mistaken when you didn't give us up to the police. You heard the voices. You knew everyone who was there.'

'And Finn wasn't one of them,' Greg heard himself say.

Josh didn't like that response.

'You knew we found something,' he said firmly. 'You must have checked on what it was after we left. Or maybe you already knew what it was? Either way, you didn't report it. You left it for Colin to find and report the next morning. I bet you didn't tell Colin you'd been there or what you'd seen either.'

Lies always return to haunt you. Lies and omissions.

'I was there and I did look. I was as shocked to see her body as you were.' That much at least was true.

'And?' Josh prodded.

'I suspected I was the last person to see Ailsa alive. So for me to report the body . . .' He trailed off. It wasn't the whole story, but it was true enough.

'So you didn't give me up, and I did the same for you. Now we both have to help Finn,' Josh said in a determined fashion.

'DI Snyder will know we're lying and he'll wonder why. Maybe he'll think it's because one of us killed Ailsa.'

'If one of us had, why would we be trying to get Finn off the hook for it?' Josh demanded.

Greg shook his head. Now they were in the region of bluff and double bluff, he was at a loss.

'Lies got us where we are now,' he said. 'I'm not lying again.'

'So you'll let them charge Finn when we both know he didn't do it?'

'Do we?' Greg said. 'Are you sure I didn't do it? Am I sure you didn't?' He paused, waiting for the next angry retort, which didn't happen.

'Look, I'll go down and speak to Caroline, if she'll let me,' he said. 'See if she knows any more about it. Maybe she's Finn's alibi for the night Ailsa disappeared.'

'You mean when she said she was yours?' Josh didn't sound convinced.

'Let me try.'

'You have until tomorrow, then I go and give them my statement, where I tell them you were there hiding in the bushes when we smashed up the hot tub. Maybe' – he thought for a moment – 'maybe you knew we were up to something and were there to guard the grave.'

Greg tried not to respond to that semi-accusation. It wouldn't get them anywhere if he did.

'I'll go see Caroline now.'

Josh nodded, his face still full of anger.

Greg waited until the quad bike took off down the hill before he went in to tell Joanne that Finn had been arrested again and he needed to speak to Caroline about that.

Joanne

When Greg left for the village to speak to Caroline, she'd immediately headed for the toilet. The morning sickness that had heralded the pregnancy had now moved to become any time of the day. Like now.

Knowing it was impossible to be silent when it happened, she had welcomed Greg's departure.

Now that it was over, and whatever she'd eaten for breakfast was no longer in her stomach, she lowered the toilet lid and splashed her face with cold water. She should, she knew, have contacted a doctor by now and got checked out. But why do that if her intention was to abort the pregnancy anyway? The truth was she had no idea what her intention was any more.

She didn't even know why she'd blurted out about a prenatal DNA test to discover who the father was. She'd read about it when she'd been researching the abortion route, and had thought how wonderful it would be to discover that the baby wasn't Richard's.

Going through to the bedroom, she lay down on the bed and, remembering how happy Greg had looked when she'd suggested the test, she wanted to burst out crying.

What a mess everything was. She'd thought that having Richard arrested would make her feel better, and in a way it did. At least she wasn't waiting for him to find her any more. Though now she was wondering how swiftly he would manage to have the charge changed to one of assault. On him by Greg, of course.

By the time Josh had arrived at the lochan, it was Greg beating on Richard, with Richard's assault on her not obvious. If Richard wove a different story . . . and he was eloquent and experienced enough to do that . . .

She shook her head to try and dispel such thoughts, but still they persisted. Greg had no real idea how powerful Richard was in his own world. Both powerful and calculating.

She placed her hands on her still-flat stomach. Even now, she couldn't believe that the beginnings of life trembled in there . . . but for how long?

She'd told Greg how she'd prevented Richard from punching her in the stomach when he had her in the shed. What she hadn't explained was what had so incensed Richard that he'd tried to drown her.

She began to relive all those moments from her opening of the shed door to find a man dressed ready to hunt. The way he'd been examining Greg's rifle rack. The instant the figure had turned and how long it had taken for her to realize who it was.

After which her terror had caused time to slow down almost to a standstill, her every movement an effort.

There had been so many other times like that with Richard, when she'd known what would happen next and had tried to circumnavigate it.

The first time was as fresh now as ever. It was the beginning of a slow and steady realization of who Richard really was under the carefully contrived exterior. The moment when sexual games became a torturous reality. When consent no longer mattered. It never had, she eventually understood.

It had only been necessary at the beginning to lull her into his fabricated fantasy.

She had learned from the best, and initially, at least, had played the same game with Greg.

Which had brought her to this point.

She had saved herself a beating because Richard had been pleased about the pregnancy. It was something he'd wanted for a long time. He'd even allowed himself to believe it was his child she carried.

That belief had got her to the car without a beating.

Then, seeing the smoke and flames of the distant fire, she'd remembered . . . that the man he'd defended had burned both his wife and children alive, because she'd been having an affair. Even though the children were his own.

The memory of that horror, a horror Richard had condoned, had propelled her from the car. Luck had been on her side, with the arrival of the fire engines, but she would have tried to get out anyway, even if they hadn't helped her escape.

After that, the dash through the woods, the triumphant feeling that she had lost him in the smoke, then the fear she too had missed the path to Ard Choille and safety, from Richard at least.

And all the time she ran towards the flames, the phrase *out of the frying pan, into the fire* replayed in her head. By the time she reached the lochan, the fire seemed so close there was nowhere left to go except into the water.

Only to discover Richard had been right behind her all the time.

He had been gentle at first. Urging her out, holding his hand out to her. She hated him then for his contrived concern, so she told him the baby wasn't his. That was what had triggered his assault. That was why he'd tried to drown her.

She had made him attack her when she might have avoided it, and Greg had almost paid the price for that, had Josh not come along to prevent him from being the one arrested for attempted murder.

She was bad news for Greg, whatever happened. He would be better off without her and the problems this child would bring.

Greg

They'd told him at the shop that he would find her here. He wondered why she had come to the graveyard. The miscarriage had happened so early in the pregnancy that Mac had neither a birth nor a death certificate. Nor a grave.

Caroline had found that difficult to bear. It was as though Mac had just been a dream, she'd said.

His response had been to remind her of the ultrasound photo they had. He'd told her Mac would always be in their hearts.

Her look then had suggested his words were hollow. They hadn't been, but they must have seemed so because of what had happened.

Slumped on the bench that overlooked the graves beyond the white fence, she was so still, he questioned as he approached if she was even alive.

On calling her name, she looked up, her face ravaged by fear and grief. When she saw who it was, he watched her strive to muster herself.

'Greg. I was glad to hear you and Joanne are okay. That man came into the shop. Said he was a friend of Joanne's and heard she was staying in the village and did I know where.' She halted there. 'I told him she was at Beanach. It's my fault he went there.' She looked stricken by that.

'It's okay. You weren't to know,' Greg said.

'I don't understand. Why did he attack her?'

'He's an ex-partner. A violent one. Stratton recognized Joanne and told him she was here.'

'God, that's terrible.'

'I didn't come here to talk about that,' he began. 'Josh told me they've rearrested Finn. D'you know why?'

'They think he killed Ailsa,' she said in a flat voice.

'But why? Why would they think that?' Greg said, now seated alongside her.

'They won't tell me. Just said they had forensic evidence from the body.' She put her head in her hands. 'What do I do? I can't tell them . . .' She stuttered to a halt, a frightened look on her face.

'Tell them what?' he urged.

She was staring at him as though reading his mind. 'Joanne's pregnant, isn't she?'

'How did you—' He stopped himself before finishing the sentence.

She nodded as though to herself. 'I suspected as much. There was something about her when she came with me that night. When the guy turned up at the shop, I suspected he might be her partner. That's why I sent him there, so he would take her away from here. From you. Even if I'd known he was violent, I suspect I would still have told him where she was. I hated – no, hate her, you see. Just as I hated Ailsa for taking you from me.'

Greg tried to process all of this, mixed up as it was with the sentence she couldn't finish.

'What can't you tell the police?' he said.

She looked at him as if he were a child, then shook her head. 'It doesn't matter,' she said wearily.

'What doesn't matter?' he demanded.

'Everything.' She rose to go. 'Josh's wee sister's over there.' She pointed in the grave's direction. 'At least she has a headstone. Ailsa will get one too now, I expect.'

'If there's something you haven't told the police – about me – about anything—' he called to her retreating figure, but she didn't stop and she didn't answer.

He sat there for a long time, trying to work through what Caroline had just said and what it might mean. Did she know something about that night that put Finn in the frame for Ailsa's murder? Was that the reason Finn had been so angry about the uncovering of the grave?

Or did she remember something about him? Something he'd blotted from his memory about that night? About the last time he'd seen Ailsa?

He tried to think and, the more he did that, the more convinced he became that Caroline was still covering for him in some way.

After Ailsa disappeared, he'd lost his wits. Drunk himself stupid. He'd been out of it for weeks. Then Caroline had the miscarriage, after which he'd run away again, gone south. Was there something that had happened during that time that he wasn't allowing himself to remember?

Something he'd buried deep in his subconscious?

You heard of people doing that. Protecting themselves from the horror of what they'd done or experienced.

The thought terrified him.

In that moment he remembered Ailsa's necklace. The one he'd kept in the envelope with the photo of Mac. Why did he have her necklace? Had Ailsa given it to him? Or had he taken it . . . ?

The clasp was broken, he remembered. How or why had it been broken?

Had he taken it from her by force or was she already dead and he'd taken it to remember her by?

He tried to find the scene in his memory and replay it, but it changed every time, like all the lies he'd been telling.

Eventually he stopped trying and reached for his wallet. Extracting Snyder's card, he stared at it for what seemed an eternity, before he took out his mobile and called the number again.

Greg

He didn't contact Joanne until he was halfway to Inverness. Drawing into a lay-by, he looked out over the loch it bordered and brought up her number.

It rang for a while, and he wondered if she was taking an afternoon nap as she'd been doing since the fire. She answered just as he was about to ring off.

'Everything all right?' he said.

'Yes.' She sounded sleepy. 'What happened with Caroline?'

'We talked. She's worried about Finn. She knows about the pregnancy.'

'You told her?' Joanne's tone had changed, as though his announcement had fully awakened her.

'I didn't. She asked me outright, as though she already knew. I wondered if you . . . she said there was something about you that night you went to her place that made her wonder,' he finished lamely.

She was quiet for a while. 'Are you coming home soon?'

He cleared the lump in his throat. 'I'm on my way to Inverness.'

'Why?' she asked, her voice rising in fear.

'I called DI Snyder. There's something I need to talk to him about.'

'They've arrested you? Was it something Richard said or did?' She sounded frantic at such a thought.

'No,' he said quietly. 'I asked to go in and speak to him. I remembered something about the night Ailsa went missing.'

The silence following his explanation suggested she didn't want to ask what that something was.

'I'll see you later,' he said.

'How much later?' she said.

'Keep me something to eat,' he said, trying to keep his tone light.

After the call had ended, he sat for a while, looking at the loch and the mountains that encircled it, remembering how he'd stopped here when he'd brought Joanne from the train. She'd taken photographs, so enamoured had she been by the view. He'd felt at the time that he was looking at it again through her eyes.

In fact, since his terror at seeing her run past the fire engine and into the woods, he'd been viewing everything through her eyes. Something that had never happened with Caroline. Even in the aftermath of the miscarriage.

He'd realized that today in the cemetery.

The pregnancy ending the way it did had provided an escape for him. One that he'd taken. But it wasn't only the miscarriage and Caroline he'd been escaping from. It had also been the memory of Ailsa.

Inverness lay huddled under a blanket of cloud that obscured the rise of the land on both banks of the River Ness and turned the Moray Firth a glowering grey. Gone was the sunshine and the light, for now at least.

It suited his mood, this gloomy city, he thought as he drew into the police car park. Snyder's reaction to his call had been difficult to read. He was interested, but not overly so. Greg had the idea that the detective had other more pressing things on his mind.

On announcing his presence at the desk, he was asked to take a seat and wait . . . and no, the duty sergeant had no idea how long that wait would be.

He tried to be pleased that on this occasion at least he wasn't under arrest, although he reminded himself that he might soon be. He'd heard nothing from Josh since his threat to reveal his presence when the grave was uncovered, but then again he'd been given until tomorrow to agree to support Finn with their lie, or else deal with the consequences.

Maybe, he mused, that particular lie wouldn't be required after all.

Eventually he was called and admitted to an interview room, just like on the previous occasion.

Snyder and DS Reid were already there and awaiting him. However, the situation felt nothing like the last time. Then they'd been there to interrogate him. Now, it appeared from their demeanour, they were merely curious to know what exactly he had come here to say.

'Mr Taylor.' Snyder scrutinized him. 'I understand you have something you wish to tell us about the night Ailsa Cummings disappeared?'

He had no idea how to say this, because whichever way he did, it would sound, if not lame, then deranged.

Eventually he said, 'I spoke to Caroline this morning in the cemetery. I realized that something had happened that night with her that I'd either forgotten or blanked from my memory. After she left, I tried to remember.' He halted there. 'You see, I'd been drinking a lot, because of Ailsa and the need to break things off with her, because of the baby. I'd been drinking at the ceilidh, trying to stop myself from going to meet Ailsa in the woods as promised. Then when I got back to Beanach I continued drinking . . .

'I can remember Ailsa walking into the kitchen. She never knocked. She always just walked in, even though Caroline might have been there. She was angry with me for standing her up. She said she'd heard footsteps approaching the fairy glen. She thought it was me at first. Then she'd realized there was more than one person and they were coming for her. Frightened, she'd started to run. They ran after her. Three men. One of them was Josh Huntly. Another was Finn Campbell.'

He no longer registered their faces. He was telling the story to himself. 'They gave up when she reached the road, but instead of heading home to Forrigan, she came to Beanach to tell me how much she hated me for leaving her there to wait alone in the woods.

'I had to hold her and tell her how sorry I was for doing that. I shouldn't have touched her, because then we were kissing and then . . .

'Afterwards, I told her that was definitely the last time we would see one another. She screamed at me. Told me she hoped the baby would die. That Caroline would die. That I didn't deserve to be a father.

'I didn't care what she said about me, but I cared about Caroline and the baby. I told her to get out.'

He halted there for a moment and then continued. 'After that it's a blur, although in the morning I had her necklace in my hand. The clasp was broken. I don't know how I got it, but I have it still. I put it in the envelope with my unborn son's picture.'

His story had come to an end, because no matter how hard he tried, he couldn't remember anything after he told Ailsa to get out and never come back.

'You think you may have hurt her?' DS Reid said.

'I would never hurt a woman.' He stopped there, realizing how untrue that was. 'I mean, I would never raise my hand to a woman.'

DS Reid and Snyder were sharing a look, which appeared to carry a decision within it.

In the end it was DS Reid who spoke. 'Mr Taylor, you are no longer under suspicion for the murder of Ailsa Cummings. We already have someone in custody who has provided us with a full confession.'

And then they told him who that someone was.

Joanne

She'd gone outside as soon as she heard the Land Rover's approach.

The sun was setting in the west, the hills turned blood red by its descent. For a terrible moment she thought they were on fire again, until she breathed in the sweet night air.

When she saw him emerge from the vehicle, she knew her fears had been well-founded. Something had happened between him and DI Snyder. Something that had drained all colour from his face, so much so that he resembled a ghostly apparition rather than the man he was.

She wanted to take him in her arms, but knew by the way he approached her that it wouldn't be welcomed. He'd retreated within himself. That much was obvious.

Once inside, he glanced about him as if checking that this was indeed Beanach, his home. As for the look he bestowed on her, it was one of surprise that she was here at all.

Unsure what to say or do, she sat down at the kitchen table and waited.

After a moment he joined her there, his hands clasped on the table in front of him. She realized with a sinking dread that they were trembling.

He's in shock, she thought, and rose to draw the kettle onto the ring, planning to serve him something hot and sweet.

Noting her intention, he said, 'I would rather have a whisky.'

She went to fetch the bottle, gladdened to hear his voice, which sounded strong despite his obvious distress.

She stood a glass and the bottle before him.

'You pour,' he said. 'Two fingers' worth, please.'

When he raised the glass to his lips, his hands looked more in control of themselves.

'I have food,' she said, trying to sound normal. 'You told me to keep you some.'

He gave her a weak smile. 'Thank you. Maybe once I've told you what happened.'

He marshalled himself, then began. 'I didn't tell you the whole story about Ailsa or Caroline, because I thought that if I did, you would leave and I didn't want that.'

He checked to see her reaction and she nodded at him to go on.

'I found Caroline in the cemetery this morning near the children's graves. She revealed she'd told Richard where to find you, hoping he would take you away from here. From me. Then she gave me the impression that because I was drunk the night Ailsa disappeared, something had happened that I'd either forgotten or more likely buried.'

He told her about the broken necklace.

'I came to next morning with it in my hand, but couldn't remember how or why I'd taken it from her neck. That's why I called Snyder. Why I went up there.'

Her heart was beating like a drum in her ears. She dreaded what he would say next, but desperately wanted to hear it, whatever it was.

'I told him all of that.' He met her eye. 'He told me I was no longer a suspect in Ailsa's murder. That someone had already confessed.'

'Someone confessed?' she said, open-mouthed.

His eyes were haunted. 'She saw me with Ailsa. Watched as we made love. She followed Ailsa when she left Beanach. Waited in the woods near Ard Choille until Ailsa came back from the campsite.'

'You mean Caroline?' She could hardly believe what she was saying.

'The argument became physical and Ailsa fell and hit her head on a rock. When she realized what she'd done, she called Finn. He buried the body where we found it.'

Even as he spoke the words, she knew that he still didn't, couldn't, believe what he was saying.

'Maybe she's covering for Finn?' Joanne tried.

'According to the police, Finn tried to claim he did it, but they said they had forensic evidence that matched Caroline's confession.'

He sat in painful silence for some moments.

'She was mad with fear that I would leave her.' He met Joanne's eyes. 'I felt that fear when I saw Richard with you in the lochan. I could have killed him – would have killed him – had Josh not been there to stop me.'

She moved behind him and wrapped her arms about him.

'I spoke with her lawyer. He says they'll take her pregnancy and state of mind into account. They'll plead an accidental death caused by the fall.' He looked up at her. 'There's something I want to say to you.'

Taking her hand, he drew her round to sit next to him.

'I don't want to make the same mistake again. I've wanted to say something since I found out about the pregnancy, but didn't because I was afraid you would think I was interfering in your choice.

'I want us to be together no matter what you decide, but

I want you to know that it doesn't matter to me who the father is, because I love this baby's mother and I'll love the baby just as much.'

So there it was.

She wasn't sure it was the right time to tell him. Then again, maybe it was the only time.

'I need to go home. Back to London, I mean. I need to make it known who and what Richard Longman QC really is. I need to speak to Lucy, my friend. I need to think clearly, away from here. From you. From this world. When I've cleared my head and made my decision . . .' She tailed off at that.

'You've booked the train already?'

'Tomorrow night's sleeper.'

'Okay. I'll take you there.'

'I don't want that. It would be too hard.' She shook her head. 'I've already asked Kath to take me and she's agreed.'

He gave a small nod. 'I need to call Malcolm, although I expect Harry may have already told him about . . .' He stopped there, obviously unable to say Caroline's name.

'If it's all right with you, I'll go up to bed now?' she said.

'Of course,' he said, the moment of intimacy they'd shared clearly over. 'I'll take the couch tonight. Give you peace to sleep.'

Upstairs now, she sat by the window. The sun having departed, there was nothing but an enveloping darkness, both outside and within.

Greg

Before she left, she'd asked him not to try to get in contact with her. That there were things she needed to do, and she had to do them alone.

'I'll call you when it's over.'

He didn't know exactly what she meant by that, but knew not to ask.

'Concentrate on Caroline,' she'd urged. 'Help her in whatever way you can. She needs you to do that.'

He had given her a promise that he would, and he was trying to keep it.

In the days following Caroline's confession, Blackrig went into shock. They said bad things happened in threes but Greg had already counted five horrors, including Ailsa's initial disappearance, the Party House deaths, the wildfire and now Caroline held in remand on a charge of culpable homicide, with Finn held too for aiding and abetting the hiding of the body.

On the day Joanne left, she'd asked if he would stay away from Beanach until Kath came to collect her. He'd been glad to do that, although he dreaded going back to the house at the end of the day to find her no longer there.

So he'd gone to the Blackrig Arms that night instead. There was something he needed to tell Malcolm personally. Something he should have done a long time ago.

Malcolm had brought him into the kitchen and dished him up a plate of stew.

'Eat first,' he'd said. 'You can tell me after that.'

When he did, Malcolm had listened in silence, before saying, 'So you've been blaming yourself for bringing the virus down here from the Party House. You might be right, but then again, so might Mairi.'

'Mairi?' he'd said, puzzled.

'She was convinced that she was the one who carried the virus from the house into the village. She had a call one night about one of the guests being ill. I didn't want her to go, but she said it was her job and she would take all suitable precautions, which I'm sure she did,' he said quietly. 'The blame for those deaths lies with the company that brought people in when it was strictly against the law to do so. Global Investment Holdings killed our children and my Mairi. No one else.' He'd looked at Greg. 'So we'll hear no more about that, because there's something else we need to discuss and it involves the future of Ard Choille.'

Earlier that same day, Greg had spent time at Ard Choille and its surrounds. Not wanting to field any questions from Colin, he'd told him to take the day off and go see Karla, knowing she would no doubt be able to fill him in on some of what had happened. You didn't work in the village pub and not learn what was going on in Blackrig.

He'd walked up via the woods with the dogs, hoping the familiar scents and sounds would calm his mind, but all he had been able to think about was the fact that Joanne was leaving and that when he got back to Beanach, he would find it empty.

Ard Choille, when he reached it, had a similar abandoned air. The endless drenching with the water cannon, followed by the torrential rain, had dislodged some of the outer wooden cladding. The windows were smeared with sooty deposits. The heavy oaken door muddied. The stag's head knocker blackened with soot.

Inside was no better. You can't drown a house and leave the interior unblemished. The entrance hall was a mass of muddy footprints that climbed the stairs with him to the once-elegant dining room and, at the top, the balcony room, which not so long ago had rung with the sound of laughter, sometimes at his expense.

Broken crystal glasses crunched underfoot as he went out onto the balcony itself. In his mind's eye, he saw the brightly coloured dresses of the women, the sardonic looks of the men. He stepped to the edge, from where he could see into the distance and to the far side of the green lochan.

The shattered blackened stumps were all that remained of what had been a forest, verdant and full of life. Beyond it, the moor was a scorched wasteland.

There would be no shooting parties enticed here for some time. The estate had no hope of recovery in the short term. So what would happen to it?

He suspected Global Investment Holdings might cut their losses and sell up, but to whom and to be used for what, he had no idea. Lord Main's dream for Ard Choille, it seemed, lay in ruins once again.

Despondent, he'd left the place to what birds remained in the woods that were still standing and, calling the dogs, set off for the hill, vowing to stay there until he was certain Joanne had gone, probably forever.

He was brought back from these thoughts by what Malcolm was in the process of suggesting, which was that they hold a meeting in the village hall to discuss Ard Choille.

'Discuss what?' he'd said, puzzled.

'The possible buy-out of Blackrig Estate by the community.'

Was that achievable? He'd been thinking only about loss and dark thoughts for so long, he couldn't imagine anything positive happening any more.

Malcolm, on the other hand, was bright with enthusiasm.

'Well, son, what do you think? Is it worth a shot? It would bring us together again. Maybe heal some of the hurt of the last five years. D'you think they'd be willing to sell? After all, there won't be any profit from the estate or house for some considerable time.' He'd looked heavenwards. 'I think the main man would be behind us on this, don't you?'

Greg

August came and went, minus the heather's fragrant blooms. September swiftly followed, when the hills rang with the roars of rutting stags and the vegetation that had survived the fire began to change the colour of the hills and woods.

The surviving birches around Ard Choille turned yellow and leaves fell to the ground like showers of gold medallions. Surprisingly, the rowans produced the best crop of blood-red berries that he'd seen in years, even the ancient ones he'd thought were past fruiting.

With no visitors to attend to, he and Colin carried on with all the other tasks of the estate. Their wages were deposited in their bank accounts, but there was no further contact from either Stratton or Chalmers.

As long as both he and Colin were paid, Greg didn't care. Plus he'd begun to nourish hopes that Malcolm's idea of a community buy-out might actually be a possibility.

On one of his many walks with the dogs, he eventually found the courage to visit Forrigan. On the neighbouring hill to Beanach, it had been the unlucky victim of the fire. Burning round behind both hills, its wind-borne sparks had caught hold on the Forrigan roof, and as the team focused so much energy and work on Ard Choille, Forrigan became a victim of that particular war.

As he got closer, he could see that the rafters had been

the first casualty, and as the flames had gained entrance, the attic bedrooms had paid the price. The helicopter had deposited a load of water on the abandoned house, in the hope of further protecting its nearest neighbour, Beanach.

He was grateful for that, but sad too at the destruction of a cottage that had stood there almost as long as Beanach had.

When he finally made himself go inside, he discovered the staircase gone, so there was no opportunity for him to go upstairs and look in Ailsa's bedroom as Joanne had done. Something that had made him angry with her at the time.

That memory made him as despondent as observing the gutted building.

Checking the time, he called the dogs and began to make his way back to Beanach and the Land Rover, intent on heading into Blackrig to be updated by Kath, who would shortly be back from visiting Caroline in Inverness prison.

Caroline had been charged with culpable homicide and held on remand, and they were expecting the date of the trial to be announced soon.

Finn they'd released on bail with Malcolm acting as his guarantor, and he was currently staying at the hotel.

Both Caroline and Finn had refused to see him, with Finn blaming all his sister's woes on Greg. Something Greg accepted.

His own brush with the law in the form of Richard Longman QC had eventually fizzled out, mainly because Joanne had decided not to press charges regarding Richard's attack on her in the lochan and, *quid pro quo*, Richard had dropped his own charge of assault against Greg.

Greg had no idea why Joanne had given up on that until eventually he'd decided to follow her blog posts as Maya

Villan, convincing himself that this still lay within the rules of not contacting her.

There he discovered that instead of charging him with the single attack, she had outed Richard for what he was – a violent, abusive partner and sexual predator – and since that moment of courage, many other women had come forward to support her claims with their own.

He guessed that exposing Richard Longman QC on the hallowed London turf he called his own had been her intention, although he still feared for her safety because of it.

The blog was without images of her, so he had no idea if she'd ended the pregnancy or not, and no amount of googling either 'Joanne Addington' or 'Maya Villan' had changed that.

'I'll get in touch when it's over,' had been her final words to him, and he still had no idea what the 'it' she'd referred to encompassed.

What was in no doubt, however, was her determination to accomplish whatever journey she'd set out on.

Driving along Main Street, he noted that Kath was back, her car parked in the drive, so he pulled in behind her. Obviously watching for him, she opened the door on his approach. 'Come away in, Greg, and I'll bring you up to date.'

It had been like this from the beginning. He had tried to keep his promise to Joanne to help Caroline in any way he could, but a visit from him hadn't been permitted. He was almost relieved by her refusal to allow this to happen. It would have been painful for them both. At least via Kath he could still offer whatever help he could.

'The date for the trial is set for—' She gave a date in November. 'As you're aware, Caroline's defence will argue that she had no intention of hurting Ailsa, only of remonstrating with her. Her sudden death caused by the fall was an accident. Mitigating circumstances will apply and you will be asked to explain what those were.' She was watching him closely. 'The pregnancy and your affair. Are you willing to do that?'

The blame, he knew, could be attributed to his treatment of both women. Even as he nodded, the same small thought surfaced again. The one that reminded him that Caroline had wished ill on Ailsa, just as she'd wished ill on Joanne.

But wishing ill wasn't the same as doing it.

And yet . . . and yet, she'd admitted she would have told Richard of Joanne's whereabouts even had she known that he would be violent towards her. Because she hated Joanne, just as she'd hated Ailsa, because they had, in her words, taken him away from her.

The truth was he'd never been 'hers' in the first place. Just as Joanne didn't belong either to him or to Richard.

Kath was waiting for his answer, so he gave it.

'I'll do whatever I can.'

'Right, now tell me, have you heard anything from Joanne?'

He shook his head. 'I keep an eye on her Maya Villan blog. She's written about the virus and the wildfire, but nothing about Ailsa.'

'Well, that story's not yet complete,' Kath said, reminding him of something he'd said to Joanne earlier in their story.

'She's also pursuing Richard and getting a lot of support from other women who have stories about him too.'

'Good for her,' Kath said.

'How's Finn?'

'Caroline worries more about him than herself. She blames

herself for getting him involved.' She fell silent for a moment. 'We all do stupid things in the horror of the moment. Things we ultimately regret. That doesn't make us bad people. Just flawed ones.'

She continued. 'You'll have to forgive yourself some time, you know. Just like we all will. We imagine somehow we'll see the bad things that are headed our way. The bad things and the good. So we can prepare for the bad and take time to enjoy the good – but, sadly, we rarely do.

'You and Caroline weren't meant for each other. You and Joanne are, despite the circumstances. My advice is to stand up in court and say your piece to help Caroline. Then get on with your life and make sure Joanne is a part of it.'

Greg

He'd read up on everything he could find that might have a bearing on the trial. What he couldn't find online, he'd questioned Caroline's defence lawyer about.

However, none of what he'd learned prepared him for what was to follow. In particular when he spotted Ailsa's traumatized parents sitting in the gallery.

He spent every day in court, listening to the evidence, until he too was called to give his version of the events of that fateful night. That, and his relationship with both the victim and the accused.

It was a sorry tale, although he felt relieved to at last tell the full truth of what he could remember.

Caroline did not look once in his direction while he did this. Yet he would have given anything to have her do that.

When it came her time to be questioned, she'd sat rigidly upright, her eyes staring as though into the past. As she began her story, she appeared to relax a little, letting the words flow as if grateful to at last say it all out loud.

'I was pregnant with Greg's baby. He'd promised he wouldn't see Ailsa again. He avoided meeting her that night after the ceilidh and went straight back to Beanach. I followed him a little later.

'When I arrived, Ailsa was inside. They were having sex. Afterwards they began arguing. Greg told her that would be the last time it ever happened. That he didn't want to see her again. That he was going to become a father.

'She was really angry when he said that. Greg told her to leave. I thought she would go back home to Forrigan. When she didn't, I decided to follow her. She entered the woods by the green loch and I realized she was going to the campsite, where her Glasgow friends were staying.'

Caroline fell silent at that point, staring ahead, her face white and drawn.

'I waited because I wanted to talk to her, explain properly about the baby. How we knew it was a boy and we were going to call him Mac. When she reappeared, I asked her not to break us up, because of the baby. She said she didn't care about that shit. That Greg liked to fuck her, not me.'

She'd halted there for a moment, her face a mask of pain, before drawing breath to continue.

'She pushed me out of the way and I shoved her back. She grabbed my hair and yanked it. I remember screaming. She told me to "shut the fuck up" and scratched at my face. When I managed to break free, she stumbled, missed her footing and fell backwards. I expected her to get up, but she didn't.

'I thought of going to Greg's place but I didn't want him to know I'd seen them together. So I called my young brother, Finn. By the time he arrived I was out of my mind, because I couldn't find a pulse.

'I didn't think anyone would believe me that it was an accident. And I was pregnant. I wanted the baby desperately. I wanted to be with Greg. It was my fault we hid her body. Finn didn't want to do that, but I begged him. I thought folk would think she'd run away again. She'd done it before in Glasgow. I'm sorry I did that. Sorry that her parents had to go through that. I'm sorry I got Finn involved. It was all my fault.'

According to the police, Caroline's story matched the forensic material they'd collected from the body. Flakes of Caroline's skin had been under Ailsa's nails. Clumps of hair in Ailsa's hands.

For five years Caroline had been carrying this guilt, knowing that everything she'd done was in the hope that Mac would be born and make them the family she craved.

The sentence was what Greg had been told to expect. In respect of culpable homicide on the basis of a minor assault leading to death, Caroline was given a custodial sentence of two years. For her attempts to pervert the course of justice by burying the body, she had three years added to that. Her time in remand would be taken into account.

As for Finn, he was given two years for aiding and abetting his sister in the disposal of the body.

Greg didn't return directly to Beanach after the trial, but drove instead to Ard Choille.

He wanted to remember the times as teenagers that he and Caroline had spent by the lochside. To remember how things had been between them back then.

An Lochan Uaine's green hue changed with the shifting lights of the seasons, but to his mind it always looked magical. A green fairy loch like the fairy glen.

They'd spent a lot of time here together. Most of every summer, even after they took up summer jobs, him on the estate, her at her family's shop. She'd had to bring Finn along some of the time. She never seemed to mind that, although he had occasionally been irked by her wee brother's presence.

When had everything changed between them?

Listening to Caroline's story of that terrible night, he could now see where all the lies and omissions had begun, both his and hers. The jigsaw that portrayed their lives – Caroline's, Ailsa's and his own – had finally been put together, and at its centre was his betrayal of both women.

Something he was going to have to learn to live with.

That, and the fact that Joanne wasn't coming back.

He turned from the loch and walked towards Ard Choille.

He and Colin had made a point of trimming the lawn until such time as the grass had finally given in to the fast approach of winter. They'd also done their best with the house. They'd got rid of all the mud and soot, although without an okay from Global Investment Holdings, they couldn't order the repairs to begin.

The sauna by the water had been destroyed by the fire; the gaping hole that had been Ailsa's grave, they'd filled in themselves.

As for the house, Ard Choille wasn't looking its best, but the villagers, having saved it from the fire, had plans for its future. They had a mind to try and achieve Lord Main's dream of a wildlife centre with the birch house at its heart.

It appeared their wish might come true, he thought, as he drew closer. For the birds that hadn't taken off for warmer climes had decided to make Ard Choille their winter home.

The balconies and walkways no longer rang with party voices and clinking glasses, but with the fluttering of wings and the songs of its resident birds.

Blackrig Revisited

By Maya Villan

The area of the graveyard where the children and their nurse are buried is surrounded by a white fence. Nearby is a seat where those who loved them can watch over them for a while.

Beyond the stone wall that circles the cemetery are the trees. The scent of pine is fresh and sharp in the December air. I'd forgotten how wonderful that scent was.

Sitting there, I imagine the burials, one after another, swift and without ceremony for fear of crowds and the mutating virus that stole their young lives.

Today, at last, the people of Blackrig will come together to commemorate those they lost. They will follow their age-old tradition of walking en masse behind a piper, from the church along Main Street and into the woods and from there to the cemetery, which wasn't permitted at the height of the pandemic.

I have chosen not to join them in this walk. I didn't know the children or their nurse. I was not here when they were taken. This ceremony, I feel, is theirs and theirs alone.

This is why I, an outsider, am here alone now to pay my respects before their arrival.

Just beyond the little graveyard, another stone has been raised. This one is for a child that was loved, named, but never born.

Mac Campbell Taylor.

If you have been following the blog on Blackrig, you will know how much the raising of that headstone means to his mother, Caroline.

My story of Blackrig is coming to an end. I will miss writing about this place, these woods, the hills that surround it. Most of all, I will miss writing about the people who call it home.

Rising from the seat, with a little difficulty because of my ever-increasing bump, I've decided to visit the green man and green woman and their assorted woodland creatures.

Arriving in the fairy glen, I can see that yet another carving has been installed during my time away. I know who it is, although I never got to meet her.

Ailsa, her long hair flowing, sits on a tree trunk, her sketch pad in hand.

Walking on through the woods, I emerge onto the road that leads eventually to Ard Choille. The folk hereabouts no longer refer to it as the Party House. It, together with the estate, is up for sale. Not wishing for any more absentee landlords, there are plans afoot for a community buy-out which looks very promising indeed. They hope Ard Choille itself will be reopened as a wildlife centre. Locals will once again swim in An Lochan Uaine and sit on its sandy shore.

My breath is condensing in the cold air as I trudge up the track to Beanach. Greg, still surprised by my return, wanted me to wait for him at the hotel, but I insisted that I welcomed the walk, after so many months in London.

The strength to fight Richard Longman QC came

because of the time I spent here in Blackrig. I thank all of you who supported my endeavours to expose him for what he was, especially the women who found the courage to come forward and add their voices to mine.

Greg predicts snow soon, possibly in time for Christmas. He says he can smell it in the air.

Acknowledgements

Firstly, a big thank you to gamekeeper Ewan Archer, who patiently answered all my questions regarding my mythical small West Highland Estate, Blackrig.

Thanks also to his wife Karen, for offering her husband's services for research purposes.

To Doug Macdonald, Watch Manager of Carrbridge Community Response Unit, for his expert knowledge on fire-fighting, and to Bunty, his wife, for her help with research.

To Donald Findlay QC who advised me on sentencing in the Scottish Courts, and to Dr Jennifer Miller, Associate Professor of Forensic Science, Nottingham Trent University, who I first met when I did the Diploma in Forensic Medical Science course at Glasgow University, and who continues to be an inspiration.

Lastly, a special thanks to my wonderful editor Alex Saunders, and all the team at Pan Macmillan for their support for *The Party House*.

Introducing Rhona MacLeod . . .

Lin Anderson's series of crime novels featuring forensic scientist Rhona MacLeod are set in and around Scotland. From the beautiful remoteness of the Orkney islands to the dark underbelly of urban Glasgow, the locations she chooses to write about play as much a role in her novels as the characters that she populates them with.

Go back to where it all began with the thrilling first novel in the Rhona MacLeod series.
Read on for an extract now . . .

I

THE BOY DIDN'T expect to die.

When the guy put the tasselled cord round his neck, grinning at him, he thought it was just part of the usual game. The guy was excited, a dribble of saliva slithering down his chin and falling onto the boy's bare shoulder. He nodded his agreement. He was past feeling sick at their antics. He lay back down, turning his head sideways to the greyish pillow that smelt of other games, closed his eyes and shifted his thoughts to something else. There was a goal he liked to play out in his head.

On the right, the Frenchman, arrogant, the ball licking his feet, thrusting forward. The opposition starts to group and there's a scuffle. Bastards. But no worry 'cos the Frenchman's through and running, the ball anchored to him, like a child to its mother. The crowd breathes in. Time stretches like an elastic band. Then the ball's away, curving through the air.

Wham! It's in the net.

The boy can usually go home now. Not this time. This time, before the ball reaches the net, his head is pulled back, then up. The intense pressure bulges his eyes, bursting a myriad of tiny blood vessels to pattern the white. His body spasms as the cord bites deeper, slicing through skin, cutting the blood supply to his brain. At the moment of death his penis erupts, scattering silver strands of semen over the multicoloured cover.

2

SEAN WAS ALREADY asleep beside her. Rhona liked that about him. His baby sleep. His face lying smooth and untroubled against the pillow, his lips opened just enough to let the breath escape in soft noiseless puffs. No one, she thinks, should look that good after a bottle of red wine and three malt whiskies.

Rhona has given up watching Sean drink. It is too irritating, knowing the next morning he won't have a hangover. Instead he'll throw back the duvet (letting a draught enter the warm tent that had enclosed their bodies), slip out of bed and head for the kitchen. From the bed she will watch (a little guiltily), as he moves about; a glimpse of thigh, an arm reaching up, his penis swinging soft and vulnerable. He'll whistle while he makes the coffee and forever in her mind Rhona will match the bitter sweet smell of fresh coffee with the high clear notes of an Irish tune.

They have been together for seven months. The first night Rhona brought Sean home they never reached the bedroom. He held her against the front door, just looking at her. Then he began to unwrap her, piece by piece, peeling her like ripe fruit, his lips not meeting hers but close, so close that her mouth stretched up of its own accord, and her body with it. Then, with a flick of his tongue, he entered her life.

When the phone rang, Sean barely moved. Rhona knew once it rang four times the ansaphone would cut in. The caller would listen to Sean's amiable Irish voice and change their view of answering machines, thinking they might be human after all. Rhona lifted the receiver on the third ring. It would be an emergency or they wouldn't phone so late. When she suggested to the voice on the other end that she would need a taxi, the Sergeant told her that a police car was already on its way. Rhona grabbed last night's clothes from the end of the bed.

Constable William McGonigle had never been at a murder scene before. He had stretched the yellow tape across the tenement entrance like the Sergeant told him and chased away two drunks who thought that police activity constituted a better bit of entertainment than staggering home to hump the wife. Constable McGonigle didn't agree.

'Go home,' he told them. 'There's nothing to see here.'

He was peering up the stairwell, wondering how much longer he would have to stand there freezing his balls off when he heard the sound of high heels clipping the tarmac. A woman leaned over the tape and stared into the dimly lit stair.

'Sorry, Miss. You can't come in here.'

'Where's Detective Inspector Wilson?'

Constable McGonigle was surprised.

'Upstairs, Miss.'

'Good,' she said.

Her fair hair shone white in the darkness and Constable McGonigle could smell her perfume. She lifted a silken leg and straddled his yellow tape.

'I'd better go on up then,' she said.

The click of Rhona's heels echoed round the grimy stairwell, but if she was disturbing any of the residents, they didn't show it by opening their doors. No one here wanted to be seen. If there was a fire they might come out, she thought, in the unlikely event they weren't completely comatose.

A door on the second landing stood ajar. She could hear DI Wilson's voice inside. If Bill was here at least she wouldn't have to explain who she was. She could just get on with the job, go home and crawl back into bed.

The narrow hall was a fetid mix of damp and heat. The sound of her heels died in a dark mottled carpet, curled at the edge like some withered vegetable. She paused. Three doors, all half open. On her right a kitchen, on her left a bathroom. She caught a glimpse of a white suit and heard the whirr of a camera. The Scene of Crime Officers were already at work.

The end door opened fully and Detective Inspector Bill Wilson looked out.

'Bill.'

'Dr MacLeod.'

He nodded. 'It's in here.'

He allowed himself a tight smile. The two other men in the room turned and stared out at her. Dr MacLeod was not what either of them had expected.

Rhona looked down at her black dress and high-heeled sandals. 'I came out in a bit of a hurry.'

'McSween will get you some kit.'

Bill nodded to one of the men, who went out and came back minutes later with a plastic bag.

Rhona pulled out the scene suit and mask, put her coat into the bag and handed it to the officer. She took one shoe off at a time and, hitching up her skirt, slipped her feet into the suit. Only then did she step inside.

Rhona took in the small room at a glance. The hideous nicotine-stained curtains stretched tightly across the window. A wooden chair with a pair of jeans and a tee-shirt thrown over it. Two glasses on a formica table. A pair of trainers on the floor beside the bed. A divan, three-quarters width, no headboard but covered with heavy silken brocade in an expensive burst of swirling colours.

The boy's naked body lay face down across it, his head turned stiffly towards her, eyes bulging, tongue protruding slightly between blue lips. The dark silk cord knotted round the neck looked like a bow tie the wrong way round. The body showed signs of hypostasis, and the combination of dark purple patches and pale translucence reminded Rhona of marble. Below the hips blood soaked into the bedclothes.

'I turned the gas fire off when I arrived,' Bill said. 'The smell nearly finished off our young Constable, so I put him on duty outside for some fresh air.'

'Did anyone take the room temperature?'

'McSween has it.'

Rhona took a deep breath before she put on the mask. The smell of a crime scene was important. It might mean she would look for traces of a substance she would otherwise have missed. Here the nauseating odour of violent death mixed with stale sex and sweat masked something else, something fainter. She got it. An expensive men's cologne.

'McSween and Johnstone have covered the rest of the room. The photographer is working on the kitchen and bathroom.'

'What about a pathologist?'

'Dr Sissons came and certified death. Then suggested I get a decent forensic to take samples and bag the body because he needed to get back to his dinner party.'

'Important guests?'

'He did mention a "Sir" somewhere in the list.'

Rhona smiled. Dr Sissons preferred analysing death in the comfort of his mortuary. Taking samples of bodily fluids in the middle of the night he regarded as her territory.

'That's some bedcover!'

'We think it might be a curtain, but we'll get a better look once we take the body away.'

'Did the doctor turn him over?'

'Just enough to tell if he's been moved. He said the left side of the face, the upper chest and hips had been compressed since death occurred. He's lying where he was killed.'

Rhona opened her case and took out her gloves. She knelt down beside the bed.

'There's a lot of blood under the body.'

Bill nodded grimly. 'You'd better take a look underneath.'

Rhona lifted the right arm and rolled the body a little. The genitals had been gnawed, the penis severed by a jagged gash that ran from the left hand tip to halfway up the right side. One testicle was mashed and hanging by a thin strip of skin.

'This must have been done after he died or the blood would be all over the place.'

'That's what Sissons said.'

Rhona let the body roll back down. The boy's head nestled back into the dirty pillow.

'Any sign of a weapon?'

Bill shook his head. 'Maybe it wasn't a weapon.'

'A biter? Did Dr Sissons check for other bite marks?'

'He muttered something about bruising on the nipples and the shoulder.'

'I'll take some swabs.'

'How long do you think he's been dead?' Bill said.

Rhona pressed one of the deepening purple patches, and watched it slowly blanch under her finger. 'Maybe six, seven hours. Depends on the temperature of the room.'

Bill risked a satisfied smile.

'Matches the Doc.'

Rhona raised her eyebrows a little. She and Dr Sissons didn't usually agree. He had a habit of disagreeing with her on points like the exact time of death.

It was almost a matter of principle. Rhona had done three years' medicine before she switched to forensic science. She liked to practise now and again.

'How did you find him?'

'An anonymous phone call.'

'The murderer?'

'A young male voice. Very frightened. Maybe another rent boy came here to meet a client?'

'Alive, this one would have been pretty,' Rhona said.

Bill nodded. 'Not the usual type for this area,' he said. 'A bit more class, but rented all the same. I'll leave you to it? Just shout if you need anything.'

She was nearly an hour taking samples of everything that might prove useful later on. After she'd finished with the surrounds, she concentrated on the body, under the fingernails, the hair, the mouth. Dr Sissons would take the anal and penile swabs.

The skin felt cold through her gloves, but with the blond hair flopped over the empty eyes, he might have been any teenager fast asleep. Rhona lifted the hair and studied the face, trying to imagine what the boy would have looked like in life. There were none of the tell-tale signs of poor diet and drug abuse. This one had been healthy. So how did he end up here?

'Finished?' Bill's timing was immaculate. 'Mortuary boys are here.' He looked at her face. 'Go home and have a hot toddy,' he said.

A hot toddy was Bill's answer to almost any ailment.

Rhona got up from the bed and unwrapped her hands. 'Any idea who he is?' she said.

'Not yet. But I don't think he was Scottish.' He pointed to the hall. Behind the door hung a leather jacket and a football scarf. 'Manchester United,' he said in mock disgust.

'There are people up here who support Man U,' Rhona suggested cheekily, knowing Bill was a Celtic man.

'Yes, but they wouldn't flaunt it. Not in Glasgow anyway.'

Rhona laughed.

'All right then?'

'Yes.' She began to pack her samples in the case.

'The Sergeant will run you home.'

He walked with her to the front door.

'How's that Irishman of yours these days? Still playing at the club?'

'Yes, he is.'

'Must get down and hear him again soon. Good jazz player. You'll ring me as soon as you've got anything?'

'Of course.'

Sean was still asleep when Rhona got back. With the heavy curtains drawn the room was dark, although outside dawn was already touching the university roof-tops. She had stopped at the lab on her way home and checked the swabs for saliva. It was there all right.

She left a note on the bench for Chrissy in case she got there first, giving her a brief history of the night's events, then she headed home for a few hours' sleep.

Rhona pulled her dress over her head, kicked off her shoes and slid under the duvet. She wrapped her chilled body round Sean's. He grunted and moved his arm over to take her hand.

'Okay?' he mumbled.

'Okay,' she said, but he was already back asleep.

Rhona closed her eyes and tried to relax into his warmth. She had been at many murder scenes, some more horrible than the one tonight. Death didn't scare her, not when it was reduced to tests and samples. But tonight was different. There was something about that particular boy. Something she hadn't been able to put her finger on. Not until the Sergeant had put it into words for her, coming back in the car.

The boy who had been abused and strangled in that hideous little room looked so like her, he could have been her brother.